# Illicit Affair the Asian Connection

Note for Librarians: a cataloguing record for this book that includes Dewey Classification and US Library of Congress numbers is available from the National Library of Canada. The complete cataloguing record can be obtained from the National Library's online database at: www.nlc–bnc.ca/amicus/index–e.html
ISBN 1–4120–1512–X

**TRAFFORD**

This book was published on–demand in cooperation with Trafford Publishing.
On–demand publishing is a unique process and service of making a book available for retail sale to the public taking advantage of on–demand manufacturing and Internet marketing. On–demand publishing includes promotions, retail sales, manufacturing, order fulfilment, accounting and collecting royalties on behalf of the author.

Suite 6E, 2333 Government St., Victoria, B.C. V8T 4P4, CANADA
Phone250–383–6864Toll–free1–888–232–4444 (Canada & US)
Fax 250–383–6804    E–mail sales@trafford.com    Web site www.trafford.com
TRAFFORD PUBLISHING IS A DIVISION OF TRAFFORD HOLDINGS LTD.
Trafford Catalogue #03–1890    www.trafford.com/robots/03–1890.html

10    9    8    7    6    5

# Illicit Affair the Asian Connection

Mike Jay

# Chapter

# I

The phone rang it was Nine on a Wednesday night, I was sitting watching some football on T.V. and I wasn't too enthusiastic about answering the phone, as I was on call out from the plant. It was a cold and dark rainy night and the game was living up to its pre–hype publicity. Picking up the receiver and listening to the voice on the other side. "Jason is that you?" For a moment I hesitated, as I didn't recognise the voice. "Yes," I said in a soft voice. "Its Jeffrey Ó' Donnell here." He was the Solicitor handling my late fathers estate. "How are you, I do hope I am not phoning at an inconvenient time?" Well I didn't wish to take away from the importance, or seriousness of the phone call. "No, not at all. What can I do for you? There is nothing wrong I hope?" "No, its just that your late father left a letter with me about three weeks before he died." I felt my mind drift back to the weeks before. "Yes, how does this concern me?" "The letter is addressed to you and only to be opened by you after his death." Strange I thought, as he continued. "I am to be in your presence when you open the letter." This was getting stranger and stranger and I passed on my thoughts to him. "By the sound of what you are saying, it seems that my father may have known something was going to happen to him?" Jeffrey responded, "This is pure speculation and I am not in the business of feeding such thoughts. But, what I did phone you for was to make an appointment with you. I thought maybe under the circumstances, a private get together, at Dun Laoghaire Shopping Centre, in the new coffee shop at twelve, tomorrow if that would suit?" Obviously my mind was now working overtime and I wanted to find out, what was in the letter, so I agreed to the meeting. "By the way, your mother is meeting me in the afternoon tomorrow in my office, so you probably want to keep this to yourself." His suggestion made sense, as she had been through enough over the past few weeks. I decided to accept his invitation. "That's fine until tomorrow at twelve then Jeffrey." My mind was now accessing the inner sensory department and working out what moves to make. Arranging to take time off work was playing on my mind and whether to take the full day or not was the question. As not knowing the contents of the letter yet, I didn't know what to do. It was strange that the letter was addressed to me and not my fathers wife Sasha? This did puzzle me.

My Father had died just about a month ago in a boating accident. Happening as it did in the Aberdeen Floating Harbour area on Hong Kong Island. It was rather strange, because he was a Sea Faring Captain and would be wary of the dangers of water and its safety, especially at night. As it happened, I was talking to him by phone from the Planet Hollywood restaurant on Kowloon that very night. Indicating that he was taking the ferry to the Central District on Hong Kong Island. My father was travelling with work colleagues and this is when the so called accident happened. This played on my mind, as I was the last of our family to hear from him. I could feel the tiredness creep up on me now, and bed beckoned. Thinking of the meeting was making me agitated and I knew from this, that I may have a restless night. Retiring to bed only to toss and turn all night and when I awoke, my head felt light. Not being in the best of shape, or form. Taking a shower, I then made some tea and toast. My next task was to phone work and telling them that I wouldn't be in for the rest of the day. Not wishing to say anything, to my mother and younger brother Jean–Pierre. They lived next door to me in the main family residence. About two years ago, I had a two–bedroom apartment built onto the existing building. From here I was able to commute to and from work without to much bother.

Sasha and my father David met while he was on holiday in Zagreb, within six months they were married. As a result, over the next couple of years my brother and I were born. They bought a house on the outskirts of Dublin and settled. My Dad was away for six weeks at a time and home for two weeks. Working for multinational trading company sailing out of the harbour of Victoria from Hong Kong Island. Sailing in the Indian Ocean, North Pacific Ocean. Calling on such ports as Shanghai, Taiwan and Macao. My memory had lapsed back to those childhood day's for a few moments. I had to leave shortly for the meeting with Jeffrey. It would take me about ten minutes to walk to the train station. Not wishing to use my car. Catching the train at eleven thirty a.m. Twenty minutes had elapsed when we got to Dun Laoghaire. Being early as I headed up to the coffee shop. In the distance I could see that Jeffrey was already sitting at a table and deep in meditation, or so it would seem. I approached with an air of curiosity. His outstretched hand greeted me. "Hello Jason, how are you keeping? I do hope everything is alright." I caught a glimpse of a letter under his paper, wondering was this it. Ordering a tea for me and as he sat down he picked up the letter. Handing it to me and saying. "This is the letter your father gave to me only last month." I was curious to find out more and why my father had left such a letter with Jeffrey. "Do you know what it contains Jeffrey?" His straightforward answer was nothing short of what I would expect. "No, but it had to be given to you, within four to five weeks of his death." Alarm bells were ringing in my ears. "How odd, it must contain some sort of time table, would you agree?" "That would be pure speculation, I don't wish to fantasise on such delicate matters". Taking the letter in my hand, knowing it was my fathers hand writing straight away. Remembering the letters and post cards that he would send me from far–flung places. Opening the letter in front of Jeffrey, as was requested. "I have to leave your presence now Jason and I am sure you would like to read it in private." "Thank you for your co–operation in this matter Jeffrey" I replied. His parting words were a small comfort that I knew I could rely upon. "If there is anything that I can do, don't hesitate to call upon me at any time in the future." I bade him goodbye and sat back down at the table. I opened the letter and began to read it. As I did my eyes began to light up. It felt like my eyes were coming from their sockets. The letter had writing on three pages back and front. I was barely through the first chapter and I knew that it would pose more questions than it would answer. I was trying to take in the contents that were being disclosed to me. My immediate thoughts were, no wonder he didn't wish my mother to read the letter. Some of the facts that were appearing on the pages in front of me were astonishing to say the least. It looked like a torrent of liberating facts, from my fathers past and present life were unfolding before my very eyes. I thought at this stage, it would be prudent to stop reading at this present time. I took the letter and put it into my pocket. Checking to make sure it was well confined inside my jacket. Deciding to get the train back to Bray and read the rest of the letter there in more peaceful surrounds.

Boarding the train, I sat by the window looking out at the sea. Thinking it ironic, that the sea could bring so much happiness and yet so much devastation in more ways than one, as I was learning now by the contents of this letter. The news that had already been bestowed upon me was the fact that my father had another wife and child in the far east, in Hong Kong to be precise. This of course sent a shiver through my whole body. What were the implications of this for Sasha, with regard to the will here in Ireland? My mother had not known of this other woman in my Fathers life and that of another child. I couldn't think straight and I found it hard to grasp the reality of the situation. I didn't want to tell them at home. My blood was boiling now, I was trembling on the train. Within myself I was trying to remain calm, trying to sort this immense burden that my father had bestowed upon me. At this point I did not know if the letter was genuine or not. Had my father been made to write a letter that did not contain the truth? These things played heavy on my mind. We had to contend with the concept, that my brother and I had a half sister. That my mother had to contend with another woman for my father's love and affection. This would be like a knife in her back, a removal of her immense

8

respect for my father, that she had. Not alone was my father bearing his inner self to me, but to contend the will, to be read in Hong Kong within six weeks of his death. These facts were swilling around in my mind, when the train came to a halt in Bray. I got out of my seat in a daze like state and walked down towards the sea front. I came to an empty seat and sat down. Reaching into my pocket, I took out the letter. I began to read from where I had stopped. It seemed that by Hong Kong law all the estate would go to the partner or sibling of the deceased. By what he was saying, the estate was worth a tidy sum. The estate did comprise of more than one property, which were of immense value in Hong Kong. Knowing then that the only way to sort this mess out was to fly to Hong Kong. I did not wish to tell them at home of the circumstance why I was going, as my brother was on the road to recovery from a two year booze induced slumber. His battle with the bottle had taken its toll on my mother. She would crack up altogether after helping him over his addiction and then finding this out about her husband. Was my father the victim of a murderer or was it an accident? These things I had to find out and see if he was in fact murdered. Respect for my father, was dwindling from my veins.

At this stage I tried to formalise a plan of action. I would phone Marjorie on my mobile, to ask her to book a flight for me to Hong Kong. Luckily enough she worked for Lufthansa, so I could also arrange to have the tickets picked up at the Airport. I could get her to arrange a hotel also. I didn't say for how long that I would be staying there. I would have asked Bill to bring me to the Airport, but he was too busy sorting out some building plans for me, so a taxi was the preferred option. My eyes turned back to the pages, a glance to the next line, what would it hold? I knew as bad as this information that had been revealed to me was, that there was even worse to come, I could feel it in my bones. My inner senses were releasing the tension from my body, I felt pins and needles all over. I thought, how could he do such a thing, to a family that loved him dearly and cared for him so much? It was a crisp Autumn day the wind was biting into my face as I looked at the pages. Was the letter genuine? I didn't know what to think at this stage. But if it was genuine, I had a right as a sibling to claim half of all his estate.

My mother had struggled for a long time, trying to bring up two children virtually on her own. Now I think it's time for her and us as his children, to gain from what was another life altogether. These rewards that he never bestowed upon us, as a family growing up. As I began to read on the contents even shocked me further. The revelations deepened with every word that had been written. Especially with the business practices or lack of them, that he indulged in every time he got a chance to. It seemed he got involved while at sea, in what can only be described as a joint venture with a Chinese smuggling ring. He had been in partnership with his other wife, in the jewellery gold buying and selling business. They owned three shops. Getting into debt, as the price of gold fell after they had taken delivery of a large consignment. It was for a figure of HK$500,000 a lot of money to come up with, in a short period of time. It seemed that the banking house which had advanced them the money desired it back rather rapidly. But the banking house, unknown to my father, was owned legally by this smuggling ring. They offered my father a monetary inducement. Obviously my father took the bait and while sailing between Tolo harbour to the port of Macao. The ship was boarded by a member of this Chinese family. He was offered money to take on board extra cargo. As he says in his letter, how do you think he came to clear his debt so quickly? The sound of a passing train jolted me back to reality. The Chai Trading Company didn't know that my father had come to an agreement with these Triads. So this was the start of their partnership, my father carrying some extra cargo that the Trading Company did not know about. My father didn't divulge the cargo or its contents, nor did he divulge it to me in the letter. Of course my mind toyed with the notion, that it could be drugs or people. I now had to get back to my place, as I was flying out to Manchester later that evening. Then the trip would lead me onto Hong Kong the following morning. Phoning Steve from the train to see if I could stay with him and Pauline overnight in Manchester. Giving work call and initially taking a week off. Approaching my mothers home, I rang the bell and Sasha answered the door. I told her that I had to go away for a week, to work at our plant in Singapore. She took the news without rancour and seemed low, she wished me a safe trip.

Proceeding to my apartment next door I then phoned for a taxi. I didn't have much time to pack. I needed my credit card and my mobile phone. I gave Steve a quick ring, to tell him what time I would arrive at. He was going to pick me up at the airport, as he was on the late shift. Luckily enough he worked at Manchester airport. The taxi arrived and I departed for the airport. As soon as I arrived at the airport, I went straight to the Bank to obtain some foreign exchange. I then set about collecting my ticket, from the Aer Lingus ticket desk at the entrance lobby. So I just had to check that my Passport was in order. I was now about to set out on a journey that may well change the rest of my life. Whether it be for the good, only time will tell. Was I doing the right thing or not?

Arriving in Manchester at eight thirty p.m. and Steve was there. It wasn't long before we got to the house. The kids were asleep and Pauline had made a cup of tea. We sat and chatted. Telling them of the unforeseen circumstances that had me going to the far East. They couldn't believe what had transpired over the years with my father. But that if I had to go and find out what was happening, then I should go with care. One of the things that they said, I took up on was to get a dictaphone while at the Airport. As they pointed out if I came upon anything unusual I could record it there and then. Later I could go back over the situation. Also that I should get a diary to write down any such incidents. We went to bed at midnight. Getting up about seven thirty a.m. and then left the house at eight fifteen with Steve to avoid the traffic. Dropping me off at number two terminal he wished me luck and I said I would keep in contact with him over the period of time that I would be there. Heading straight to check–in and leaving in my luggage. I then proceeded to the departure lounge, once inside I remembered what they had said about a diary. Entering one of the paper shops, to see if they sold diaries. I could see that they had some in stock, so I put my hand down to take one. I felt the tingling sensation of another hand on mine. I quickly released the diary and stood up. A soft gentle voice carried in my direction. "Oh I am sorry, I didn't see you there." My attention was drawn to the beauty of the woman in front of my eyes. "That's all right, you can take that one there, as you can see there is plenty more." She stood back for a moment and looked directly into my eyes. "How kind of you, are you sure you don't mind?" I could feel my heart pound a bit faster, "No, not in the least, go ahead." I followed this up with an old saying. "Great minds think alike." Her response was a delight to hear. "Yes, but do you know the follow up to that?" I immediately retorted. "I am afraid I do." We both laughed aloud and looked at each other. I went back to acquiring a diary and a paper. Suddenly the silence was broken by the sound of breaking glass. Pieces of glass were scattered over the floor. This elegant and smart looking woman that I had bumped into a short while earlier had let fall an ashtray. "I didn't mean to drop it," she explained. What else could I say, only agree with her. "I didn't think you meant it. These things happen. At least it wasn't too high a price." Her calm demeanour had caught my attention. "No, I suppose you are right, it could have been a lot worse and a lot more expensive on me." I went back to paying for the items I had in my possession. The mess made by the broken glass, was already being cleaned up, as I paid for my paltry lot. Walking towards the departure gate, knowing it was gate 132, flight CX 270, it would be another hour before take off. So seeing a coffee shop on the way down, I decided to indulge myself. I sat down at one of the tables on the periphery of the coffee shop. I could see this gorgeous looking woman that I had met in the shop and she was heading straight for me. I thought to myself, is there a sign over my head saying here I am? She ventured forward and asked if I would mind if she sat beside me. "No, certainly not, in fact it would be my pleasure". I had told myself that she was a welcome intrusion into my circumstances. "Allow me to get you a cup of coffee, or tea?" "Its all right really." "No, I insist what shall it be?" "If you must then, tea will do nicely." I got up to head for the counter. Her voice followed in my direction. "By the way my name is Phoebe." Nice name I said to myself. "May I say that's a gorgeous name, where is it from?" "You know I really don't know." Her soft voice had a calming and appealing effect. I wondered if she was a psychologist, or maybe something in this line. "Well that doesn't change the fact that its a gorgeous name." I introduced myself at this stage. "My name is Jason, how do you do Phoebe." I stepped up to the counter and

acquired her a pot of tea. "Where is your destination Phoebe?"
She seemed to hesitate for a moment. "I am going to visit my
sister in Hong Kong. Where are you off to Jason?" My heart
nearly leaped into my mouth, with excitement. I had to sound
cool and calm, so I said in my deep voice. "I am also off to the
far east to Hong Kong actually." "That's nice, we are going in
the same direction, it's a warm part of the world to be in at this
time of the year." "Have you been out there before, to visit your
sister, Phoebe?" She smiled with those lovely white teeth. "Yes,
a year ago, she has been working out there for the past three
years." "It must be nice for you, having someone there." "I
suppose so, I never thought of it like that." Deciding to massage
the moment as best I could. "I think having to wait for the plane
to take off is the worst time." Her response was something I
could latch onto. "I agree with you." I quickly followed on.
"She will be glad to see you then?" "I do hope so." The tea was
now making inroads into my bladder. "I have to go to the toilet,
excuse me for a few moments." I got up and headed for the
toilets. On my return, I saw Phoebe with a pen in her hand and
writing in her diary. I had to take advantage of the situation. "I
hope you are only writing the juicy bits and you aren't leaving
anything out?" She smiled and gave me a glance. One of those
glances like a naughty schoolgirl, for me to know and you to
find out? It was time to go to the departure gate. As we neared
the gate a Cathay Pacific representative announced the departure
of flight CX 270. "That us Phoebe, maybe we will get to talk to
each other on the flight." Entering the plane I headed for my
seat. Not wanting to seem unduly interested in the whereabouts
of Phoebes' seat, I tried not to glance in her direction. But as we
were both heading in the same direction, I couldn't but see her
in my vision. When she reached her seat, she turned and waved
to me. I nodded my head in response. Drawing closer and
closer, I looked at my seat number. Virtually being beside her
now, I again checked my seat number. It turned out that we
would be sitting next to each other on the flight. "That's a nice
coincidence, maybe its faith Phoebe?" I remarked. She laughed
as she followed up with her reply. "Who knows, it may just
be?" We both sat back into our seats, waiting for the jet to take
off. "Would you like to sit near the window?" I said in my

gentlemanly manner. "No, its quite all right Jason, I prefer not to watch the ground move from under my feet." Within several minutes, we were up in the air. Floating across the skies, towards Amsterdam for a fuel and cabin change. Stopping for a half hour stop over, without getting off the plane. It was nice to have someone to talk to on the flight. Phoebe was now being the inquisitive one. "Who are you going to visit in Hong Kong?" I was relaxing in my seat, when this straight to the point question, was thrown at me in an unobtrusive way. "It's rather awkward and complicated at the moment." This was the best I could come up with. "Well, you know things are not always as bad as they seem at first." Her mature statement was a gratifying remark. "You seem to be speaking from experience?" I looked into her eyes. "Lets just say I have thought things were worse than they were and not given any desire to approach things in any other way." Phoebe was a young woman in my eyes at any rate. Maybe in her late twenties, or early thirties. She seemed to be older and more mature than her appearance would have you believe. Having a young face, blond hair, grey eyes, a small nose, light complexion and a bright energetic smile. Underneath her calm exterior, may lie a heart of beating passion, a woman scorned possibly. Beginning to drift back into my own troubled life. What was I going to do when I got to the hotel, in Hong Kong? Whom would I see? Whether to go straight to this woman and her daughter, confront them, was an option. These things were revolving around in my mind. I must have looked agitated, because at that moment Phoebe`s voice displaced my thoughts. "Is there something wrong Jason? If there is you can tell me, I won't breath a word to another soul". Thinking for a few moments, and not knowing this person. If I tell her, she won't know who I am talking about and I need to get this off my chest. The words just came pouring out, the letter I had received. Telling her of the contents, the predicament my father had placed upon me. This was not normally my style, but then again I had never been put out on such a limb before. Without knowing it, I was expunging the fear, that I may be divulging some dark secret that may revisit me with a vengeance? What had come over me anyway, had this good looking woman seen inside my very soul. Phoebe listened to my story without

14

interruption. She then gathered her thoughts, for a few moments.

When she spoke, it was with a quiet calm relaxing and gentle twinge in her voice. "I think you should first go to the most obvious place and that is the Public Register. Register as a family sibling documenting your legal status, to claim for your late fathers share of the estate." I thought this indeed did make good sense. It also allowed for the possibility, in the event of something happening to me, that another member of my immediate family could follow on the claim in my place. This idea does allow me to plan a course of action and it did have its merits. I also wished to get a copy of the report of my father's death. Hopefully it could give me some leads, to the people who were with him on that faithful night. Smiling to myself inwardly, another outlook gave me a better perspective on my situation. Not only did this intervention lift my emotions, but it also made me feel better in myself.

# Chapter

## II

We were now coming into land, descending within the view of the skyscrapers protruding above the skyline. The sea with its galaxy of Chinese junks ferrying with their cargoes to the many outlying islands, ancient hamlets and fishing villages. Competing with the criss–crossing ferries and air–conditioned Cruise Ships that frequent Victoria Harbour. The multitude of the masses, mingling on the surface of the sea, is certainly a sight to behold. As we glided down from the heavens above, we were carried on a wave of expectancy and arrived in Hong Kong on a sunny Saturday morning. It would take another half an hour, to get through passport controls and baggage reclaim. Coming out to the arrivals hall and Phoebe's sister Jill was there to greet her. Jill was introduced to me. They were heading out to the outskirts of Kowloon and offered me a lift, but I had to decline. As I had a taxi picking me up.

Phoebe had given me her phone number, so I said I would contact her later and bade them farewell. The taxi journey didn't take to long. The mixture of old and new buildings complimented each other. Noticing the mass throng on the streets succumbing to western influences, as the McDonalds that we passed. Many delightful young Asian women in their western dress did brighten up a tired and weary traveller. I booked into the Park hotel and took a shower. I then came down to take a stroll in the afternoon sunshine. I stepped out onto Cameron road it was a Saturday afternoon. The Public Register office had closed at twelve thirty, and the papers would have to wait until Monday. I walked up to the main thoroughfare on Nathan road, as I wanted to phone home. Remembering the time difference, I would have to phone later that evening. Finding myself in the Tsmi Sha Tsui district, with many shops and eating places. I knew from the letter that the main shop that this woman and her daughter lived in was not far from here. By pure chance an advertisement board had caught my eye and on it was an ad for The Jewellery Kingdom Group. This was the group that my late father had a majority share in. A lot of chop sui out of that. I wondered if my father was just a front for this other group, or did he and this other woman run it themselves, as a going concern. Questions were coming, but would I ever get the answers, only time would tell. I began to stroll down Nathan road. Gathering my thoughts, a shop in the Hyatt hotel caught my eye. It was a Jewellery Kingdom shop so I decided to go in and have a look around. See what my late father had going for him out here. Barely had I stepped inside the door when an assistant was there to greet me. I pointed out that I was only looking, but this means nothing. The persistence got to me, so I had to abandon the petty attempt to see if they sold anything other than jewellery or gold. Within my eyesight it looked like three employees were employed and they seemed to be expert at selling. But these people did not interest me, that episode would come later. Plenty of questions began to pop into my mind. Like, what if they were selling some other products under the counter? I wondered to what extent my late father was involved in the operational partnership with these Triads. How did these people go about doing their business. Did they have business offices here, which was a cover for their real trade. They trade in misery, trade in peoples lives. Ferrying vulnerable people to a promised land, which they didn't care, or it mattered little to them, as long as they received large sums of money for their illicit trade. I stood outside the premises for a short while, looking at the overall picture it painted in my mind. This was my late fathers and none of us back home, ever knew, ever suspected such a thing. My mind couldn't comprehend his actions. Was it the lure of the Orient, the mystery that surrounds it. Now to try and figure a way, how best to approach these two women, but these may be questions that I may have to find the answers to myself. I came out to a cascade of colour and a fascinating array of illuminations. These were the historical array of past and present virtues, that we from another Continent have come to share with the Orient. The symbols of the dragons and other animals, of all kinds of shapes and sizes, were transcended onto the buildings facades. These being lit up by varied coloured lights, the contrast was beautiful, it was like a Christmas scene. I had forgot it was Chinese New Year. I came to the junction of Moody Road down onto Chatham Road, I could see the hotel in the distance, it melted into the skyline along with the rest of the skyscrapers. When I reached the entrance of the hotel, I could see the receptionist retrieve a letter from a hardwood table to her right hand side. As I got closer I could see it in her hand. "Mr. Byrne, you have a message. It was left in a short time ago." She handed it to me. It was from Phoebe, this was a surprise. She wanted me to join herself and her sister Jill, for a meal at Jill's apartment. The temptation was appealing, but I had to phone them and decline. I was very tired and needed some sleep. The effects of the heat, had taken its tool on me and Phoebe understood. It was good of her to offer in the first place, I had told her I may see her the following day. Checking the restaurant, it was still open, the allure to have a bite to eat rumbled inside, but I knew it would upset my stomach. Declining not to indulge at this stage of the night. Searching for a public phone. My attention was drawn to the right hand corner and its contents. I had a prepaid phone call card with me. I dialled the number of the house in Ireland and it took awhile for any tone to be heard. When it did ring, the tone seemed to be busy, but I held on for a few moments and it rang through to the house. Sasha answered the call. "How are you Jason? How did the trip go? I do hope well?" I didn't wish to tell her I had bumped into a woman on the way out. "Fine no problems but it was a long and tiring journey." Her inquisitive sense came to the fore. "Do you start work tomorrow?" For a moment I had forgotten what I had said to them back home about the trip. "Yes in the afternoon, I hope to have a better understanding of the situation then." I felt bad about withholding the truth from her. Wishing to get off the phone now, as I didn't

18

want to answer too many awkward questions. So saying I was on my way to bed. Telling her that I would phone her tomorrow. Then I put the receiver down and swivelled on my heels, to see a cascade of colourful reflecting on the building opposite the hotel. My body was now feeling the effects of the time travelling. Pointing myself in the direction of the lift. On entering the lift, I could feel my body get heavier and heavier. When I entered the room, I didn't waste any time in undressing. Feeling sleep take over, I fell into bed. Hitting the pillow within a minute my eyes were closed. I must have woken at five or so. Seeing the light of the morning come shining through to my room, I turned over and fell back asleep. I got up at nine thirty and took a slow shower. The water hitting my body and the droplets running down my frame, it felt like an oasis in the dry sand. Taking my time going down to the restaurant for something to eat. My choice an orange juice, an omelette with fine herbs, croissant and tea. After I ate, I noticed a tourist display unit in the lobby, one of the trips appealed to me. Taking the brochure up in my hand and reading it. The peak of Hong Kong, South China Sea and surrounding areas. Deciding to find my own way to the summit. It was now ten forty five on a Sunday morning. I stepped outside and it was a lovely day, temperatures in the low twenties and the throng of people seemed never to cease. Strolling down towards the HK Space Museum on the Sailsbury road. I knew this was the spot, where the ferry to Central District departed from. Catching the ferry, which made a connection with the open air double decker shuttle to the lower terminus, for the assent to the peak. The view was spectacular, as we made our way up. The sight from the cable car was a perspective I hadn't anticipated. It was a peaceful journey and it brought with it a serene and thoughtful setting. Many of the local population appeared to be visiting. When my eyes caught sight of the public phone I decided to call the hotel. Now I was glad I had done so. Phoebe had left a message for me. The receptionist read it aloud over the phone. Could I meet her in the hotel at two that afternoon and we could take a trip out together. My emotions lifted my spirits. Drawing myself away from the spectacular and outstanding view, which was a wonder to behold. I caught the next cable car down to the terminus. Knowing the ferry had a regular time table to keep. Catching the ferry, I landed back in Tsim Sha Tsui district and began to walk back towards the hotel, but I decided to go to Kowloon Park off Nathan road. Having a spare half hour before I was due to meet Phoebe. Venturing inside, local musicians and mime artists where order of the day. These being complimented by the appearance of lovely looking women of Asian complexion. The community spirit was much in evidence. It was time to move on and I ended up on Humphreys Avenue, leading onto Prat Avenue and across Chatham road. The hotel was visible from here and in the distance a silver car caught my eye. It pulled up a short distance from the hotel and I could see Phoebe exiting the car. Being in a position that she could not see me. I was hidden behind a parked bus. Standing there for a moment and watching her enter the hotel. I took my time, reaching the hotel and as I entered I saw Phoebe sitting in a chair in the lobby. Walking in her direction, she must have noticed me in the reflection of the mirror. Rising from her chair she swivelled around, her eyes widening as I approached. "Jason, how are you? I do hope you had a good nights sleep?" She seemed to be very relaxed. "I think so, I must have awoken early and went straight back to sleep again." "Are you here long? I hope I haven't kept you waiting?" Her calm manner, seemed to radiate confidence. "No, I just got out of a taxi." This was strange as I had seen her with my own eyes, get out of the silver car, that pulled up a short distance from the hotel, with her inside. I am sure it must be a close friend she did not wish me to know about. Phoebe suggested that we go visit Man To Temple on Hong Kong Island. Thinking this a splendid idea. Her appearance was a pleasure to see, as she looked very well in her short tennis skirt with matching socks, runners and a light cardigan, if a breeze blew up! We set out in the direction of the harbour, along Chatham road, but this variation in Phoebe's explanation of how she arrived at the hotel bothered me. Not that it should. As we walked down the road I remembered what Steve had said about a Dictaphone recorder. So I thought now might be the right time to purchase this item. Suggesting to Phoebe that I wished to acquire a camera for my brother, and at the same time she wished to purchase some items in a nearby pharmacy. This worked out to my satisfaction, as it gave me enough time to purchase the Dictaphone with tape and batteries. On emerging from the shop my eyes were drawn to the silver car in the far off distance. It was well concealed behind some parked cars. Continuing down Chatham road I showed Phoebe the camera, asking if I could take photo of her. She duly obliged. So when it came to taking the photo I made sure to position her in such a way as to include this car in the background. It seemed to have two occupants. Nearing the harbour now and we could see that the ferry for Wan Chai was about to depart. We had to make a run for it, laughing all the way. I said to Phoebe that we just made it by the width of her big toenail. We both smiled and I thought to myself that she wasn't as forthright as before, was something the matter? Maybe the car. Upon sitting down I could see the car turning around and heading back up Salisbury road. I was sure now that this was the same car that dropped off Phoebe earlier on. I looked around once again and it disappeared.

We headed towards the Wan Chai ferry pier, it was pleasant and not too long a journey. Phoebe was noticeably quiet and this was unsettling me somewhat! "Is there something wrong Phoebe?" Her low key tone, just didn't fit the normal outspoken her. "No, no what makes you think that?" "Well it's just that you seem quiet." Her demeanour did seem dull and less enthusiastic, than the usual Phoebe. "It's just the long journey is only hitting me now". I thought to myself that's possible, I'll let it go at that. Arriving at the pier, we disembarked and headed up Fleming road in the direction of the tram terminus. This would give us the connection to Sheung Wan district. The temple was on Hollywood road, not far from the tram terminus. Catching the tram and exiting, we found ourselves climbing Man Wa lane. It was a hilly climb up towards the temple and the surrounding shops mostly sold ancient artefacts. This of course, if one was to believe every shop unit who portrayed its wares. We mingled among the many visitors that craved to find that special artefact. I was glad of the opportunities to move in and out of the shade. Phoebe was a bit of a amateur art collector, and there was many a fine piece from which to choose, from what I could see. Then again I wasn't up to the mark on modern art, or the ancient

Orient at that. Phoebe said she liked some of the pieces and maybe the two of us could come back some other day and try to find a painting that she liked. I was flattered, that she had me in mind when entertaining such thoughts. "Of course, that's one of my strong points, I am known as the Vangough of the Electronic division, I carry my pencil always on my other ear." Phoebe laughed at the thought, mind you in a subdued way.

We entered the temple and from the moment you entered you could feel the humble surrounds that you were in, the peace, quiet and tranquillity made you feel in awe, of the humble beginnings that they had struggled from. It is one of the most important temples in Hong Kong, it is dedicated to the God of Literature and the God of War. It is like an oasis of historical reverence which embodies its subjects with particles of light on a journey through time. "Have you ever been in a more peaceful place Jason?" "Not in a long time, you feel like staying here, not letting the outside world encroach!" Knowing that we had to leave soon, entering the light from the scorching heavens above, the multitude of the masses exceeding its limit, comes too near for comfort. Heading for the modern day shopping mall, in a renovated Edwardian building to suit the modern day consumers. There were many small little hamlet like shops, selling knick knacks. We seemed to have covered a great deal of distance in a short space of time. My legs were tired now. "Are we going to eat soon Phoebe"? I was at that stage where you wish to sit down. "Yes in a short time." This while she was engrossed in some paintings, I said. "My pallet is overflowing only for the thought of my gastronomic embellishment." Her response was a lot like the old Phoebe. "Oh trying a bit of the old blarney then I see." "You don't mind hurting my feelings then I see." This was me being sarcastic. "Is that meant to make me feel sorry for you". The veil of the shadow that I felt hung over her, seemed to have lifted from her head. "You could say that, its just that I am hungry, are we going to eat yet?" I was getting to her. "Oh why not, if I don't I am sure I will hear about it, for the next while." So I managed to drag her away from the intriguing ramblings of her favorite pastime. We made for the nearest restaurant, it was now six thirty on a balmy evening, when we sat down to eat. "What are you going to eat Phoebe?"

Looking at the menu. "I think I will have the Steamed Rice I am watching my figure." "I also am watching your figure and may I say it is a gorgeous figure at that." "Are you trying to pay me a compliment Jason." Feeling now on ground which I could compete with. "Let there be no doubt about that Phoebe, you look very well to day." She smiled, at least I can make her smile now and then. I once again broached the point I had made earlier "Are you sure there is nothing wrong Phoebe?" This time she slowly and calmly began to unfold. "My Sister Jill had a slight encounter with some strange people this morning." This was not what I had wished to uncover. "What sort of encounter did she have?" Not seeming to be unfazed by what had happened to her. "Well it was about you actually Jason." When I heard this, I immediately straightened in my chair. "What about me Phoebe?" She now focused more on my attention. "These people suggested that it would be wise if we did not help or give assistance to you while you are here in Hong Kong." My internal emotions were raging, but I did not wish to show this to Phoebe. "Em, who knows that I am here and why I am here?" She quickly interjected. "I have been talking to no one about you. Only to Jill that is, maybe she said that you were here and someone overheard her in work." I was now curious as to the whereabouts of Jill's place of work. "Where does Jill work Phoebe? Is it for a Chinese company?" She didn't flinch an eyelid, when she answered. "Yes she works for a Trading company here in Victoria harbour." I could feel my stomach churning up inside. "That's interesting what the name of the company?" Funny that her next answer did ruffle my curiosity. "I don't know off hand Jason, why is it important?" Surely you would know where your sister worked, especially if you were visiting her and collecting her from her place of work. Maybe I was over reacting. Now being more curious to know, who drove her to the hotel this afternoon. "Who were the people that gave you a lift to the hotel this afternoon Phoebe?" She seemed surprised, that I knew about the car. "How did you know that I was given a lift?" Being quick to respond to her remark. "We all have our own little secrets." Wishing to see her facial response. "Why did you say that you arrived by taxi?" Looking down to the floor, not wanting to face me, she responded. "Because they were the men that Jill had a run in with." I sat back in my seat, wondering what I should do. "So they made sure I was out of the way for the day, I wonder why?" It is wise that we remove ourselves from here and head straight back to my hotel." "Why, do you think they will have been able to gain entry into your room?" "With these people you don't wonder you just know that they are capable of it!" "What did they say when they left you off at the hotel Phoebe?" "They just said to take you out for the rest of the day to Hong Kong Island". So they had planned this all along. Now I had to wonder had Phoebe anything to do with it. "O K, you better grab your things and we will go?" Heading back to the main terminus to catch the tram back to Wan Chai ferry pier. It wouldn't take us that long before we could get the ferry back to Kowloon. It was eight thirty in the evening, when we got on our way to Tsim Sha Tsui. Twenty minutes later we were disembarking. No point in rushing to my hotel room, what would that achieve. I am sure they had a look in my room! They will find what I wish them to find, but nothing about what I am about to do.

# Chapter

# III

In the letter my father left, he gave me the name of a very good friend of his, whom he said I could trust. In any event this person would take care of anything that I needed. This would seem to be the best time to get in touch with him. By the looks of things I may need some transport, or he may be able to find the people who are behind this. It looks like I may need him sooner that I thought. Hopefully he can arrange to have the documentation that I have in my possession and which is required, as documentary evidence, along with my Affidavit installed in the Public Register Office without the others knowing about it. That's of course presuming that they have taken the bait? This is something I had not told, or was, I about to tell Phoebe? On the day I flew to Manchester, I had Jeffrey draw up an Affidavit stating that I was David's son. This was also to confirm, that I was heir to any Foreign Estate that may arise. As Jeffrey was a Commissioner of Oaths, I thought it advisable, to have this stated at this time. Having a good friend Kevin, who is involved in the computer industry make me two copies each of my Birth Cert., and the Affidavit. I even found it hard to detect which were the genuine article? Placing a copy of each, in a satchel in my suitcase. The original documents were kept on my person at all times. My fathers sudden and to my mind unexplained death, caused me to revaluate my own personal safety! So caution was my byword. We entered the hotel from Chatham road, it was now eight fifty five. The interior of the lobby had some guests that were checking in and some who were checking out. As we strode towards the reception desk, one person in particular, caught the corner of my eye. The chair he sat in was at an oblique angle and could see the entrance and the reception desk. I could see from the reflection in the mirror on the wall, that this person was watching our every move. Not wishing to alarm Phoebe, so I said nothing of our friend. "May I have key No. 72 please?" "Certainly sir, oh there is a message also." This caught me by surprise. She handed the message to me. "Thank you, when did this arrive?" "I took it in myself, it was at six fifteen." Taking the envelope from her I put it into my pocket. Then we both headed for the elevator. I turned around and could feel eyes following us. As we headed up to floor No. 3. I said to Phoebe, "You didn't see our friend in the lobby then? She looked at me. "No, where was he?" "In the chair to the left of the reception." She said nothing more, which I found unusual. As we arrived on the third floor, the doors opened. The couple inside the lift, were in a passionate embrace. It certainly threw us both off the immediate task we were focused on. They were laughing as the elevator doors closed, the mind boggled. "They seemed to be enjoying themselves, would you agree Phoebe?" "Yes that was my impression also Jason!" We looked at each other and smiled. In the distance we could see door No. 72. Approaching the room with caution and trepidation. I put the key in the door and opened it, not knowing what to find. There didn't seem to be anything out of the ordinary, not on first sight. "Jason, can you see anything moved or disturbed?" These words came from the mouth of Phoebe. "No, not that I can see, wait till I look in my suitcase?" Looking in the case, and on opening the satchel I found papers removed. "It's not here so my hunch was right, they took the bait." I now took out the envelope that was left at reception for me. I read the few lines that were on the paper, he left his phone number. "Is it from the friend your late father had told you about ?" "Yes, it's the message I wanted to hear about." I need to phone him tonight, but not from the hotel. I thought about my mobile phone for awhile, but thought the better of it. I knew they would be using scanners here. Phoebe was standing up well to the ordeals of the day and I told her so. "Your keeping

26

your cool, I have to admire that?" If you're up to it we still have to contact our mutual friend here. It will have to be somewhere else rather than here, but where? My contact actually lived on Lantau Island, about thirty minutes away by ferry. I needed to give him the original papers so as they would be registered. To get out of the hotel, without our friend in the lobby seeing us was our problem. "I think we should go down to the lobby, ask for a taxi, make sure this person hears us. Then stepping outside and hopefully attracting his attention and make sure our friend follows me?" "What then Jason?" "I think you should have the taxi, wait up the road at the junction of Prat Avenue. I can double back by Cameron road to you in the waiting taxi? If we can do this then we have a chance of getting the papers to him, without our friend in the lobby knowing. So it has to be done right, form the start. Do you agree with me on this Phoebe?" "Yes, I think that is a plan that can work Jason!" We had scarcely time to sit down and we were off again. "I will need a drink after this tonight, I know that much," I followed up. "I don't drink Jason, but I will join you." Was Phoebes reply. "That's good to know anyway Phoebe." I closed the door to room No. 72 on our way out. We turned to walk towards the elevator, still wondering was there any other way we could make our departure any less noticeable. Approaching the elevator, I noticed a door handle, without a keyhole. Mmm, thinking to myself, could this be what I think it is? Pressing the handle, it opened onto a small balcony. I stepped out, looked down the twenty odd feet or so to the ground. A fire escape ladder was attached to the balcony, it went down to within about three feet of the ground. This is the opportunity we were looking for, as it gave us the exit without being noticed. "Do you think you could make it down the ladder Phoebe?" "Why, do I look like I can't cope?" "Far from it, but some people are afraid of heights." Her reply was strong and decisive. "Well, not me, let's go." She stepped out onto the balcony, then onto the first rung down. I followed and we were on terra firma within a few minutes. Looking around we could see no one in sight. This was the back lane leading onto Granville road. It was now nine fifteen. Our objective to find a public phone, so I could contact our mutual friend. Coming to Nathan road I had remembered seeing a phone box earlier, so we headed up towards McDonalds and you could see the phone box in the distance. Entering the phone box, leaving Phoebe outside, watching to see if she could see the person from the lobby of the hotel? I had my prepaid call card with me. I phoned the number that he left on the envelope. It rang twice before it was answered. There was a strong commanding voice on the other end. "Who is it please?" "Its Jason here, I wish to meet tonight, would this be possible?" "O K, I will see you within the hour, down by the old Train station. Oh, by the way Jason do you know you have a visitor in the lobby of the hotel?" "Yes and we have managed to avoid him tailing us". "I see you have some of your fathers attributes then." "Its nice to hear that from you, Sun Yat Sen as I know how much my Father respected you, for what you could do." He bade me good bye. "Well, I better depart soon, as I will see you within the hour." The phone went dead. Putting the receiver down, I walked outside. "Well, what's happening then Jason?". "He should be here within a short time". Her somewhat flippant remark, threw me off my stride. "What's a short time, fifteen minutes, twenty or what?" "No, but within the hour". She seemed more interested in her stomach, than what might happen to us. "Lets go to MacDonalds to get a cup of tea then." "I don't think that would be a wise decision, do you? Not with our friend maybe hovering around?" "Maybe you're right, well lets get a cup of tea to take out." This seemed a more realistic idea. "O K, that sounds fine." We crossed over the road and into MacDonald's. I ordered two teas to take out. Making our way towards the old Train station, down by the Culture Centre. This wasn't too far from the ferry pier from Lantau island. Managing to hide behind some crates and ropes all from the ferries that were tied up to the pier. This was kind of ironic as we were opposite a Police Station. Thinking how well we both did, to get out of a tricky situation. But this was only the start, how are we going to get back to the hotel, without him seeing us. "It seems like these people, want your share of the business Jason and don't mind who's feet or should I say toenails they step on." This situation seemed not to bother her. "You are right there Phoebe". My instincts were curious as to Phoebes presence here. "Where exactly are you from Phoebe?" Her rather smooth accent was hard to pinpoint. "From a small town in Cheshire, that's in north England." My internal gut reactions were rising again. "Oh, I know that's where Cheshire is situated Phoebe. What's the name of the town"? "It's called Cheadle, have you ever heard of it Jason?" I knew the place very well. "Yes I certainly have, as I have a cousin living there." "You have, well imagine we may have passed each other in the street?" That thought had never entered my mind. "Yes, that's a possibility, maybe we were destined to meet." "Look Phoebe, you don't have to help me anymore, if you don't wish to." "I know that Jason, but I do wish to." What had happened didn't seem to faze her. "Your not only saying that, just to ease my conscious?" "No, not at all". Her eyes were like a beacon to me, the bright spark that kindled the embers burning inside. "Have you ever been to Ireland Phoebe?" "Yes, only the once, that was a long time ago." "Well, I will have to remedy that, as soon as I am finished here." Her eyes lit up. "What do you say Phoebe, will you by my guest if we manage to extradite ourselves from this situation?" "Yes, I would like that Jason." We both smiled at each other taking the time to divulge a small bit of the inner feelings, we had for each other.

Then reality struck, our attention was drawn to the harbour area. Hearing the sound of a thudding engine coming from the water. Approaching the water front, you could see the swell of the waves, flow up against the pier. Then from under the pier, up sprung a well built man causally dressed in black. It was hard to make him out, he certainly had the right idea of black to camouflage himself. "Jason, I hope?" "Yes, Sun Yat Sen, happy to meet you!" His extended hand greeted us both. "This is my very good friend and confidant Phoebe." "Pleased, I am sure.?" He was much bigger than I had imagined. Tall for a Chinese man and broader. He spoke with authority. "Have you got the papers Jason?" I removed the envelope which I had strapped to my body. Handing him a well concealed body wrap from around my waist. Unfolding the envelope I gave it to him. "This is the papers you require, please take good care of them!" "You know I will do that." I have some friends, in the Registration department. These will be within the safe confines of that department early tomorrow morning. I won't stay much longer

Jason." With that he was about to make his way back down the ladder and onto the waiting boat. "Remember your friend in the hotel, he will be watching your every move, so go carefully." "We will do that Sun Yat Sen, thank you for coming." Being quietly more confident now having done the right thing! "Oh, by the way, they had searched my case and found a copy, of each of the documents that you have. So they hopefully will think they have the originals." His confident words were a comfort to me. "Lets hope so anyway, it gives us more breathing space. I will say goodnight to you both now, until we meet again. I will contact you Jason, when the deed is done." "He didn't hang around that long, did he Jason?" "No I suppose it's in his nature to be circumspect, don't you think?" Her shrug of her shoulders was an indication of her lack of understanding of the delicate moment, or was it. "I suppose so, I don't really know." It was now ten fifty five and getting back into the hotel without being seen, was our next problem. The fire escape ladder was no use, as it didn't reach down to the ground and besides the door wouldn't open from the outside. "Well Phoebe, how do you think we should get back in?" "That's a good question Jason, what do you think we should do?" I tried to rack my brain. "If I only knew." Beginning to walk in the direction of the hotel. Phoebe turned suddenly and said. "Why not come and stay with me, at Jill's place?" I was now thinking of leaving my belongings in the hotel. Thinking why not, they have already looked through my cases. "I have no objection to that Phoebe, in fact I am looking forward to it!" Both smiling at each other. "I had better phone Jill first to check if she is at the apartment." Making our way to a public phone. It was one of those old phones on the side of the street. Trying to ignore the sound of the traffic was the biggest problem. She picked up the receiver and dialed the number. It rang five times, before Jill answered it. I could here Jill's voice in the background. "Well that's no use as there is someone there and she doesn't want us to go back there." "It's strange, it's as if she doesn't want us to go back, know what I mean?" "Maybe its someone that knows of me or someone in connection with work. Didn't you say, that Jill worked for a Trading company." "Yes, but what has that got to do with it." I told her my thinking on that situation. "It may be the same one, that my father worked for and someone is asking about me." She nodded her head in agreement. "That might be so Jason, who knows." So we now had to go back to the first problem of how to get back into the hotel. As we were walking up Nathan Road, a thought struck me. "I may have an idea." "What is it then Jason?" "How about if we phone for an ambulance and say there is someone very ill in room number seventy six and when the ambulance comes, we skip in by the side door. What do you think Phoebe?" "Well its certainly worth a try, but how do we get in without being seen?" "When the ambulance personnel come to the lobby, they should cause a commotion, by asking for the room." Then we can come into the lobby and go up the stairs to the side." "Well, it's the only idea in town at the moment so lets go to it." I could see the hotel International, on the way down to the Park hotel where I was staying. From here you could see the lobby of the Park hotel. A good vantage point, to make the call for the ambulance. Stepping into the lobby of the International hotel, I walked to the public phone. From this point, I picked up the receiver and dialed for an ambulance to come to the Park hotel room number seventy six. We stayed close to the window, looking out onto the Park hotel. Within a few minutes, we could hear the wailing of a siren, it was getting closer and closer. Now having to be prepared, for to make a run for it to the other hotel. The ambulance got closer, we could see it approaching the hotel. Crossing the road, to just outside the lobby of the Park hotel. Seeing the person that was keeping a watch on us, stand up to see what was happening. Watching the ambulance pull up to a screeching halt outside the hotel. Two people go out and ran inside to the reception desk. They were making gestures towards the elevator and a crowd began to gather around. The person who had shown so much interest in us was also a spectator. This gave us the chance to slip into the hotel without been seen. Heading straight for the side stairs and up to floor number three. We could hear a lot of noise from the corridor. The ambulance crew must have woken up the people in room number seventy six. Hearing them say that they had just got off a plane. We stepped out of the stairwell and into the hallway of the hotel. Making our way to my room without much fuss. I opened the door and we both stepped inside. A sign of relief, left both our bodies like a tyre being deflated. Phoebe threw her arms around my neck, it was a warm feeling! Her every feature pressing against my body. The tingling of my body became a rushing flow. Our lips met, the soft caress, that warm embrace, the passion let loose was now in full flow. I had to draw back, but not wishing to. Remembering that the person in the lobby, may now consider, that we had arranged for the ambulance to come as we could get out of the hotel. So I knew that we had to show our faces. If only for a few moments. I could hear, "Do we have to Jason?" "I am afraid so, I don't wish to go down either Phoebe, you should know that." Her look said it all. "I suppose if we have to then." I caught Phoebe by the hand and walked out the door. It felt like I was walking on air. We came down to the lobby, it was now eleven fifteen. Stepping off the elevator, my attention to this not very elusive person in the lobby chair watching our every move. In his hand a mobile phone and was clearly talking to someone on the other end. On his feet and out of his chair, but on seeing us, the beads of perspiration he wiped from his forehead. Removing the phone from his ear, he looked in his own way pleased to see us. Our objective the bar for a drink. I knew Phoebe didn't drink, but I still bought her a cocktail. Lifting my glass, "Here's to today. I happily shared the company with you Phoebe." She returned the compliment. "Thank you Jason, may I say the same." Telling her, that I bought her a drink. "By the way, you have a cocktail." She simply lifted her glass in return. "Well I will drink to that." I watched her sink it in one go, now I was sorry I bought the drink. Within a few minutes Phoebe was beginning to sway and feel very tired. "I guess I will have to take you up to the room." She started to laugh vocally. I knew then she was away in a world of her own. Reaching over I took her by the arm. She virtually was unable to put her arm around my neck. I had to catch her hand to keep her from falling down. We must have looked a right sight, me dragging her across the lobby to the elevator. Not exactly what I had in mind, or come to think of it, I didn't think Phoebe had either! Not anticipating the end of the evening what would occur. We got to the room and I had a job trying to open the door. Eventually we entered the room and I put her on the bed, she was virtually out cold. I slept on the sofa.

The alarm rang, it was nine fifteen on a sunny Monday morning. Feeling groggy, as having slept on the sofa and not very well at that. Phoebe was asleep in or on the bed. I wasn't quite sure, but soon found out. She roused holding her head. "What hit me?" Her first words were that of a seasoned taker of the dreaded demon drink. "It's called a Singapore sling and you went through it very fast." Her eyes were nearly twirling around in their sockets. "It's a very potent drink, isn't it Jason?" "It does have a certain aroma to it, I can still feel its effects." Phoebe was still disorientated, while asking the time. "What time is it? I hope not too late". "Nine fifteen, to be precise." Her mobility was a sight to behold. "Do we have to get up this early?" I thought to myself, do I need to bring her with me? Then it seemed as my inner instincts took over. "I am afraid so, just in case something goes wrong with the papers." She really didn't seem all that interested in our exploits. "All right, I will freshen up now and later I will take a shower, when I get back to Jill's place." My mind was awash with conflicting answers. "Not knowing if the papers are in the possession of the State Registrars office is the worst part." Now in a more positive mood as I suggested we go down to the restaurant. "Come on Phoebe, let's get something to eat." Her reaction to my suggestion was typical of a person who had consumed too much alcohol. "You certainly have not lost your appetite since you came, at this moment in time I really don't feel like eating." Managing to resume normal power to her otherwise wretched body and mind. I encouraged her to take a pain killer for her head. Heading for the elevator, we saw the couple in a passionate kiss from the previous evening was stepping off the elevator. We were securing our, or should I say, Phoebe's delicate body to the hand rail of the elevator. Managing a little smile to myself. Stepping out into the lobby of the hotel, a quick glance at the clock above the receptionist. It was nine thirty five and our watchdog was sitting there. Looking smug in his seat, but little did he know of our encounter. Watching us from across the lobby floor and into the restaurant. He was now talking on his mobile phone. I wondered whom he actually was talking to?

Was it the Triads that my late father had dealings with? Sitting at a table nearest the window and ordered some breakfast. As we sat there, a messenger from the hotel came in and gave me an envelope. This took me aback. I immediately opened the letter and took out its contents. They made me smile openly. Phoebe was very interested in why it made me smile. "What's in the letter Jason?" "The package we left in safe hands has now reached its destination. This is at least one less factor to contend with. This, what I hold in my hand, is an official receipt of that said document. So my sibling rights are an issue, that these others will have to contend with now." Phoebe's desire to be excited by the arrival of the receipt was entwined with her desire to have a proper rest. "I am glad that you have got this far and I am sure it is only the beginning." I myself was worried on the legal end of things. "Hoping that it goes alright for me when I show up at the Public Registrars, especially as I am not from this country. I will assume that they will have to check out that my birth certificate, my passport and the affidavit I have enlisted in their possession." "That will take a few days to sort out Jason." Seeing a smile come over Phoebe's face, she had something devilish planned. We both sat and enjoyed our breakfast, in the glare of the sun. This was a good start to the day. "Are you going to go back to Jill's to take a shower?" She lifted her eyes and thought for a moment. "Yes, are you not coming with me?" My heart jumped like as if awoken. "Of course I am, you hardly think I would let you go there alone." My immediate thoughts turned to our friend in the lobby. "We better order a taxi for the journey to Jill's." Getting up from the table, we moved to the reception area. Seeing our shadow take a keen interest in us and I just said to myself, what if he knew where we were going? The thought just melted form my mind. Asking reception to order a taxi and to pick us up outside the hotel. The day itself was gorgeous. We both sat on the small veranda, looking onto Nathan road in glorious sunshine. It would take fifteen minutes for the taxi to come to collect us. As we sat there looking at the mass throng passing us by, I thought, no wonder my father stayed in this part of the world, with the weather and beautiful sights to see. Mind you, a lot of these beautiful sights were women. Phoebe wished to go to a shop not far from the hotel. Wishing to purchase some mints, as she hadn't washed her teeth that morning. Crossing to the other side of the road and entering a small shop. It seemed to sell everything. Imaging that you could purchase whatever you chose to within reason. The people were very gracious and patient. As we came out, we caught sight of a taxi pull up at the hotel entrance. Then I noticed our shadow come out and talk to the taxi driver. Feeling this a strange thing to do. He clearly didn't see us across the road. I didn't know what to do, whether to get into the taxi or not. If we got into the taxi, was he going to bring us to some far off place, arranged by these impostors? The decision had to be made on the spot here and now. A passing tram solved the immediate problem. I grabbed Phoebe by the arm. "Come on, let's get this tram." We hopped on it and took off in the direction of the apartment. "I thought you called a taxi?" She said with a dismissive tone in her voice. "I did, but our friend the shadow, had a word with the taxi driver." Her concern seemed to be more about the situation we left behind, rather than the new one created. "This way he will still be back at the hotel waiting for us, it gives us some time." This certainly seemed to disturb her. I carried on with the attempt to win her over. "I think this a better bet than the taxi Phoebe." "Alright, but I want to get to Jill's to change and have a shower." For a moment, it's as if she didn't with for us to escape the clutches of our shadow. "We are going to do that now." I said in my deep voice. "Its just that we are going to get there, in a different mode of transport." This didn't register with me and besides, what difference would that make. "My head isn't the best Jason." I suppose that could be the answer, I found myself saying to an inner dimension of my mind. She had put her hand to her head. "It doesn't look the best either." Her child like expression did her justice. "Why do I not look all right, what's wrong? Is my hair a mess, do I look too fat?" "Nothing its just that you look tired that's all." She shook her head in agreement. "That I certainly am Jason, but not from what I thought I would be." A pleasant thought entered my mind and stayed there for a moment. "We were heading up Canton Road on the tram. My mind was awash with simmering thoughts, festering and mingling among my positive frame of mind. How did I get into this mess, it was my fathers fault. You are becoming paranoid with looking all around you, perfectly innocent people, going about their daily business. I found myself watching to see if they are looking at me for any prolonged period. Why was I doing this? The problem here was, the fact that we stood out being from Europe. So no matter what I felt, it was obvious that people would look intensely at me or Phoebe. I really didn't have an idea or know what I was really looking for. Trying to put what was actually happening to us to the back of my mind. So I chatted along the way about the things that we were going to see and do. This I don't think made an indentation on Phoebe's impression of me. Having a good view from the top of the tram. I looked to the rear to see if we were being followed. Nothing seemed out of the ordinary. Deciding to pass by the apartment block just in case there was anyone lurking outside. As we passed by, no unusual people or things were to be seen. It looked like we would disembark here. This was Mong Kok station and the apartment was a short stroll back. It would give us an opportunity to case the apartment as we approached. Making our way to Dundas street. Phoebe had written down the combination to the electronic entrance gate. She pressed some buttons and the gate began to swing open. Once inside we both sighed with relief. It was a short but still an awkward walk to the entrance door. We were inside the building now and heading up to the second floor. Glad that I didn't have to leave the paperwork into the Public Registrars as this was bad enough. Approaching the room and opening the door, we entered. A bright, well decorated lounge, with some interesting wall mounted pictures. It was clear that the occupant, Jill, had good taste. Phoebe was about to take a shower. "I'm going to take a shower, will you put on the kettle Jason?" "Sure, where is the kettle? Oh I see it." I pushed the button on the kettle and turned on the switch. I then returned to the lounge again. Looking out the window, I could see the entrance gate from here. No one to be seen, so I began to take an interest in the pictures on the wall. Are any of these valuable? The sound of the kettle boiling caught my attention. As I approached the kitchen I noticed some post on the small table beside the TV. The post was lying face up, the name caught my eye. I was focused upon the name in the window box of the letter. But it didn't seem to correspond with the name Phoebe had told me was their surname. In fact it was a man's name. A mister Tung Yuen, who was he? A mystery man in Jill's life that Phoebe didn't know about. This was interesting. Then came a ring on the apartments intercom system. I ran to the window and could see the same chap from the hotel. He was with someone who seemed to me like a more important person.

Phoebe came running out. "Who is that?" I glanced as she approached with a bath towel around her body. "How should I know, but that shadow from the hotel is with him. I think you should dress Phoebe." She ran back inside and jumped into some casual gear. I then saw the person with our friend the shadow from the hotel, phone someone on his mobile. The next minute I could see him from the window, press some buttons on the gate. It began to slowly open. "You have great eyesight." I knew at this stage it was time to remove ourselves from the apartment. "Get a bag if you can with some clothes in it." She was more worried about the items she wished to bring, than the situation we were in. "I haven't unpacked my weekend bag yet." "Well, grab that and lets get the hell out of here." The two men were now heading in our direction. Opening the door of the apartment, we walked out into the landing. Knowing that we needed to make up as much time as possible. "Let's get down to the first floor anyway." I was virtually dragging Phoebe behind me. When we got to the first floor, the sound of the front entrance door opening could be heard. This stopped us in our tracks. What to do next? Looking along the hallway, all I saw were some doors. "Damn this." I tried one, it wouldn't open. They were getting nearer and nearer, you could hear them walking up the stairs. I tried another door it opened into a small storage room. I grabbed Phoebe from behind and pulled her inside and shut the door quickly. I put my fingers to my mouth and made a silent gesture. I thought, just in the nick of time. Hearing them pass by the room brought a gasp of breath. They seemed agitated and talking loudly. The sound became faint, this was our chance. Taking Phoebe by the hand and walking from behind the door. Quickly stepping on our tiptoes we made our way to the entrance door. Reaching the door in good time, opened it and out into the daylight. Phoebe fingers pressed the buttons on the exit gate, it opened. We spirited ourselves as quickly as we could down towards the tram station. My mind was rumbling with inner thoughts. What bothered me mostly was, who did the guy phone to get the combination of the entrance gate? Was it Jill? I had no time to dwell on that thought for the moment. We had to get far away from here. Catching the next tram. "Did you see the person who was with that shadow Jason?" "Yes, I saw him from the window." "What did he look like?" "Very smart looking, casual dresser with black long hair combed behind his ears." My internal thoughts were telling me he looked like a business man. "Why Phoebe, would you recognize him from my description.?" "It is hard to make out their features from that distance. They certainly were heading in our direction. For a moment I thought that they were acquaintances of Jill's." Her remark threw me off my line of thought. "Why do you think they came to the apartment Phoebe?" "They may have had some kind of bugging device hidden in the room." Her theory was something that I hadn't taken into account and then she added. "That's how they probably knew where we were." "Very interesting, have you done this sort of thing before?" Her smile was refreshing as we sat on the tram. "Is the apartment rented out to Jill?" Her strange face was a sight to behold. "I don't know, I think it is owned by the company she works for." It had me thinking, was Jill at the heart of the Triads operation? I wouldn't think so, I doubt if they trusted anyone but themselves. "There was a bill there for a mister Tung Yuen. Does that name ring a bell Phoebe?" "No, can't say that I ever heard Jill talk of him." My mind was now running amuck. "If they have placed a bug in the apartment, this is probably the way they find the routes of the shipping company. Would Jill have access to these routes?" She thought for a moment. "I doubt it, I don't exactly know what she does there."

Finding ourselves heading back down Nathan road. I needed to phone Sun Yat Sen, to find out what was happening with regard to the Public Registrar office. First I wanted to visit the mother and daughter, to find out what they knew about all of this. So we made our way to Hankow road, where they lived above the shop. Not knowing if I was going to walk Phoebe into anymore danger by going there. "Where are we going to now Jason?" "The jewelry shop." "Is that wise?" These words coming from Phoebe's mouth. "That I don't know, we will only find out by going there." Hopping off the tram we headed for the junction of Peking Road. In front of us stood the shop of jewelry Kingdom. It was a well know brand shop in Kowloon. We crossed over form our side of the street, to the entrance of the shop, my heart began to beat that bit quicker. Was I now going to meet the other woman in my late Fathers life? I got a dig in the back, "Lets get in there, I don't wish to be exposed out here." She was right. So opening the entrance door to the shop and as soon as I did, a shop assistant came towards us. But before the assistant could greet us, a voice carried over her head. "Leave these people to me, I am expecting them." I was caught on the hop. I didn't know what to think. A young beautiful looking Asian woman came towards us. "Jason, I think and your friends name?" I didn't know if it was a wise to tell her that, but it popped out. "How do you know who I am.?" "As we say in this part of the world, there is more than one way to skin a cat." She bowed and clasped her hands together. We reciprocated. "Please follow me." Entering a most delightful room. Its many varied paintings and tapestries were a sight to behold. I knew who would find themselves at home here. There was another room leading off this room and who or what occupied that space? There seemed to be a figure sitting at the large table. As we approached the room, this figure became clearer as we drew closer. A even more distinguished woman sat at this table. A voice came from the person that led us into the room. "This is my mother." I walked forward to see a instant warm face, of full cheeks, dark green eyes, long flowing black hair and a beautiful smile. The woman got up from her chair and walked forward to greet me. Her outstretched arms swung around my shoulders. I felt the immediate impact of the woman that I had never known. Her genuine warmth eased any such fears that I had. "I have waited for this moment for a long time Jason, your father was very proud of you." "How did you know I was coming?" "We both know a mutual acquaintance." I was not thinking straight. "Who is this?" "You know the one called

Sun Yat Sen!" "Yes, I know of this person." "Well this person is my brother and was a very good friend to your father." This eased my mind even more. She introduced Susan as her daughter and my half sister. I introduced Phoebe as my friend and my confidant. Some tea was brought in from the outer room and laid on the table by Susan. We were asked to sit at the table. I couldn't believe that I was sitting down to tea with the woman that was in competition for my late fathers love and affection. Did they know who was behind the people following us? "Have you, or do you know, who is behind the events that have just accrued?" "Let us just say that I do know of someone whom would be capable of such an action." Her very calm and relaxed manner was what I expected. "It is a family group, which your late Father had some dealings with. They want to take over the running of the entire group." She came straight to the point. I tried another tack. "Of course it would be a great outlet for their trade, whatever that may be, would it not?" "Yes, I believe this is the way they think Jason. They had a person ready to step into your shoes, only we beat them to it. They won't be able to do anything until after the will is read." I thought to myself, is there anything that I can do personally to avoid these people. "By the way Jason, the will, it is to be read on Friday. Enough about the present, now we look at the past." I saw Susan get up from her chair and go to the next room. On her return, she was holding in her arms what looked like some photo albums. This is what she must have meant, by the reference to the past. "Before we continue Jason, I will insist that you and your good lady friend, stay here with us in our humble home." I thought for a moment and decided to decline the offer. Then this gracious woman pointed out what had been bestowed upon us in the last twenty four hours. Reconsidering the invitation and succumbing to the idea. "Well if you put it that way, I don't think we could say no." "Your bags will be picked up from the hotel and your bill paid later today." I sat back and wondered how I had let myself be talked into this situation. I guess my late father had felt the very exact same. This woman in front of me was a skilled negotiator and clever at switching the situation to her advantage. I was sure she had to do this all her life, as regards her living in the climate of survival they had to endure.

40

The photo album was opened in front of her, she beckoned me to come and see. In front of me, was a black and white picture of my Father exiting from a ship in Hong Kong harbour. My eyes lit up. "Who took this?" "If you look at the picture, ahead of your father is my brother. His name is Sun Yat Sen, I believe you have already met." I thought to myself this is how my father met this woman. "Your father and my brother sailed on the same ship. My brother brought him to Lantau island where we lived at the time. He was a handsome man and I wanted to be in his company." I had a small glance at what greeted my late father in those earlier days. "Your brother still lives on Lantau island, is there any more of your family living there, or is he the only one left?" Her deep and thoughtful answer was etched on her face. "Yes, I have some more family there. My brother was the main money earner at that time he had a good job and traveled around the world. He would send us postcards from far off places, as I am sure your father sent you, Jason." "Yes, indeed." I thought what would my mother think now. Me sitting down to tea with this woman. Phoebe was rather quiet for her. "Is everything alright with you, you seem quiet?" An interjection came from Susan. "That is a beautiful name you have, it is very exotic. Where exactly does it come from? Is it East European?" "That I do not know." "We hear this name sometimes on the television shows that we receive here from Eastern Europe." Then Susan walked towards Phoebe. "I do hope that Jason stays here and of course your good self." She had pre–empted my reply and I had to make this clear. "I haven't said yet, that I will be staying with you here." "This of course is entirely up to you Jason." Wishing to make sure they understood me. "Yes, it is indeed." I thought it a good moment to take a walk. "Myself and Phoebe will take a walk. I may talk and decide if we stay with you here. We will take in some of the shops and return later to confirm if Phoebe and myself will stay or not." Stepping out into the shop and heading for the exit door. As we walked towards the door, a faint voice said. "Be careful of anyone following you both." I took her advice and we slowly edged our way to the door that led us onto Peking road. Training our sights up towards Nathan road. A sigh of relief came from both of us. "Well, what do you think of them Jason?" "I am not so sure, it's hard to know." Phoebe was cautious when she spoke. "I didn't know if you wanted to stay or not, that is why I said nothing back there." "What is wrong Phoebe? You don't seem yourself?" For the first time she made a very personal remark. "They don't seem to like me, I can feel it." She may have been right, as I was engrossed in the total reality of what was happening. "Don't you think maybe, that they are more cautious of you, because you are not a family member. It may take them a little time to come around, otherwise they wouldn't have asked you to stay." There was no splitting hairs with Phoebe on this. "They asked me to stay, because of you Jason." "That may be, but don't judge them, as I can't either in such a short spell of time." "That's a fair comment Jason, only time will tell." "Well, where are we going to stroll to Jason?" "Lets have a look at some of the antique shops, what do you say Phoebe?"

# Chapter

# IV

The sun was beaming down, I could see on the far side of Nathan road, some antique shops. Pointing over to the shops, we made for the nearby pedestrian crossing. There were many objects of delight, that Phoebe was interested in. She would pick up a piece and show it to me, asking my opinion. My limited knowledge, curtailed me to the few, but helpful assertions, that I imparted to her about its charm, its colour, its texture, and its very pleasant appeal. This seemed to satisfy her and made me feel good. Inwardly, I ran away with myself. Thinking maybe I did know something about these pieces. She told me, that some of these pieces looked like they came from the Han Dynasty. Being curious, as how she spotted this? "There is a small mark at the base of the object, this is what you look for". I was impressed by this information. "But how can you tell if its a fake or not?" "This is where you study of the subject comes in. Before I came out, I took a course in the famous Chinese Dynasties collections. Learning what to look for." She knew what she wanted. "Thinking ahead I see Phoebe." "No harm in that." Sure there was no reason to phone Sun Yat Sen. His sister would have told him, of my position. By now, we or should I say Phoebe, must have looked at every item in the shops. It was now four forty five, on a sunny Monday afternoon. Wondering had my bags been picked up from the hotel. "What are you going to do, stay with me at their place or not?" She was still very agitated by the two women. "I think at this stage, I would rather stay at Jill's apartment for the time being". Not being surprised by her choice. "If that's what you wish, then so be it. Do you think we could go for a cup of tea now?" "Why not, I have looked at all of the pieces I was interested in." Her interests in these objects were a fascination to me. "You must have looked at everything in the shops." We both laughed and began to walk, in the direction of a café I had seen earlier. Sitting at a table in the open air, getting some sun and a hint of a slight wind in our faces. "It must be hard to keep track of the many Dynasties that seem to be around us." "That's the beauty of searching through such pieces. You get a feel for the different items, that each province provides us with. It is of course a labour of love that creates these pieces." Her enthusiastic approach to the subject she really liked, was an amazement to me. This seemed to bring a energised Phoebe back to her strongest and most amiable self. "You very much like dabbling in this field, don't you?" Her eyes would light up as she spoke about the subject at hand. "Will you come out to dinner tonight Phoebe?" Her thoughtful deliberation caused me to anticipate her to decline the proposal. "Why yes Jason that would be nice. Had you anywhere in mind?" I was now back up and running again. "Maybe the Aberdeen Floating Harbour area, there is a great selection of places to eat." She again looked into my eyes and seemed to foresee my thoughts. "Is that the only reason Jason?" Quickly demonstrating my objections to her thinking anything else. "Of course why else. I want to take a gorgeous looking woman out to dinner and hold a deep and meaningful conversation with her." "It isn't the fact that your late Father was killed in that area?" I could see by her demonstration of the workings of her mind, that she had deep understanding of the ability to, reach inside and take a piece of your inner mind and quickly dissect it. "Well it may have something to do with it. It gives me a chance to see the area, that this so–called accident is supposed to have happened." Her ability to be calm and understanding was a refreshing factor in her make up. "All right I will come to dinner with you, but you have to be careful." I at least had captured her attention for the evening. "Are you going back to Jill's place?" She was persistent in her determination to exercise her right to stay at

Jill's. "Yes I think it wise for me. It will give me a chance to find out if there is any listening devices there." I thought her a very stubborn woman, but then when didn't you come up against a stubborn woman? "You also be careful Phoebe." Our eyes met and we looked at each other, searching for that look of approval. Stepping out onto the pavement, as Phoebe needed a taxi. Throwing my arm up in the air, trying to capture a taxis attention. Suddenly one pulled in and she got into it. "I will see you this evening at eight, at Jill's place, if that's all right?" This was a parting that I wished didn't have to happen. If she would stay. "That's fine, until then." The taxi was out of sight, before I moved on. Not wishing to go back to the shop for some time. So I took a stroll back down Nathan road. The rush of people to their destinations, left me in a quandary. Do I follow on with the expectations that I have bestowed upon myself or do I quit and leave my late fathers character in the hands of others. This was a deep and dutiful decision I would wish to leave till later. Guessing that I would be waiting for an answer for a long time. Looking for signs, as if there is a path to follow. When you feel alone in such a situation, your off beat thinking becomes a constant companion. Glancing quickly behind me, as I pulled my head back to its rightful position, thinking I caught a glimpse of Phoebe. This must have been my imagination. Why I just put her in a taxi. This person was going into a small stairway entrance at the side of a shop. But I had just seen her go off in a taxi. I think my eyesight must have been playing tricks on me. Needing some place to sit down and think. Another cup of tea or a drink maybe. Wishing to keep my head clear for later that night. In the current situation, I think that the wise thing to do, is to take a cup of tea. So a cup of tea it was. Seeing a café opposite the entrance I thought I had seen this Phoebe enter.

I went inside the café, sat down and a waitress came and took my order. Needing to draw up a plan for myself sit back and take a look at the situation, from an outside point of view. Where am I going? Whom do I know and how long do I know them? These people were in my life only within the last two days. This was a lot to take in. My inner feelings were in a quandary, as I was in a different environment and their approach to settling things, were much different to mine. What if the letter had been written under duress, I had only paid a glance at this situation. Are these people really who they say they are. How do I know, where can I find out? Just because they have a photo with my Father along side of them, doesn't say they know him, or, that they are good and close friends. Questions were flowing now that I had not thought of before. Being in a more relaxed and rested state now. Maybe getting over the Jet lag. New and even more sinister questions were lurking in my mind. What if Phoebe already new who I was? This idea had never occurred to me before now. What if she was working for someone who wanted information on me. These questions were frightening me. Was my mind playing tricks on me? But these were questions that I would have to ask myself over and over again. The chance meeting at the airport, was it stage managed? Phoebe's sister Jill, just happens to be working for the same trading company, that my late father worked for. Were these mere coincidences, possibly so, but very close together. What about this Chinese mother and daughter. Against that I never met them, only through a letter that my late father has supposedly written. I think the same for these as for Phoebe, they may only want to find out information for their own purpose. There is a lot at stake here. These shop units and the property that goes with them is worth a lot of money and hard currency means a lot here. Who ever controls these units, has a great advantage for the products they sell or even the value of the properties. Am I in danger also, from both these parties as well this Chinese family. I really do need a plan of action. First, course of deed to find out if the woman and daughter are who they say they are. Hopefully I could find this out, by going to the Births and Death registrars office. This should have her name and daughters name if she was my late Fathers wife. Little did I know, that I would end up searching to see if these people were involved with my father or not. Yet in the background is the question of Phoebe. Well you know the old saying, keep your friends close, but your enemies even closer. Here am I, sitting in a café half way round the world wondering if the people I am involved with are really trying to do me harm. It is not a very comforting thought, I can assure you. But these are problems that with proper mental intellect, can be overcome. Am I being to suspicious, I think not. As I sat looking out at the world from over the brim of a tea cup, flashes of my late father crept into my mind. Like the times he would come home from being away and always bring something as a gift for me and my younger brother. Those days have long passed but the thoughts still linger and remain clear in my head. A thought just struck me, did he or this woman choose the presents he gave us for Christmas. Since these revelations, lots of little things have sprung into my mind and they are now in danger of turning my world upside down. What will be the final outcome? Glancing up the road once more, out of the corner of my eye, I caught sight of Phoebe stepping out of an old but somehow modern building. That's strange she said she was going back to Jill's place. Obviously she knows more people here than she is letting on. My curiosity was getting the better of me. So deciding to take a walk up by this building and passing by. Number 74 Kimberley road. No name on the building. It somehow gave the impression of being derelict. I called my mind into question, am I sure this is where Phoebe stepped out of. The answer was yes, but what would she be doing in such a run down place. The mystery got deeper and deeper. I could look up in the telephone book the number of the building I suppose. Was this building a front for some other business. There seemed no point in me hanging around, as I wouldn't know what to look for. Should I tell Sun Yat Sen of this development. This is the tricky bit, who to trust if anyone at all. If I tell him and he along with his sister and daughter is working for themselves. Where does this leave me? Where do I look for help, is there anyone that I

can trust. Best thing for the moment, is to say nothing. In keeping this to myself, I at least have maybe the jump on the others. Deciding to head back to the shop. My mind was awash with revolving questions. It was becoming a very heavy burden to carry. These troublesome thoughts, had now taken the form of a headache. So I called into a pharmacy, on the way back to the shop. Some pain killers were the order of the day along with a throw away camera. These provoking deliberations were not helping me move in the right direction. But then the answer to this did seem elusive. My inner feelings told me not to stay at the shop. So deciding to keep the room at the Park Hotel. I phoned them at the shop, to tell them of my decision. The phone was answered by Susan. "Its Jason here Susan, is my luggage collected from the hotel yet?" "No", came her reply. "Why do you ask Jason?" "I am going to have to decline the offer of accommodation after all." There was a silent pause on the other end of the phone. "Why Jason?" "Its on a personal level, but I do appreciate the offer. Will you tell Anita Mui the news from me. Hopefully I shall call around tomorrow, if that's all right?" "Yes Jason, we will look forward to that, until then, we wish you well." Putting the phone down, not knowing what they thought. I made my way back to the hotel. There was no shadow there this time. Feeling a bit more relaxed. This was not to say, that I would drop my guard. I purchased a newspaper at the front desk and took the elevator to my floor. Sitting down in the chair I began to read the paper.

The headlines jumped up at me. Triad Boss trial starts. Hong Kong's most wanted Triad boss, went on trial yesterday, accused of murder, blackmail, smuggling people and explosives, drugs and armed robbery. How would I judge these people surrounding me now? Are any of the people whom I have met, involved with individuals in the paper? That is the big question now. Reading the article, I noticed that there was a recurrence of one or two names. These names were based on secret societies, from the late eighteenth and early nineteenth century. One of the names was Sun Yat Sen had a very familiar ring to it. The article was a graphic detail of modern crimes, committed without thought of who they killed or maimed, or who got in the way. I would have to collect Phoebe soon. Who was she seeing at that address? This will have to wait, so I left the article there. Phoning the lobby to have a taxi pick me up at seven forty–five. I then took a quick shower and this made me feel much more relaxed. On coming down to the lobby, the taxi was waiting. Telling the driver where to go. We arrived at eight on the button. Getting out I asked him to wait. Pressing the intercom button and Phoebe answered. "I will be down in a moment". It was several moments. By the time we were leaving the apartment, it was eight twenty. When I was waiting for Phoebe, I noticed a car that I thought was familiar. Then it came to me, it had a British sticker on the small side window. This was the very same car, that was parked at the entrance to where Phoebe visited earlier that day. What was it doing here? We made our way to the Aberdeen Floating Harbour area. The lighting was spectacular as we strode down the pier. Finding an intimate table in a secluded corner of the restaurant. It gave us the spectacular view over the harbour area. "I must say Phoebe you look fabulous tonight." Her eyes lit up. "Thank you Jason, you don't look to bad yourself." The waitress came over and took our order. "Jason, I have something to tell you." This didn't sound too good, I didn't know what to expect. "Does it have something to do, with the visit you made to that seedy place earlier today?" The look of surprise on her face, as she pushed her body back in her chair. "How did you know about that place?" "I noticed you enter it when taking a stroll down the road. I also remembered a car that had been parked there. It was also parked outside your apartment block this evening when I called to collect you." At the same time she seemed very calm and collected as she was forthcoming with an explanation. "I think it only fair, that I tell you a story that includes you Jason. Let me say first off this situation is most embarrassing for me. I work for a certain organisation, that helps track down Foreign criminals, such as the Triads." This was pretty heavy stuff to me. "What has that to do with me? I don't have any criminal connections, or do you think I have?" "But Jason you were a bystander till the other day, is that not true in your late Fathers business?" "Yes, but why are you telling me this now. I have nothing to hide. I am not the same person as my late father." "As I said, I work for an organisation called the NIS. This is a British Customs and Excise Department and we investigate fraud, drug trafficking and also people trafficking. Unfortunately for you Jason, your late Father I have to tell you, was involved with a Triad Family that we are investigating. These are the very same people who are connected with some of these offences, which I am sure you have read about in the newspaper. We believe that they are trying to take over the group of properties that your father and his partner own." I was curious how much she knew about the mother and daughter. "Tell me is this woman and daughter involved in this so called racket to?" Her answer did nothing to relieve my mind of the fears I had about them. "Not that I am aware of. Why, do you suspect that they are involved in something, other than running the shops?" "No, I was just curious Phoebe that's all. What do you hope to gain, by telling me this." The answer I felt, would be as much as a disclosure, of her knowledge of the workings of the Triads, as opposed to the real facts about my late father. "If you succeed in claiming your late Fathers inheritance, you will be in a position of power in this organisation, without you being aware. This influence you will have, may sway the company to go in a new direction. I mean away from the path it is on now. We in the NIS, (National Investigation Service) want to bring to justice, the exploits of this one particular Triad family. This family export drugs, people, counterfeit goods, gambling, guns of all calibre's and cigarettes to the British mainland." This was definitely heavy stuff we were talking about here. My mind was trying to take in the facts, which she was throwing at me. Trying to stand back and say, of course these are the facts which suit her. "So what would you have me do, if I am to believe you?" I am sure she will have some well versed explanation of how I will be able to help stop the plight of these drugs being pushed upon them. Of course helping to create a climate where people in society in Asia, can leave in peace, not fear, from these demons. "If you keep us informed of what there plans are." Her elusive answer did nothing to over burden my guilt. In fact it hadn't any such effect, so I pressed on with a question. "Phoebe why are you telling me these things, do you think I will come in contact with these Triads?" Her no answer left me with no illusions as to the outcome of the path I was taking. My late Father, had not only given me a poison chalice but, also put my own life in danger. Phoebe indifference to this left me somewhat cold. "I am afraid you will come into contact with these characters Jason, not by means you choose. As I have said they had an arrangement in the past with your late father." I wished to convey to Phoebe that I had no intention of hanging around Hong Kong after the will had been read. "But I don't intend to be around here after the will had been read. My wish to go back and bestow on my mother, some of the financial gains that my Father had declined to do in the past." Her soft and soothing voice, was unconcerned by my slight outburst. "That may be so, but I am sure they will not look favourably on this in their course of action. You see, they want your share or they wish for you to assist them in continuing their lucrative trade." My direct question again to Phoebe, as regards to the two women, might steer me in another direction. "Are Anit–Mui and daughter heavily involved in this Triad family you talk about? Or are they involved in any part of the organisation?" She definitely was not committing herself to a full disclosure of all the facts at this point in time. "We don't know, that's why we need you to keep tabs on them for us." The waitress bringing our main meal interrupted us. To be honest, this was a welcome intrusion. The night was quickly and easily evaporating into a melting pot of tangled ideas. If I was to believe Phoebe, I was now stuck in the middle of an international criminal investigation. Questions were being asked of me, as though I knew the answer. Where does this leave me if I decided to help this so–called NIS department. Who would protect me, who could I call if I needed assistance? These questions were popping up over and over again. If I knew what to do, that would be fine. Not being in Ireland, I don't have the assistance of friends. I only have this person who is sitting in front of me to communicate with. What if she isn't who she says she is? This was turning out to be a much more devious situation than I had anticipated. Which way to go was a very demanding process? I either had to put my trust in Phoebe or not. Almost sure that each country had something to loose, but which one could I trust the most.

My mind was now in a greater quagmire and I was afraid of overloading it. We finished eating and the conversation was a far more serious occasion than I had hoped. It was time to depart from the harbour area. The restaurant called a taxi. The time was now one thirty in the morning, we were bogged down in nitty gritty elements of the future role I had to play with this Triad family. Not having a chance to view the spot where my late father had this so–called accident. We headed back to Jill's apartment. The evening had been revealing in one sense. I now knew a little more but could I believe what I just heard? Phoebe works for a British surveillance service. I am the pawn in the middle of an International drugs gang, and God knows what else, an elaborate trade by a Triad family! No, my father didn't tell me this would be the outcome of his legacy. Now I find out these others from England are trying to put this Triad gang out of business. That doesn't fill me with great confidence. It had now just occurred to me. Say if this Triad family decided to get rid of me after the will is read, who or what can stop them. What way can I protect myself of such a thing happening? Being in the NIS doesn't make them invisible and they also can be killed. I asked Phoebe if she knew whether my father was murdered or not. She huffed and puffed, but didn't give me a straight answer. So I was left to draw my own conclusions. Making our way to the taxi and about halfway through the journey, Phoebe put her head nestling on my chest. Her child like charm began to shine through. "Do you still like me after what I just told you Jason?" I sat and contemplated for a moment. "Why of course, it's my fathers fault that I am in this position now." She told me that it was comforting to hear me say that. Gently I put my arm around her shoulders and let her nestle into my body. Now I felt in a relaxed state of mind. As we approached the apartment, Phoebe asked me if I would like to come in for a nightcap. Without hesitation, I accepted the invitation. Looking to see if the car I had seen earlier was anywhere to be seen. It was a soft and hazy night, with a gentle breeze in the air. We strolled from the taxi towards the apartment and in the distance you could hear the sounds of the night. We entered the apartment at two minutes to two. A quick glance at the clock above the fake fireplace in the lounge. "What would you like to drink?" She asked. "I don't mind, something with ice. A whiskey?" I walked over to the mantelpiece, where there were some miniature pictures hanging above the fireplace. As I looked at them, I could see that one of the pictures had been removed. From what I suspected it must have been some sort of family picture. Why had it been removed? Not that this would bother me, but maybe it had fallen. The question now entered my mind, as to how would I be able to check out that Phoebe worked for this NIS Department. I doubt if she carried a calling card. If I am to believe her, I will need a lot more convincing. Her story is plausible. She came back in with the drink for me. "Are you not having anything to drink yourself?" "No, I am tired, it has been a long day."

Putting the glass to my mouth, the tingling of the ice cubs hit my lips was like a velvet cushion caressing my tongue. "Well, here's to the future, what ever it may hold." She smiled and I looked in her eyes. That same smile had caught my attention the other night. I knew there and then, that I wanted to take her in my arms kiss her and caress her. Slowly I approached her, wondering if she felt the same way about me. I stretched out my arm, put it around her waist and kissed her. She responded by pressing against my body and slowly tantalising me with an even more equally and seductive kiss. Her lips pressed against mine, the fusion of our tongues, the tingling sensation, when our bodies pressed against each other. "Jason, I wanted you to do that from the moment we met." Thinking to myself, so did I. "I didn't know, I would have been happy to oblige." We both laughed. "Jill is due home any minute, so we will have to delay our passion till tomorrow." It was hard to break away from her arms. One more quick kiss, to see if this was truly happening. Feeling that tingle flow down my whole body. Our arms parted and she had phoned for a taxi. I found myself now on my way back to my hotel. Having time to think on the way back in the taxi, but trying to think straight in these circumstances was easier said than done. Where do Anita–Mui and Susan come in to this scenario? It can wait until tomorrow. Just wishing to sleep now. It was a strange sensation, but I had a pep in my step as I got out of the taxi. Having a good look inside to see if my shadow from the other day was back on duty. No appearance, so I swiftly strode to the reception desk and picked up my key. No messages this time.

It was a gorgeous sunny Tuesday morning, the light protruding through the curtains. What is going to happen today? Triads, NIS, where will it all stop, or, is this just the beginning? Look what my father has got me into. We falsely assume, that we live our lives free from these monumental distractions. Trying to work out if I inherit my father's major portion of the business? Does this automatically make me a leading international smuggler? Will I be the target of other Triad families? Really, I am damned if I do and I am damned if I don't. Being in a no win situation at the moment. I can only cope with what is thrown at me, by virtue of how best to respond from a given situation. That choice may be out of my control and this makes it all the more dangerous, if I am backed into a corner. Not knowing what side to take is the biggest fear. Which one of them is telling the truth? Getting out of bed. It was eight fifty when I decided to take a shower. Feeling refreshed now and proceeded down to the lobby. Wishing to purchase a newspaper before I had something to eat. The unfolding events of the Triad trial was a concern, as it seemed that it was possible the same family may be involved with my father. Purchasing a paper, the headlines read "Government official bribed". Reading the small print. It stated that an official in the Department of the Marine, had passed on information to these Triads. Reading on, it said this person informed the family so as to pinpoint the accuracy of the positions of ship movements. These Triads could then plan their strategic movements and deliberately board the ship while at sea and remove their valuable cargo. It seemed all very well organised. Thinking then, how does Sun Yat Sen know these friends in the Public Registrars office? It certainly bears some resemblance to what my father was engaged in. I found it hard to believe, that Anita–Mui and Susan didn't know what was going on. After having some breakfast, I wanted to visit them in the shop. My thoughts were distracted by the influence of Phoebe and what she was up to. I needed to phone Sasha at home. I sat contemplating what was in the article in the paper. At that I extracted myself from my chair and walked to the public phone on the corner of the road. The phone rang at the house and they were all right. I told Sasha that I may be here for another while. Not wishing to say too much over the phone. It might be a good idea if I dropped into the local police station, to enquire about my fathers so called accident. So I decided to go to the police station and hopefully gain some insight into his death.

Making my way out of the hotel, a woman caught my eye. She had striking features like most Asian women and seemed to be staring at me. This puzzled me as I hadn't noticed this sort of behaviour before. Then a thought struck me, did she know me? Looking behind me to see if anyone other than I was there. No, well I suppose I shall still have to wonder. Was she working for this other family? Not knowing who to trust. Hearing my name being called. "Jason, is that you?" Getting nervous I looked around and this stranger that I had spotted on the far side of the road, was upon me. "It is Jason, isn't it?" My response was slow and cautious. "It all depends on who is asking." Her clear voice and precise pronunciation was a noticeable feature. "Let me introduce myself, I was a good friend of your late father. My name is Sally Yeh." She bowed and put her hand out to shake mine. "How does this friend know of my father?" Her strong but yet gentle manner drew my confidence out. "I had known him through business and also as a personnel friend." She appeared to be talking from deep within her conscious mind. "I was also in the jewellery business and your late father bought his jewellery from me. I am in the wholesale end of the market." Her words I felt, were that of a woman who had a profound understanding of my father. Suspecting that this woman was a very special personal friend of his. Now beginning to wonder how many special friends he had in this part of the world. Trying to draw her out to see if she knew of these other people in his life. "What do you want with Jason then? It appears to me that there is so many people that you could not trust and sometimes its hard to know which way to turn." Once again, she portrayed a positive and confident manner in her response. "Well, speaking for myself, I assure you that I am not in league with any such characters." My inner feelings were telling me that it was worthwhile listening to her. "That's good to know, but I still have my doubts. She asked me if she could talk to me in a private manner. I had the time and there is no harm in listening. So I agreed to the invitation. Thinking to myself, does everyone here have a double barrel name. "Will you join me in some tea?" She pointed to a small teahouse. "Certainly, if this is the place you wish to speak." We both sat down at one of the tables on the fringe of the traffic. When the waitress came and took our order, Sally–Yeh began to reveal things of my father. These unsolicited, verbal, intimate and personal details, would only be known by a very close, knowledgeable and intimate friend. She told of the times, when my father first entered into the jewellery business. Asking how long did she know my late father. "I must have known him in this region, for at least ten years. He, or should I say, they are one of my best customers."

I wondered what she knew of this other business with the Triads. "Did my Father always deal with the jewellery end of the business?" "Yes, he phoned in, or he would personally call in to see me, constantly increasing the amount of units which they required. Business seemed to be going exceptionally well." I was curious to find out just who they were. "When you say they, whom do you mean?" She was slow and deliberate in her answer. "I mean Anita–Mui and your father. Never having much dealings with her." By the sound of what she was saying, she hadn't much time for Anita–Mui. "How was the business doing in sales terms, when my father died?" She did seem to have a knowledgeable insight into the business. "Oh, I would say it is in the top end of the list for sales in this area. That is to say as a group, with combined sales for all the shops." Sally Yeh had given me trinkets of selected information. So I decided to inform her of exactly why I was here. I wished to gauge her reaction. "I am here to inherit his majority share of the business." I could see her dissecting my words. "Your father was a calculating person and was always one step ahead of his Asian family. If you are successful, you will inherit quite a tidy sum. Are you going to continue on with the business? If this is not an inappropriate question?" Fishing for information I could sense her inquisitive nature. "That I do not know, I suppose I could sell my share to Anita–Mui. Do you think she would be in a position to purchase such a share?" I noted with interest, that she did not wish to commit herself to any side. "That I couldn't say, but there are many who would be glad of the opportunity to acquire your share of the group." I now wanted to enquire about my father. "Did you see my father before he died?" "Yes and I was talking to him." "Did he seem alright, or did he seem agitated?" "He did seem nervous, like he was always looking over his shoulder. Why, do you think it was more than an accident?" She was now gauging me, by the question I was asking her. "Well, put it this way, he was careful where water was concerned." She was interested to see if I had faith in the local police. "Have you been to the police yet?" She took a keen curiosity in my reply. "No, I was just about to give them a visit. I don't know if they will give me, or they are capable of giving me any further information on what happened to my father. Its something I have to do, at least I have to find out what the official stance is on his death." Her advice was a welcome addition to my inner state. "Be careful whom you speak to." "Yes, I see by the article in the paper at the moment, you wouldn't know who you are talking to." She nodded her head in agreement with me. "Yes, this is true, be wise in the face of adversary. If you need anything, or need some personal assistance in the ways of our traditions, don't hesitate to ask. Or if you wish to phone me, here is my phone number." She appeared to be genuine. "Do you know of the one called Sun Yat Sen?" Her hesitation was there to see in her face. "I have heard of the one you mention. But this only through your father and he did not go into any great detail. To me your father had reservations about his so called friend." Sally Yeh was certainly giving me an insight, that was not forthcoming from Anita–Mui. "Do you think it wise of me to trust him while I am here?" This question would draw on her loyalty and possibly question her own stance. "That I cannot say. You would be wise to keep your own council on such delicate matters." She was not to be drawn on which side of the dividing line she would take. "I understand, I am imposing on you too much. Please forgive for my inexperience in such delicate matters. I am not sure of the ways of your country." Her glance and warm expression set me at ease. "That is quite alright Jason, we all have our own ways of dealing with unpleasant quandaries. While you are in my country, you should visit the Island of Lamma. I do think that you would find something of interest to you." Is there more there to discover about my father? Is she sending me a signal to visit the island? I thought a more direct approach would be suitable. "Why do you wish me to visit the island?" The passion in her voice was plain to hear. "I come from the island, it is beautiful and a tight family knit community. Your father paid frequent visits there." I felt there was much more here than I could make out. To visit an obscure island on a regular basis must have had some attraction. It could hardly have been another woman and maybe this woman in front of me. At this point, I calculated that anything was possible where he was concerned. Sally Yeh was one more mystery in an ever more demanding plot. Where was this equation going to lead? Was there nowhere that he had not touched? Sasha at home, wouldn't have been able to cope with this. The many varied characters that he had taken on board in his worldly travels, would have taken a great toll on my mother. Did he get caught up in the intrigue of avoiding the powerful state machine of the Chinese Government, or simply the more realistic aims of making as much money as he could. My own belief at this point in time was leaning towards the latter. But then again, you always tend to think the worst in these circumstances. I decided to ask Sally Yeh a direct question. "Did my father know someone on the island?" Her sheepish answer was a way of making me more interested in visiting the island. "That is for you to find out Jason. I think you will learn more about him, if you do visit the island. You alone can be the judge of what you find there. It may help resolve some of the harsh thoughts that you have about your late father." These words penetrated my brain. I suppose if it was possible to find any form of positive contribution, it would lift my weary heart. "May I say Sally Yeh, you seem to know much about my late Father. As much as any person I have encountered so far." She looked at me with a questionable gaze. "That may be so Jason, but there is good in all of us, if you only look for it." Her contribution was common sense as usual. "Very wisely spoken." Thinking it prudent, to visit the island as soon as possible. "You have me searching my brain trying to picture what way my father acquitted himself on this island." Her vaguely implied answer was a source of intrigue to me. "Good Jason, at least you are not jumping to conclusions. It is now up to you to search out a more fuller picture than you already have. I have to bid you farewell for the time being. Remember Jason, no one else would have told you of this. By the way, I recommend that you don't mention this to the woman and daughter." She left me in no doubt, that these two women were not to be trusted. With that, this fine featured woman with her long black hair, was walking away from me within the vanishing mire of a populous crowd. She had left a card with her phone number on it, along with a message saying, phone me if you need anything. Taking it in my hand I turned it around. There was an address on the back of the card. This address was on the island of Lamma. She was determined to have me visit this island. This person whom had just breezed in and out of my life, left me with an air of optimism. Not all was doom and gloom. Contemplating my next move when I got a tap on my right shoulder. "Hallow Jason, how are you today?" It certainly was a surprise to see her face. "Fine and how are you keeping Phoebe?" My mind was scrambling this information it had just been furnished with into some sort of order. Do I tell Phoebe or not? As I sat there the burden became heavier. But I didn't know what to expect on this island, so silence was the benchmark I had adopted on this matter.

Although Anita–Mui and Susan were in the background, why didn't my father tell them of this island. "Have you planned anything for the day Jason?" What do I say. "I thought about going to one of the islands." It seemed strange to me that Phoebe was always around just after I had talked to someone of interest. "Were you keeping a close eye on me?" She didn't like the question asked of her and plied on with her own follow up. "Do you mind if I tag along?" "Not in the least, the company would be great. Have you heard any more about this Triad family?" There was a stillness in her voice. "No, but I am concerned for your safety Jason." "Well, that's good to know." I retorted. She also in my mind, was keeping tabs on me. "You have to be careful of these people Jason, they are dangerous. The NIS are monitoring the chief suspects in this family. We will need your help Jason to expose them, if we are to force the hand this Triad family. Not alone will it benefit you, but the people who are suffering at their hands." I must say she was good at promoting the NIS. "No need for the speech Phoebe." She tried to brush it aside. "Now Jason, where did you say we were off to?"

# Chapter

# V

**W**e headed in the direction of the ferry terminal. Getting to the Central District Outlying Islands Pier and looking at the bulletin board, I suggested we go to Lamma Island. Phoebe had no objection. Purchasing two return tickets to the Sok Kwo Wan village. The next ferry was leaving at eleven thirty. It would be a short wait. We boarded the ferry with many more day trippers. Our trip was pleasant and enjoyable. On our arrival, we discovered that there were no cars or buses. So one had to use a bicycle or use ones feet. "It's a good way to get around, free from the traffic, but endure the mass throng of the people. I doubt if one could ever feel alone in this part of the world." The multitude of people gives you very little space to hide in. Although when it comes to solving crimes no one can be found. It had taken about forty five minutes over on the ferry. The sun was beaming down and the water was calm, it was very relaxing. We sailed into a small hamlet, you could see the hills from the ferry. On disembarkation, we had a pleasant stroll on the pier by the restaurants. Passing a Tin Hall Temple on the way. You could appreciate the history attached to the island. We came upon a path that ascends up into the hills. This gave us a spectacular view of the jagged cliffs. At this point we decided to lie in the sun. The features of Phoebe lying beside me, encroached on my thoughts. I turned towards her and at the same time she turned to me. Our eyes gravitated towards each other and our lips succumbed to the melting pot of passion. The constant flow of people did in fact encroach on our passionate entanglement. We parted form our warm embrace, to the discreet vision of sober contentment. "What are you thinking about Jason?" "It would be nice to hold you in my arms without so much company in our midst's. What do you think Phoebe?" "Yes it would be nice alright Jason. It would be nice to say the things I would like to say to you also Jason. I am interested in what you would say to me." Her inquisitive mind always working. "Well Phoebe, for one thing you look beautiful to me and you have a way of capturing my inner emotions through your eyes. I feel that I can talk to you and you respond without words." She thought for a moment. "That's certainly deep and something to say Jason." I was getting sucked into the vision I was seeing in front of me. My thoughts weren't focused on the immediate problem of finding out where this address was on the island. "I could stay here for the rest of the day, but we should get back to the village." "Yes, maybe its time to do that Jason, but we will have to catch up on where we left off at a later stage." "I agree with that Phoebe, we will catch up on where we left off."

Smiling, we dragged ourselves to our feet, the sun was beaming down from the blue sky above. The village itself wasn't too far away. In my mind, I was beginning to focus back to the task in hand. Number 37 Kai Shun road, to be exact. This was my chance to investigate the subtle questions that Sally Yeh had neatly unravelled in my mind. As we came back to the outlying houses of the village, my eyes began to scour the immediate area for this road. Knowing I was close to finding out more facts about my Father. Noticing the name plaque of the road we were approaching. It was the road which was my target. "Shall we stride up this road Phoebe?" "Why not?" Her voice echoed. It was a narrow lane type road, with wall front gardens as entrances. You could not see directly into the front gardens, without jumping up to take a peek over. As we walked up this road, I saw number 37. The house that Sally Yeh had left the address of. From afar it didn't seem any different than the others. But when you got close to it, it became apparent that it was different. Some children were playing in what looked like a courtyard. Also on the side of the front pier was a plaque stating it was an orphanage. This had me thinking, what had my Father to do with this place? We strode on our way for something to eat, without Phoebe knowing the secret I was withholding. It looked like an oasis for the young people that lived there. It would be prudent to phone Sally Yeh later and ask her to explain what significance the orphanage had. All sorts of thoughts were running through my mind. In the distance were some craft shops to our right and I could see Phoebe's eyes light up. "Do you mind?" "No, not in the least, come on." Walking in the direction of the craft shops. "Haven't we rambled a fair bit today, don't you think Phoebe?" She seemed relaxed. "We have and we haven't finished yet." Entering our first craft shop. I counted about ten when we were coming up the road. Indeed, it looked like we hadn't finished walking yet. It was getting late in the day, as we strode out of the last craft shop. "The ferry will be leaving soon Phoebe, so we better make our way back to the pier." She looked disappointed. The orphanage was still playing on my mind. Boarding the ferry at five thirty that evening. Phoebe had bought some gifts to bring back after this assignment was over, or so she said. She was thrilled, as she thought she had a genuine piece of history in one of the vases she bought. We were sailing out of Sok Kwo Wan harbour, when Phoebe turned to me. "There is something I want to tell you Jason. Our intelligence is telling us that some members of this Triad family, may try to abduct you." I looked at Phoebe with my mouth open. Why was she telling me this now? "They may try to force you to sign over your share of the business to them. We believe that this is a renegade section, trying a solo run." "I feel very solo now. Do you think it may happen?" "We really can't tell, I am afraid. So you have to watch your back from now on". "Its more than my back I have to watch." Came my reply. "You will have to be careful of who you talk to." "Does that include you Phoebe?" She smiled. I still wanted to go back to the island later that night, but this new information stopped me in my tracks. Was Sally Yeh a decoy to lure me onto the island? I would find out later that night. Trying now to decipher which thoughts would hold the right move for me. Why now did Phoebe tell me this news? Was the NIS trying to keep me in a fish bowl? Trying to starve me of any outside influences. They wished me to be a prisoner of their whims. Well not for me. I decided that any interlopers would be treated with respect, but that I would be the person making up my mind. We approached the ferry pier in the Central district. We were both tired. I could see the car from the NIS was stationary at the exit gate. Keeping a close eye on Phoebe and me. This could cause me a problem later that night. "Well Phoebe, here we are, back on dry land once again. I am going to have an early night, I am tired from the walking today." "I think I will do the same Jason." We walked to my hotel from where I phoned for a taxi. All the time the NIS car was discreetly in our shadow. The taxi arrived within five minutes. Phoebe headed for her destination. The car was still there as I walked for the elevator. Entering the room I noticed the chair had been removed form its usual position. Closing the door behind me and I was startled to see Sun Yat Sen sitting in the seat. Controlling my emotions I quickly quipped. "I see you don't need a key?" He just passed off my remark, as if nothing had occurred. "Such consequences are of minor detail. I am here on a more delicate matter. The one named Phoebe is in fact a NIS agent." "What is a NIS agent when its at home?" I threw in for good measure. "Then you are telling me that you do not know of this?" I was surprised by his remark. "That is precisely what I am telling you. How do you know this anyway?" "We have our sources." I wondered what their sources were saying about me. "Tell me, who is this we?" His cautious, but reserved attitude did not astound me. "That again is of now concern to you." He certainly could be abrupt. "What does NIS stand for?" "It is an agency for the British Government." I was more curious and pushed the notion. "Precisely what kind of agency are you talking about?" His evasive answer was causing me some concern. "It's an agency that you do not wish to know about." I think I had thrown him off course with my quick reactions to his questions. At least, it didn't seem that I had known that Phoebe was an agent. "How did you come by this information?" "We have people working in many areas." I thought to myself, I bet you do. "What does this have to do with me?" "Well it's what she, or who she is after is our concern." "What do you mean?" "Jason, she may be after some of the people I am connected to." "This surely is a problem for you." "This is where you are wrong Jason. It includes you, as she has befriended you, now why is this?" "This is news to me, I don't know." "You better not, or it could be a nasty bit of trouble for you." Sounded like a veiled threat. "What do you mean by that?" He didn't stand on ceremony. "You can work that out for yourself." I wanted to know how much they knew about Phoebe.

I felt I had pushed as far as I could, otherwise I would reveal my hand. "You watch your step with this Phoebe. I wish you to tell me anything that may occur out of the ordinary." "If you insist." His demanding voice was a constant reminder that I was on his territory now. "I do Jason." Wondering who was the person giving Sun Yat Sen inside information on NIS agents. It might be an inside agent, Phoebe may be in danger. I must tell her later, that they know of her secret. Obviously they were worried enough to send Sun Yat Sen to warn me. His voice once again took advantage of my left eardrum. "I must depart now Jason. When the need arises I will see you." With that he vanished from my sight. It was imperative to keep a low profile later tonight. Heading down to the restaurant, with the sound of the warning from him playing in the back of my mind. Here I was going to make plans to execute my disappearing act later tonight. I now knew that Sun Yat Sen and his colleagues, would be keeping an eye on the NIS agents and more than probable, on me. Those very agents would be outside tailing me later on. I wanted to phone Sally Yeh. So I took a walk up to Nathan road and phoned her from the public box there. Dialling the number I heard the receiver being lifted on the far end. I needed to be careful to whom I was talking to. "Is that you Sally Yeh?" I said gingerly. "It is I Jason, where are you phoning from?" There was a silence on the other end of the line. Then came. "I was waiting for your call." Was she physic I wondered. Then I got to the point of my call. "Will you meet me later tonight on the island?" My request didn't ruffle her. "If you so wish, Jason." "If it would be possible, I would like to meet you at eight forty five, if that's OK?" "I don't see a problem with that." She sounded a little apprehensive, but then again why wouldn't she be. "I will meet you at the orphanage, at that time then, and try to keep a low profile." The other end of the receiver went dead. It had been a sharp short conversation she didn't hang around. Was there an eavesdropper to our conversation, this I wondered? Seeing the car that had tailed me earlier, parked at the far side of the road. It had two occupants in it. The time was now seven thirty and the ferry left at seven forty five. I had scheduled to meet Sally Yeh at eight forty–five. Now to get on the ferry without them following me on board. Deciding to cut through the Central Park, this would mean that the people following me would either have to drive the car and one would have to follow on foot. Thus I will have a better chance of undoing their tight hold on me, by splitting them up. By the time they realised what was happening, I was half way through the Park. This gave me the extra time I needed to catch the ferry. Just making it onboard as it was tugging out to sea. Seeing the gangplank being removed from the pier as the NIS agent came screeching to a halt. He threw a paper on the ground in disgust. It felt good to be able to out–manoeuvre two professional agents like that. I was now on my way to Lamma Island. The vanishing lights of Kowloon disappeared from my sight. It was a calm night for sailing. The gentle thudding of the engine against the caressing ripples of the water made for a serene crossing.

It was eight twenty, when the lights of Sok Kwo Wan came into view. I only hoped I knew what I was doing, meeting Sally Yeh alone. We entered the horseshoe harbour on time. So was I about to uncover another chapter in the jigsaw of my father's life? The one he so conveniently left behind, when he came home to Ireland. I guess only time will tell. When the ferry came to a halt and we disembarked, I waited for all the passengers to file past me. I just wanted to make sure, that I was the last one leaving the ferry. If Sun Yat Sen had sent someone to follow me, they were doing a good job. Walking past the many culinary delights of the harbour. To many what looked like gastronomically fulfilled paying customers were in abundance. I knew I needed to get my bearings. Taking my map from inside my jacket, I pinpointed the way to the orphanage. The streets were dimly lit. The drizzly surround of mist didn't help matters, especially when it came to vision. Catching a glance of a figure in the distance I hoped it was she. She moved quickly and greeted me with a smile. "We meet again Sally Yeh." "Yes

Jason, but this time on my homeland. I feel a bit safer here and more secure." I was curious bout her fear. "Why is this, do you not fear for your safety?" Her remark now put me in fear. "I am afraid, there are many paths to cross." "Has the death of my Father brought you anguish." "Yes, in many ways, as regards the orphanage. You see Jason, your father paid for the day–to–day running costs. This was a burden I, nor the local community could bear." I was now inquisitive, "Why should he do this?" You could see in her face, that she had lost a guardian of her wishes and dreams. "He felt it a duty and with the extra money he was making on the side, that it was a good cause to support." I threw in a slight twist, to the story she told. "Of course with a little persuasion from your good self." She looked annoyed, as she further explained her liaison with my father. "It took a lot more than that Jason. A lot of people on this island, barely eke out a living on the land, so they are forced by the harsh realities of life, to supplement their earnings. This may be to join a Triad gang. If they get caught, they may spend the rest of their life in prison. These children that you see here, are abandoned by their mothers, and they have nowhere else to go. We provide an education, food and shelter for them. Now with your father dead the prospect of the orphanage closing looms nearer." "How can I help in this matter?" "If and when you inherit your father's share of the business, you can then by your own choice, decide to grant a monthly payment to keep the orphanage open. This can come out of the profits of the business. A lot of the kids fathers, that are in jail, worked for the Triad gang that your Father did business with. He felt it his duty, to provide for these children." The Triad family didn't seem fit to bestow upon their own foot soldiers, a decent way to live. "So will you at least think about what I have said, with regard to the orphanage, Jason?" I knew I had to listen to this well–intentioned woman. "Yes, you have my word on that." I felt an internal bond with what she was doing. I was now inquisitive to find out what they knew at the jewellery business about this. "Do they know this at the Jewellery shop? I mean, about what you do here?" Sally Yeh obviously didn't wish to over expose the community on the island to any further encroachment from the Triads. "No, your father kept this a secret. He and I felt it wise that the local

community had suffered enough from the hands of the Triads."
I felt enough courage now, to approach her with a more intimate
question. "Along with a lot of these things, what was your
relationship with my father?" Her straight and frank answer
caught me by surprise. "We were lovers, he would visit me on a
regular basis. As I have said, I sold jewellery to him. That's how
we met. Enough of this, it's now the orphanage I care about.
You must not judge your Father too harshly, he had a good side
to him." I was finding out his, but it was on the far side of the
world to where his first family were living. "So it would seem."
I was now discovering a part of my father that little was known
about. In a short time I had to head back to the mainland soon.
"I will think seriously about what you have asked of me Sally
Yeh. My intention is to leave now." "Be careful of how you go
Jason, take great care." "I will Sally Yeh and you do the same,
until we meet again."

I drifted off into the misty night. Learning something more
about my late father. The pier came into sight, I could see the
reflection of the lights on the water. Hearing the hum of the
engines I knew the ferry was ready for boarding when I arrived
at the pier, with a slight chill in the air as we departed from the
island. Having a greater understanding of the people that lived
there. This had me thinking in a slightly different light about my
father. He might not have been as harsh, as I had judged him
to be. We were now entering Victoria Harbour. Finding myself
wondering if the two men from the NIS were still there? No
sign of the car in the immediate vicinity. It was ten thirty on a
Tuesday night when I was stepping off the ferry from Lamma
Island. Feeling a heaviness in my legs, it had been a tiring day.
I caught a taxi to the hotel. It was with surprise that Phoebe
was in the lobby of the hotel when I arrived. "Are you alright
Jason?" "Why shouldn't I be?" What did she know. "This is
news you don't want to hear. We had two agents tailing you
tonight." "Really, did you?" "You know we did, where did you
disappear to?" Her attitude was now somewhat unpleasant.
"That, I am afraid is my business." She didn't seem pleased
with the attitude I was taking. "Well one of these agents was
found about half an hour ago, with his throat cut, lying dead in a
back alley. He was assigned to following you Jason." This took

me completely by surprise, I didn't know what to think. "What does this mean, Phoebe?" "We are sure that he was tortured and we are not sure how much they obtained from him." "What sort of information are you talking about here Phoebe? I hope you didn't tell him that I knew, that you were a NIS agent." "No, you do not have to worry Jason, of course not." Contemplating whether I should tell her of the earlier visit. "I had a visit earlier, from Sun Yat Sen. He knows that you are a NIS agent. He also asked me if I had known of this? Obviously telling him no, then this happens." "What time did this occur Jason?" "It must have been around seven to seven fifteen. I got the impression that they knew you were after someone in authority. But didn't know how much you knew." Now trying to recall what was said. "He said they had people discreetly placed." "This is no surprise. I had better not be seen with you Jason, as they may have people following me. Do you know if they followed you earlier tonight?" "I didn't get that impression." "OK, I will leave through the side entrance. I will phone you here at the hotel later. Don't mention anything about what has transpired tonight on the phone. If you are asked, keep it uncomplicated and simple. Is this clear Jason?" She must suspect that the phone is being bugged. "Yes, just like a casual conversation." "Precisely, keep them off the scent Jason, watch yourself, its getting rather dangerous out there." This is the second person today to say this to me. "I will be alright Phoebe, don't you worry." With that she was gone. It was even more confusing. Not really knowing who to trust. I was now feeling nervous, more nervous than I had been. Heading up to my room and wondering if the same scene, would greet me as earlier tonight. I opened the door with trepidation. But seeing the chair in its rightful place put me at ease somewhat. Hearing the news of the murder of the NIS agent had me on edge. Deciding to take a quick look around the room. This I did. Having bought a paper earlier, I sat down and began to read. The trial of the Triad bosses was still headline news. It seemed they had disposed of some of their competitors on a nearby island. A certain island jumped into my thoughts. The phone rang in my room and I jumped. What the hell am I doing, its only the phone. I picked up the receiver feeling uneasy. The sound of Phoebe's voice on the other end, came as a relief. "Did you get something to eat yet?" I really couldn't focus, I fumbled for the right words. "I managed to grab a bite in the restaurant at the hotel." She persisted in her question. "What did you have to eat then?" What did I have to eat then! What sort of a question was that! I said under my breath. "I can't remember", hearing myself say. Thinking this was a pointless conversation. Does she know what she is saying? Were these unknown assassins outside the hotel right now? If they could take a life without a whimper, surely it wouldn't bother them to take mine. The questions were rolling around in my head. What brought me back to reality was the sound of Phoebe's voice on the other end of the receiver. "Jason, Jason, are you there?" "Yes, I am sorry, my mind was somewhere else, what did you say?" "Will you be going to the Public Registrars office tomorrow, Wednesday? I thought the authorities have to verify your registration?" "Oh yes, it had slipped my mind. I have an appointment at ten fifteen in the Foreign Affairs section of the Department." Her invitation came at the right time. "If you like, I will accompany you there?" Thinking it might be wise to have someone on my side. "Yes, that would be good of you." "I will meet you at the hotel in the morning then." "That's fine, until we see each other in the morning then." I put the receiver down. Not knowing if I would get any sleep this night. It was eleven fifteen when I slipped under the covers. I surprised myself, by the amount of sleep I did actually get. My eyes unlocked at seven thirty, it was another warm and humid day. I lay in the bed for a short while, and then a shower freshened me up. I didn't know what the day ahead held in store for me, and I didn't fancy finding out.

It was eight o'clock on a sunny Wednesday morning when I pulled up the blinds of the hotel window. Knowing I had to go to the Public Registrar office, for ten fifteen this morning. Phoebe didn't say what time she would call to the hotel. On the way down to the restaurant, I looked about for any unwanted attention and headed straight to the paper vendor on the far side of the road, to pick up a daily newspaper. Acquiring one, I headed for the hotel restaurant. Ordering some Chau Mieng with egg, orange juice and tea. As I sat there reading the paper, the reality of the trial of the Triads hit me. They did have a powerful presence in society here. I wondered if Sun Yat Sen was making a play to control the jewellery shops. He knew enough about my fathers' practices, to engage in a partnership with his sister. It would explain his presence in my room last night. Reading the trial notes, it seemed putting money in the right government officials' hand, was half the battle. If the NIS is involved, it means that there must be a significant abuse of power by officials. Noteworthy amounts of illegal contraband substances must be getting into Britain. This of course presuming that none of the NIS agents were involved in any wrongdoing. Contemplating these unusual circumstances before Phoebe arrived. Arriving by taxi, in the background a car was following. "Are you alright Phoebe? This must be a shock for you all." To be honest she really didn't seem all that put out by it. "Yes, it has us all on edge. Let's me and you take a walk Jason." We walked in the direction of Nathan road. The appointment was in the Tung Sun Commercial centre, on Hong Kong Island this morning. Having to make our way to the ferry. It would leave from the Tsim Sha district. Phoebe told me how she had feared for her own life. "I may go back home Jason, it is getting very dangerous here." "I feel the only way to defeat these pariahs is to put them away for a long time. Would you agree with me Phoebe?" "Yes, I do agree with you Jason." Here was me telling a professional, how to confront her dilemmas. Funny enough I didn't feel out of place saying these things to her. "These Triads thrive on fear, that's how they maintain their stranglehold on power Phoebe. Who better to be in a position than you". Her response was rather distant. "I know this Jason, but I fear for us all." "I am sure you are not the only person with those fears Phoebe." "It has become a much more dangerous a situation than was anticipated. I will help you in as far as I can." "You can get out now Jason, without any recriminations." I was here on a mission and I intended to carry on, until I'd seen it through. Wishing to let her know this. "I am in it up to my neck and I am here to stay. My father asked me to contest this reading of the will, because he knew that this Triad family would try to take advantage of the situation. In doing so they only create more orphans." Now I may beginning to reveal maybe more than I wanted to. "The other night when I slipped away from the hotel, I went to Lamma Island. My father with the help of a friend set up an orphanage. This is for the children of the members of the Triads, who have been put in jail. The children have been abandoned by their mothers, because their fathers may have to serve life in prison. The orphanage will have to close, if I don't provide the funds. They don't know anything about this in the jewellery shop." "We in the agency, don't have anything in the files about this orphanage." Now I had realised that I had furnished her with information that she didn't originally have. "No, why should you? It wasn't a moneymaking operation. It was his way of putting something back into the community. The Triads didn't bother doing anything for their own loyal community." "So there was a compassionate side to him." "Is there not that side to us all?" "Not with these Triads Jason. May I visit it with you?" She seemed to know a lot about these Triads. Being somewhat caught off guard with her request to see the orphanage, but I didn't see any problems. "I don't see why not. I will make arrangements for us to visit soon. It is not in my hands". We made our way to the ferry, getting there just in time to catch it. It was now nine thirty, we sailed out of Star Ferry pier. "Have you read the papers in the last few days?" "Yes, do you mean the articles on the Triads?" "They have held people hostage for money, so just be careful Jason. Don't bury your head in the sand." The ferry sailed into Wan Chai Ferry pier. Docking at nine fifty, time was on our side. I thought if Phoebe was right, they might try to kidnap me at a future date. Where did Sun Yat Sen come in, this puzzled me. I was sure that they wouldn't let me stroll into the shop and let me have a say in the running of the business. We caught a tram to the Wan Chai station. It was a short walk to Lockhart road. The building was a throw back to the bye-gone days. But once inside, the modern facilities jumped at you. We made our way to the Foreign Affairs section. Approaching a hatch, I knocked on it and a pleasant looking woman peered out. "May I help you sir?" "My name is Mister Byrne, I have an appointment to check if my registration is in order. There is a reading of my late fathers will in the next few days. "Will you wait there for a moment please sir?" I sat back down in the wooden chair provided. As Phoebe and myself were the only people in the room, we sat and looked at each other.

It was a hallow room, with scant furniture. An odd picture, of the seafaring days gone by adorned the walls. Phoebe and I didn't want to say too much, in these intimidating surrounds. We started to chat about the weather, when suddenly a woman's frame appeared from behind the hatch and quickly disappeared again. Was there something wrong with my application? This thought ran through my mind. Was my passport in order? The feelings emanating from the room were not good. The situation was exasperating to say the least.

"Mister Byrne." The name came floating over the counter. I stood up and said, "Yes." Then a stern voice echoed in my direction. "Will you come this way please?" This in my mind didn't feel good. Asking me to step behind the doors of power, what evil atrocities had befallen on the poor mortals that had gone before me? My heart was beating faster now, with every step I took. Then the door opened, I stepped through, glancing at Phoebe as I disappeared inside. In front of me sat a poker-faced man in a dark suit. His sallow face hid the power it transmitted to me, his quarry. He had black hair, combed back with gel, craggy nose and deep eyes. Not the sort of person you would nominate for a portrait. His lips were thin and his smile wiry. I sat in the chair ashen face in front of his desk. He resembled a headmaster in school. "Mister Byrne, is it your first visit to our country?" I replied with the hint of a tourist, "Why yes it is." I found myself folding my arms. "I see you are the son of the late Mister David Byrne. Owner of the Jewellery Kingdom business." "This is correct." This may mean that they accept my legality and the reason I am here. "I see you are here to contest the estate of your late father." The paperwork which you deposited with our office is in order. There are some legal matters that need to be addressed. These are being dealt with as expeditiously as possible." I was curious to know what legal matters. "Which legal matters are these then?" "Most of the profits must remain in this country. If you live outside Hong Kong, you will only be allowed to repatriate some fifteen percent of the profits in any one year." Trying to keep the money in their country. "I see, and if I don't agree to this?" "If you decide to forego this legal requirement, we will set up a trust and from this trust a percentage of the profits will

72

be forwarded to your account. Of course this account will have to be set up here in this country. If you set up an account of your own accord and channel the profits into this, well, let's say the percentage you may repatriate will be greater." "I see you are well drilled in this line of monetary illusion." "That may be the way you wish to see things. You have to understand, that I come across many such cases each year." Covering all their options I see. So what he was really saying was that I couldn't take the money and run. "You will have to sign a legally binding document. This will commit you to the appropriate structure of the monetary fund. Is this clear with you Mister Byrne?" Well it looked like I had no other option. "Yes, may I think about I it for a few moments?" "Why yes, if you wish to confer with your friend outside, please do so." "Yes, I would like to do that at this time." With that I left the room. Telling Phoebe of the financial restrictions. She said that this sort of scenario is a common mechanism in Asia. Taking this to mean that I should procure the deal. Looking at the long term projections it might be wise. It will mean an annual or quarterly income to the house back home, to help with medical or other such debts that may occur. Anyhow, I may still have the option of selling my share to a local entrepreneur. I walked back into the office and agreed to sign the official document. This gentleman introduced himself as Mister Yip Fong Wah and handed me the document. I signed on the dotted line. The deed was done. As soon as I had signed, then seeing that he was preparing to give me my documentation back. But there was one difference, an added copy of my official authenticity document, this would bestow on me the equivalent right, as Anita–Mui and Susan. When it comes to the reading of the will, therefore I am a benefactor. Thanking the official for the documentation and bad him good day. It wasn't the outcome I had expected, but then not everyone will be happy. Obviously, my father had known about these drawbacks before he had his will drawn up to include me. Now beginning to think that his business partners were wary of him. As I was now sure he was of them. They may suspect me of playing his game now he wasn't around. It seemed, that he was always trying to be one step ahead of his business partners. As we can see, he had a good reason for this. The fact that he is no longer with us. I must see if he left any diaries. These I am sure, would contain many fascinating facts logged in some sort of chronological order. Wishing now to leave these premises as soon as possible. Phoebe was rather quiet as we made our way to the tram station. Telling her that I must phone the shop, to see if my father had left any personal belongings with them, for me. "Why is this Jason?" "What if my father had been thinking ahead, as I suspect he had. I know that he did keep many journals and diaries. Say if in this diary, the facts of his many transactions and the people he met were logged. Then say, beside these names, monetary figures were pencilled in with the amount and the date and place of these meetings. Would that not be a case scenario, for say killing him?" "You may have a point Jason, I never thought of him ever having any such written proof. If this were the case, it would not only implement the Triad family, but the political friends they bribed. It would give your father in their minds, a hold over them. So your theory could hold up to scrutiny Jason." The slight breeze was a refreshing welcome to the humid conditions. We were now on our way back to the mainland. I didn't know why I hadn't thought of this concept about my father earlier. But many things were now beginning to fit into place. My father's death may have been because of the knowledge he retained and the threat he posed. Not wishing to go to the shop without an excuse. I am sure they would be very interested in the outcome of my legal application. So this would be the ploy that I would use, to call on them. We set out for the shop as soon as we came ashore. Telling Phoebe, that I would be happier if I tackled this situation alone. She accepted this with some misgivings and said she would visit one of the stores opposite the shop. Entering the shop and as soon as I did, Anita–Mui appeared in front of me. Where did she come from? Out of thin air, I thought. "Greetings again Jason, I hope your news is in keeping with your wishes." "I could have wished for a greater outcome, but you can't always get what you wish for." How did she know so much? Had she the ear of someone in the Public Registrar office. "You must have bush telegraph here then?" "Many minds make light work." Its whose minds they have to call on worries me. "I would like to ask you Anita–Mui, did my father leave any personal belongings with you, for me?"

74

"If I remember rightly Jason, his satchel was deposited to his solicitor not long before he died." Little did she know, this was the news I had hoped for. Always thinking that he had left some notes regarding his business. Of course, this will only come to light when his will is read. I will have to wait till then to find out. I just called in to see if he had left anything in your possession. "I will say good day for the moment Anita–Mui." "As you wish Jason, you know where you may find me."

I walked out the door and left them with something to mull over. Phoebe appeared in the distance. As I walked in her direction I felt a shiver run through my back. I wondered now what they were thinking back in the shop. Does Jason know more than he is letting on? It was strange, having them wonder what I knew about their situation. Up to now they kept me in the dark. Telling Phoebe what had transpired, she asked me was it a wise move. "Is anything a wise move? I don't know if it was wise, but it felt good." "You know, this may give them enough ammunition to warrant your kidnapping. Say if the satchel is deemed to be in your possession and it may be thought by them, to have something to do with the business. It will have the effect of making you a target." She knew that is what I wanted them to think. "Undoubtedly, it will make me a target, but maybe that's what I am aiming for." "I think Jason, you may be playing a very dangerous game." She was probably right, but I wished to find out more about how my father died. "Well, they won't try anything at the moment." "Why is that Jason?" "If they did, they know that the NIS is keeping tabs on them. So where would they hide?" "I suppose you are right, as you don't have the share of the business yet. But one of the individuals in the group, may see you as a bargaining chip." "Em, I never thought of that situation." We strolled back down towards Nathan road. The sun was beaming down I was warm and thirsty. "What about a drink Phoebe?" Her eagerness seemed a bit over the top. "I don't see why not." We headed for the nearest hotel. Stepping into the lobby and headed for the bar. A beautiful looking woman stood in front of me, she dropped her bag. I stooped down to pick it up. She appeared very interested in me, thanking me and politely kissed me on the cheek. How charming I thought. That's when it must have happened.

Phoebe was nowhere to be seen. She had vanished. I looked around the hotel several minutes, but to no avail. Thinking she might have been called away suddenly. I was reaching for straws. I feared for her safety. Whom could I tell? The NIS was out, as I had told Sun Yat Sen I didn't know if she was an agent. And besides, how could I contact them, they hardly advertised in the local telephone directory. Then I thought why not Sally Yeh. There was no love lost between her and Sun Yat Sen and Anita–Mui. I found a phone in the hotel and called the number she had given me. There was no reply. She may be at the orphanage, or more likely out dealing in the jewellery trade. I felt I could trust her. She is the person that persuaded my father to finance the orphanage. In my mind, I deduced that she was a good natured person. A person you could call on, if you were in need. Well I was in need now. Where would they take Phoebe? At least if I had Sally Yeh on board, I might stand a chance of finding her. I will assume they have taken her, so as to bargain for the portion of my fathers business. It looked like someone other than Sun Yat Sen and his friends may have taken Phoebe. Recalling Phoebe saying about the possibility of a gang member, making a play for control of some of the territory of the family members, already involved in this area. Another gang member may be behind this O K. I would have to find Sally Yeh. If I go to Lamma Island and she is not there, I would be wasting valuable time. But what else can I do. So I headed for the ferry terminal. There wasn't another ferry for three quarters of an hour. I would call into the shop, to see if I could suss anything out there. I headed for Peking road, thinking of what they may know. Then I thought, say if it was them that had Phoebe removed and they did the same to me? This slowed the rate of my tempo and I quickly turned in my tracks. I was now heading for the ferry terminal, my original objective. In front of me stood a small craggy faced man, smoking a rolled cigarette. In his hand he held something what seemed to be a letter. He pushed it in front of me. I hesitated. Then taking the envelope in my hand. With that the man vanished. Opening the letter straight away. My first name was printed on the front of the envelope. It was a partial note from Phoebe and it read :– Jason, do not agree to anything that these people wish of you. I am fine. I thought what a professional under these trying circumstances. There was a footnote to the letter, very different writing on it. Thinking this may be the real message it bluntly stated :– If you wish to see Phoebe (Alive) again, you will follow the instructions below. I read the three very simple facts that they wished me to comply with. The main one being, when I inherit my share of the business, they will contact me at my hotel with further instructions. Presumably to dictate their intention of removing my majority share for the Phoebes` life. So it did initially regard my inheritance. Knowing I had to do something. Sally Yeh was a lifeline that I hoped I could depend on. Only time will tell. I could see the ferry terminal looming in front of me. A quick look around to see if I was being followed. It didn't look like it, but just to make sure. I began to cross the road into oncoming traffic. No one else following and I made it to the other side without anyone following. Entering a shop immediately off the pavement. Standing inside for a moment, looking back towards the path I had just weaved through the traffic. Nobody following in my footsteps. Thinking that I could ask Sally Yeh if my father left any diaries with her, or did she know of any? Boarding the ferry, I glanced over my shoulder, closely looking for any interlopers. We departed the Star Ferry pier at one forty five, I knew this would be a long shot, if she was at home or at the orphanage. But it would keep me away from the mainland and out of prying eyes. Then I thought, what if my father had shown the satchel to Anita–Mui, knowing that she would tell Sun Yat Sen. Using that satchel as a decoy. Where would he leave the real one? I might be heading in the right direction after all. Don't forget, I hadn't known this person existed until yesterday. She may hold the key to Phoebes release. My brain was again beginning to flow with ideas, mainly of ways of extraditing Phoebe from the dangerous situation she was in. If I hadn't have come, none of this would be happening. But then, I wasn't to know that I would meet Phoebe. Just try to think of ways of getting her out of this mess. The ferry journey gave me time to succumb to the mechanics of the situation. If it turns out, that Sally Yeh has the original satchel and it contains what I think it does, then I can use it as a bargaining chip for Phoebe's release. Too many ifs and buts at the moment. I have to find out if she has a satchel first. We were nearing the harbour of Sok Kwo Wan. Little did I imagine, that I would be back to appeal for help from the person that is appealing for help from me. It was two thirty earlier that day when I passed the orphanage. Knowing that Tin Hall Temple was on my route. If Sally Yeh is not at the orphanage, I will try her apartment. Previously she showed me the general building that her apartment was in. Arriving at the orphanage at two forty five. I stood outside, trying to rearrange in my mind the approach I would take. Entering the courtyard with apprehension. There was a chain hanging from a bell. Pulling the chain and the result it gave a pleasant chime. A stern looking woman appeared in front of me. She had the look of a woman who would quickly stop you in your tracks if the need arises.

"My name is Mister Byrne, I am a friend of Sally Yeh. Could you please tell me if she is here in the orphanage now?" A very stern answer emerged form the voice box of this bland woman. "No, she is not." Straight to the point. "I don't know when she will come." I will try one more question. "Do you know if she is at the apartment?" She certainly wasn't giving anything away. "This also I do not know. You should try the paper seller at the entrance to the apartment." I thought, a strange thing to say. "She will get mail there. It's beside the restaurant." "What restaurant?" "The one with the two birds on it." "The one with the two birds on it, do they fly away if you come near?" She burst out laughing. HA! HA! HA! HA! What I said must have been very funny. "No, No, sign with two birds." Beginning to see the irony in my answer. The woman stepped from the hallway and beckoned me to the entrance of the courtyard. She pointed in the general direction of the village. Thinking there must be more than one restaurant, with a sign with two birds on it. I began the walk towards the village. The sun didn't bother me so much now. It must be the fact that I had so much on my mind. That everything else is duped into forgoing, the realisation of the impact of the sun on ones body. Waving to the woman as I moved on. My thoughts were jumbled again. Catching a glimpse of the sign with two mallards on it. This must be the one. There was a paper seller outside. I went over to him and asked if he knew if Sally Yeh was at home. He seemed bemused by the question. "You are looking for her in what capacity?" This stunned me, the man in front of me was not a paper seller. If he was then I was a china man. A slight cough came from my throat, I cleared it. "I am only asking you if the person is at home at this present time." His uneasy presence was unsettling me. "I am not aware of her presence here at the moment." "Thank you good bye." I left the immediate area as quickly as I could. Was there someone else looking from afar. My mind switched to the woman at the orphanage. I could leave a message there for Sally Yeh, for her not to go back to the apartment. The woman there was genuine. The person I had just spoken to, was far to sophisticated to be a paper seller. The watch around his wrist was solid gold. He looked and sounded agitated, when I asked was she at home. This was not the actions of a constant beacon, that would greet you with a cherry smile. Far from it, quite the opposite. That person would have tried to tease me out, so as to engage me in conversation, to find out whom I was and what I wanted. Maybe I would make a good agent in the field, after all I only hope that the partner I would have, would be Phoebe. This person didn't seem to be from the NIS either, they would be more subtle. Whom did this person work for. Was Sally Yeh the target of someone else, rather than the kidnapper of Phoebe. This person did know about Sally Yeh and my father. Then suspecting, that he or she may think that she has some form of documentation. This is a dangerous situation for Sally Yeh and myself. This person who is behind the kidnapping, is closely involved with the people on the ground. I suspect that he or she, may have known that my frather did keep some sort of documentation. With regard to his business transactions and with the people he was dealing with. This I suspect means that the person knew my late father well. As far as Sally Yeh was aware no one at the shop knew about her or the orphanage. It doesn't look like they know about it or they would have someone watching. I could leave a message there. Arrange to meet her on the mainland. There was no one in sight when I approached the orphanage. Pulling the chain to ring the bell and the same woman came out. "May I leave this message with you for Sally Yeh?" I had written on it for her to phone or contact me and for her not to go to the apartment, as there were people watching it. She took it from me. The orphanage was vanishing from my sight as I made my way to the ferry pier.

# Chapter

# VI

I jumped on the ferry to the mainland. Kowloon was bustling with people, when we docked. Where to go and what to do, constantly rang in my mind. How else could I help Phoebe. The reading of the estate is going to be heard on Friday, only two days to do something. I felt the need to acquire my mobile phone and Dictaphone. So I found myself heading back to the hotel. It was now five thirty and finding that I constantly looked over my shoulder. My feet were laden with the body of a man, who was bereft of any ideas. How to get Phoebe out of her incarceration. Maybe Sally Yeh will have some ideas, lets hope so. I entered the hotel and while walking across the lobby I noticed the public phone. I automatically went straight to it and rang the orphanage. The phone rang and on the other side a woman's voice answered. "Hallo, this is the person who left a note for Sally Yeh." She knew whom I was and remembered me. "Oh that man, yes I gave her the note." "Did she say anything to you, regarding the note I left?" "No, she left straight away." At least she had received it. I had left my mobile phone number on the note, so she could contact me. Hopefully she hadn't phoned in the meantime. Heading straight to the room and peered out the window. Two occupants sitting in a car opposite caught my attention. They were there for the purpose of following me. I could slip away by the side entrance. Collecting my phone and Dictaphone, I again walked back to the lobby. Waiting for the right moment to exit the side entrance.

A minibus was pulling up to the front entrance. This was it. As the people got out I slipped out. My aim now, to get in contact with Sally Yeh. I also left word in the note for her, to meet me in Planet Hollywood at seven thirty this night. I needed to get away from the prying eyes of the streets. So I went down towards the quay area. Still keeping a constant watch on my back. Noting the H.K Culture Centre and the Chinese Arts and Crafts Centre. A good place to spend a few hours. These buildings also overlooked Planet Hollywood, so I could see if Sally Yeh was coming. Finding myself on Hankow road and I crossed over to the far side. Being able to see the jetty of the ferry from Sheung Wan District on Hong Kong Island would dock. For her to get to me here, she would have to change ferries on the same island. It was a good vantage point and I could go to the Terminal Shopping Complex, when it closed. Wondering what part Sun Yat Sen and his sister played in this plot. Staring out into the mass throng, when a familiar face caught my eye. It was Sally Yeh, she was early, in the wrong building. Maybe she was doing the same as me, keeping a watch and brief to seek out interlopers. I watched her enter the building and she headed for the left luggage section. She seemed to hand in a ticket. A small bag was passed over the counter. She took it and walked across to one of the seats in the café. She went to the counter and came back with a tray. After placing in on the table, she proceeded to the toilet with the bag, taking longer than normal in the toilet. What was in the bag, documents? When she reappeared from the toilet, she headed straight to the left luggage section and handed the bag back in. Then she sat back down at the table. Should I approach her, I didn't think so. Maybe her presence here was for the purpose of meeting someone other than myself. This is when my doubts set in about her. I watched as the culmination of time crept up on me. Striking while the iron was hot. So I decided to approach her. "Sally Yeh here you are." She jumped with surprise. "Jason, you scarred me." Noticing how taken aback she was, to see me there at this time. "I didn't mean to Sally Yeh, are you O K." "Yes what has happened, how come you are here at this tome?" Doubts were creeping into my mind, as if I should tell her or not. "Someone has kidnapped Phoebe." "What do you mean?

82

Why would they want to do that?" I thought it was plain. "Because of my inheritance." "I don't see the connection." Obvious to her it wasn't as plain as I thought. "They have threatened her life, if I don't give them my share of the business. They left, or should I say a messenger gave me the note with these words on it." She read the note. "Yes, but what connection has Phoebe to you." I could tell by this, that she didn't share the same appeal for a friend in need. "Well lets say, we are more than good friends and I wouldn't like to see anything happen to her." "When did this, so called kidnap take place and where?" "It was this very morning. In some coffee shop, I can't remember they gave me a note, stating not to tell anyone." Thinking I would throw in the character outside her apartment. "There was some stranger outside your apartment, that's why I left the note." Do I tell her that Phoebe is a NIS agent or was I going to far, as it was? "Also I must tell you that Phoebe is a NIS agent." "What is this NIS?" "It is a British Customs and Excise enforcement agency. They are here trying to catch and expose the Triad bosses. Those who run drugs and contraband into England. It seems that these people want a greater share in the business going to that country. My thinking is they had my father killed so they could achieve this aim. Guessing they didn't reckon I would come along and spoil the party." "Do the NIS know that Phoebe is in such trouble?" "Not that I am aware of, I haven't informed them." Sally Yeh recognised the delicacy of the situation. "This is a very delicate matter indeed." I then put a straight forward question to her. "Do you know anyone that can help?" "I may know one or two, who could help in such a situation." "I think Jason, the first thing is to find out where they are holding her. It may be on one of the islands." At least she was thinking of coming around to the idea of helping me. "What do you suggest we do Sally Yeh?" She looked at her watch. "It is now seven, I will phone some people. I wish you to go back to the hotel, so as not to draw to much attention on yourself and onto me. I will phone you on your mobile, when we are ready and we may have to move quickly." I wasn't all that hot on waiting in my hotel room. "Can't I come with you?" "Not at this point in time. I promise I will phone you, when I know something." With that, I know it was time to go. I would leave the building first. Gradually making my way towards the exit and out into the throng and disappeared exceptionally easily. At least something was happening and I had an air of expectation about me. Was it the right thing to do? Letting Sally Yeh know. Who else could I trust. Walking slowly up Nathan road. The lights of the night, were blazing in all their glory. It certainly wasn't the way I was feeling inside. The situation was hard to fathom and what would be the outcome? Would it be even more hazardous in the next few hours? Waiting for a phone call, in my room. I felt there must be something I can do on my own. Now recycling in my mind what had gone before me, feeling something can be done. The NIS office, the old looking shop front. Deciding to head there, without changing pace. Trying to find the road, it was near Mcdonalds. Slowly approaching Mcdonalds, there was a side road running down its north side. Hilwood road, I can vaguely remember. The last time I visited this area, was in daylight. My footsteps seemed to get louder the further down the road I walked. Like an echo reverberating off each wall. The road wasn't that well illuminated. I could why the NIS had an office here. Then it struck me, what am I going to do here. Not wishing to tell them that Phoebe was kidnapped. They might storm the wrong building and have her killed. I stood looking at the entrance door and pondered whether Phoebe's future would be better served in Sally Yeh's hands, rather than the NIS. I would phone Jill to see if she had heard from her. Phoning the apartment but received no answer. Thinking that I may go to the apartment. Once again I turned in my tracks and headed for the train station. Catching the first train out to the district where she lived. Walking to the exterior of the building, I saw that there were no lights on in the apartment from where I stood.

Just as I was about to find a place to sit and watch the building a noise came from the entrance gates. It was the sound of the electronic gates opening. A black jeep appeared from the building. It had all its windows blacked out. You could catch silhouettes of two women and two men in the back of the jeep. I knew I had to follow this vehicle. Able to hail a passing taxi telling the driver that I wanted to follow the jeep as soon as it pulled away. He had no problem with this request. Encouraging him, with an extra cash bonus if he tailed it to its destination. Its surprising how money melts inhibitions. The jeep pulled up to a halt. A large figure got into the jeep from the opposite side. My heart began to beat faster now, as we drove off after our quarry. "Don't lose them, whatever you do." He shook his head in response. "No, I am good driver, you don't have to worry." Thinking now that they might have Jill as well as Phoebe in the jeep. It was travelling at a steady pace, not suspecting that it had company. It started to manoeuvre down side streets. Slowing down so as not to draw too much attention to the taxi. "Keep them in sight, at all times." "This I will do." The jeep began to pick up speed. "Do you think they have spotted us?" The driver had a flair for this sort of thing. "No, they are free of the city now." Finding ourselves passing Sha Tin Racecourse. I only hoped we were not going into mainland China. Then the jeep pulled off to a side road. Thinking if we should go down this road? The taxi driver was now on new territory. "Do you know what's down there?" He did hesitate and I couldn't blame him. "I remember it as an old mine, it now closed". This may have been there resting place, their layer. "All right, will you write down where we are. I mean the name of the road and the district we are in.." "I no write down this place, it to dangerous." "Well, how am I going to find this place again?" "I bring you back, if you pay many dollars." Maybe not so much afraid, as a money spinner for him. The sway of the mighty dollar. I will try tease him out somewhat. "Do you know of the one, called Sun Yat Sen of the Jewellery Kingdom." "This name I have heard before, he is the one called the enforcer." This was definitely news which I didn't wish to hear. Was Sun Yat Sen freelancing or working for the Triads. Now I was very, very, weary of him. "You might as well take me back to where we started our journey from."

This depressed me, not knowing which one of the protagonist may be involved in her kidnapping. They may have both joined forces. Which outcome do I now plan for? My main aim now, to get in contact with Sally Yeh. I tried another question. "Do you know of the one called Sall Yeh?" "Yes I know of this person. She is from the same island as I am." Well at least this was encouraging news. "Could you try to find her for me? It is important, I need to get a message to her." He was quiet for a short while. "I will look for her, if you request me to?" What does this mean, request me. I thought of the obvious, money. "Yes, I would like to request that you, for a small fee help find Sally Yeh. Is this the kind of request that will be taken seriously. "Then I would be glad to help you." My mind was slightly adverse to this type of inducement. "If you find her, tell her that Jason is looking for her urgently." As we approached the hotel, I looked to see if anyone was waiting. The taxi driver was sharp. "I see you have company." Pointing to two occupants sitting in a car, parked overlooking the hotel. "I have seen these before." Now even more curious as to whom they worked for. "Do you know who these work for?" I was looking for a glimmer of hope, a name that I could respond to. "These work for the one who pays the most money." The light dimmed inside again. I left the departing taxi driver with these words ringing in his ears. "Find her and give my message to her."

Stepping from the taxi in full view of the car opposite I was soon ensconced in my room, I took a shower. I had heard nothing from Sally Yeh since I had talked with her earlier that night. It was now ten forty in the evening and time was running out. As I sat down to dry my hair a thought came to me just out of the blue. Why do these thoughts strike after the event. I don't even know the name of the taxi driver. I don't even know the taxi company he supposedly works for. Yes, you heard me right, supposedly works for. If he doesn't work for any, whom could he work for? My heart was in my mouth now. Feeling the pounding of my heart in my chest. Did I give the only people in the world, that I shouldn't have, the name they wanted. I could feel my stomach, churn inside. If he did work for this Triad family, Sally Yeh was now in great danger. Having to do something to redeem myself, if this was the case. Grabbing my jacket, which had my mobile phone in it. I walked down to the lobby and out onto the street. Looking for some landmark, to gauge a sense of direction. I began to walk fast, as my pace had a purpose to it. Approaching the junction of Humphreys avenue and Carnarvon road. As usual there was plenty of traffic about. The car that was following me was now stationary. This was an opportunity to circumvent a false move on my behalf. Finding myself on Nathan road. I strode across the road while the traffic was moving. The occupants in the car, where unsure of what to do. One of them jumped out and began to follow me on foot. Heading down the side of Kowloon park, I heard the screech of tyres in the background. Looking around to see the taxi of earlier that day opening his rear door. "Get in, they come after you." My thoughts sprang alarm bells. Am I going to run into the hands of my pursuers? Was I willing to take that gamble? Seeing in the distance the car pull up along side the person on foot. Knowing it was time to make that decision. I jumped into the rear of the taxi and we sped off. The other car was in hot pursuit. The taxi veered to the left and I catapulted to the right. "Can you lose them?" "This is my intention, I am doing my best." The pavements flashed by as we drove at death defying speed. We were now heading into the countryside. I promised my God that I wouldn't get involved in anything like this again if we got away. Travelling at great speed on narrow roads and the diminishing City lights were now way in the background. "Where are we going?" "Its not far now." As he swung around the wheel like it was an everyday occurrence. "What's not far now?"

Visibly slowing down, were we in a different district. There was no pursuing car now. The taxi driver knew the area well. I only hope this is an area where Sally Yeh is holed out. It seemed that pursuing car had thought twice about following us into this district. Had I crossed the threshold of their limits? The taxi stopped outside a white bungalow. A rare thing I thought in this area. "You go in, you see." said the driver. He was very insistent. This didn't exactly fill me with confidence. Opening the door of the taxi I got out. My slow monolithic pace towards the house, belied the fear that cloaked my emotions. I opened the wooden gate that led into the garden. The house had recently been painted. You could tell by the smell. Or was it the smell of fear. Putting my hand on the wooden frame of the door. It opened and I gingerly walked in. A small demur man greeted me and pointed to the right. I took this to be where the those who held the power congregated. Steadying myself for my entrance. The old man looked on with amusement. Walking in to a picture, of four people sitting at a table. All old men apart from Sally Yeh. She was a beacon to the wise old men. My emotions rotated between good, bad, up and down. A voice came from the one with the thinning moustache. "Are you the one called Jason?" At this point in time I hesitated. "Yes, that is me." "Why do you come here?" Where was I to start? "I came to ask your help, to find and help me free a very close friend of mine. This person is being held against her will, somewhere in the surrounding area." I now waited for a sign of their intentions. "If we help you in this matter, how will you help us?" This felt like a game of questions and answers. "This is a good question. Maybe Sally Yeh could think of something that would be of benefit to your community." I looked for any sign that would give me an inkling, of the direction they wished for help in. "You do speak words of wisdom for a young man." Taking this as a compliment and guessing I must have been doing something right, if he was to say this to me. "I would rather say survival, as this is what I wish for myself and my good friend Phoebe." There was a pause and then some laughter. Sally Yeh beckoned me to her side. Whispering in my ear, "You did very well Jason." I felt very good inside. The principal old man, had a beard along with his moustache. "These people you see here, are the Elders of our district on the mainland. Our elderly as they are now, moved here many years ago, to survive the harsh realities of precious little food and no work on the island they left. This has changed now, but they still hold the respect of the people in this district." My mind could imagine what depths of despair these people had to endure, all those years ago, similar to Ireland. "What can I offer these people in return for their help?" "I am in the process of setting up a Medical Centre and we do need a doctor to call each day." "Yes how can I help in this situation?" "What we do need is the monetary increments on a monthly basis. This would allow us to have a doctor visit our premises on a daily basis. The money is a small sum and hopefully could come from your forthcoming inheritance, I mean from the profits. It is something you take for granted, were you come from, is it not?" I had to dig deep to find the words that gave me great heart from their willingness to help me, all be it, through the elements of a medical centre. "I have it in my power to help you and this I will do." Sally Yeh turned to the man to her right and whispered in his ear. The old man then took my shoulder and said. "You have chosen the way of the good Samaritan." I thought this ironic or was it the words of a wise and travelled man. "I have told Sally Yeh, that I will provide an allowance, to have a doctor call here on a daily basis, in your Medical Centre." Sally Yeh and the old man looked at each other and started to gesture. I didn't know if this was a good or bad sign. Knowing that this decision, would sway the pendulum in either direction. "We have listened to your suggestion and we are in favour of the help you ask of us." My heart soared, the cloud lifted from over my head. I had a light to walk towards. Wishing to inform Sally Yeh of the situation which I had encountered earlier that day. "Sally Yeh I think I may know where they are holding Phoebe." She looked at me curiously. "This is the place to start then, Jason." We paced into another room and she called out a name. Within a minute, the taxi driver with whom I had such a avid encounter, was in our presence. He looked at me and grinned. "So you know where she is then." He was at home with the people in this area, as was his confident reply. "Yes, that's why I have friends in the right places." I was now anxious to get things happening in the search for Phoebe. "What can we do to free Phoebe?" "What we do know is, that a Triad Family, in collaboration with Sun Yat Sen and his sister are behind this deed. They obviously want to cut you out of the picture and take all the profits for themselves." I was annoyed at the way they were going about it. "This may be Sally Yeh, but they didn't have to involve another person, did they?" "This may be so Jason, but the fact is they have and now we have to redeem this situation. These people don't care who they involve, as long as they get the money." "Sally Yeh can we work on a plan?" She seemed calm and relaxed in these surrounds. "We are trying to formulate a strategy at the moment Jason. The area which you found yourself today, is a well guarded vicinity, unseen by the untrained eye. We have a person out scouting this region at the moment. He will be back later in the night. It is wise that you stay here for the moment." She pointed towards a door. I walked over and into the room. It had a bed, some water and a jug, to wash with. Very simple and very basic. "I see you already expected me then." "You have met John Woo, your taxi driver." I looked over at him and he bowed his head in respect. I nodded back in courtesy. "When do you think we can do something to get her out?" "When we have a proper plan in place. We need to cover all the aspects, these are not amateurs." At this point, I decided to retire to my bed. I tried to get some sleep, but had a repeating dream of Phoebe calling for help. I awoke to the sound of a humming bird outside the window. It was seven thirty on a Thursday morning. I must have dropped off at some stage, during the middle of the night. Opening the door to the kitchen, to find three people sitting around the table. One was Sally Yeh, along with two well built men looking at a sketch. My guess that one of these men, was the person who was out scouting the locality where I had encountered the jeep. Moving towards the table I looked at the sketch which lay on the table. "What are these positions?" Now pointing to the red dots, that were stuck in sections on this sketch. "These red dots are positions of guards, who patrol the area." At this point, the two men got up from their chairs and choose to exit the room. "They are going to get some sleep, it will be a long night ahead." At this point John Woo walked in and went straight to the sketch. He gazed at it for a moment and turned to me. "You come with us later?" Nodding in affirmation and I said. "Yes, are we able to go in from the sides?" Pointing to what seemed like breaks in the line of their defence. "Yes Jason, that's what we are planning for." It was Thursday morning, one day before the reading of the will. "Hopefully we may succeed in liberating your friend Phoebe from her captures."

The layout of the undulating hills, made it a bit easier to approach the premises without being noticed. The terrain that would confront us, was wet and marshy. This would cause a problem for the haste we could approach the building. "Surprise would be our goal, right Sally Yeh and the wet marshes doesn't help in this matter." "No certainly not Jason, but we may have a solution to that." I pondered what that may be. "You will have to wait and see. I have to go into Kowloon, so I will see you later Jason." With that she was on her way out of the house. The morning was going at a snails pace. I watched as the Elders and the young people of the community, helped each other to bind and weave the panels, for the medical centre. There was a strong bond between the two generations. I had plenty of time to think, while marooned amongst the contours of the landscape. The locals, along with the Elders, were helping to erect the prefab walls. These units were to be the new medical centre. In a country of so much and so many, there was little purpose to share from the top. It dismayed me, to see children abandoned and the locals hardly able to survive, in this great technological age. This is the very place the Triads recruit their factions from. Then they leave them to rot, if they are caught carrying out the Triads business. That's why there is so many abandoned children. I had time to sit and think of what I may do in the future. This place and the effects that were happening to me, gave me a wider issue to focus on. I was brought back to reality, by the sound of a falling wall unit hitting the ground. I could see that they needed a supervisor to overlook the job they were doing. Walking over while they were all pointing fingers at each other. I gestured to them that they were putting the wrong unit into position first. They looked at me as to say, who the hell does he think he is. I pointed to three of the people helping, to get hold of the wooden unit. They obliged and we hoisted it in the air. It was now in a standing position. I got them to sink their end of the partition into position first. Then I grabbed two more unwilling participants, to hold the other side. Then with a little force and much brawn we shored this end into its rightful position. They all clapped and my back got it as well. It was a good feeling I had inside. I then set about helping, with the other fixtures that needed to be completed. It seemed that no matter where in the world you are welcome to help and share in other peoples misfortunes. This whole exercise does help to generate a commarady among the locals and a pride in what you can achieve. It binds people together, something which is now sadly lacking in my own country. When the money rolls in, the pride rolls out. I was glad now, that I had some time to give to these people. Seeing why Sally Yeh had put so much time and effort into her community. The time had passed quickly. A car approached from the laneway. It was Sally Yeh, she had a person with her. When this person got out of the car, you could feel his presence. He had a aura that said, I am here to help you. He was a big man, six foot, well built body, but no excess fat. It was all muscle. To me he reminded me of a wrestler. Sally

Yeh brought him over for me to meet. His outstretched hand, the size of a shovel, grabbed mine. I thought he was going to crush it. Luckily he stopped short of doing that. "Jason, this is my brother Cho Yun." From what I could see, you would want to be foolish to go up against this giant of a man. "Pleased to meet you." He bowed his head in respect. I acknowledged this and reciprocated the gesture. Was this man going to be the jewel in our crown

Had we the array of personal now, to push for Phoebes rescue? Was I only fooling myself by the judgement I was making. "Jason my brother will be invaluable to us." I looked at him and I thought that straight away. "I am sure he will, if I was to go by his frame alone, he would send shivers up and down my spine." "My brother is a student of Buddhism and is a high priest of Po Lin Monastery, on the Island of Lantau. He has earned the respect of the local community, this by way of his acts and of his prayers for this community." He will be feared by the Triads because of his reverence. They will also see him as a man to fear because of the curse he could bring on their heads." I thought this must be a symbol in their religion. "Will they believe in this Sally Yeh?" "Why yes, most of them. The majority of these people, will have been brought up to believe and fear such a priest." I wondered if Sally Yeh herself believed this. So I decided to ask her out straight. "Do you believe this?" Her reply was strong and confident. "Without a doubt, I do not ask the imponderable." Thinking to myself, well I think I would. "I am glad to hear this Sally Yeh." My mind lifted with the belief that Sally Yeh showed in the outcome of her brothers appearance here. "Of course there is one more piece of news that figures in what I have to say." This sounded more positive than I expected. "Yeah, what is this?" "Well how should I put it. Em, Cho Yun is also gifted at self defence. In fact I would say, that there would be no parallel within these Islands." This did change my appreciation of him. "Now this makes a difference to me. In fact it is a major difference." "So you see Jason, all is not as gloomy as you may make out." I bit my lip and said nothing. "What makes you think it is not as bad as I make out?" "My brother is like a beacon in the night, he goes where others have floundered. He reaps the rewards of the teachings, he has learned." This was turning out to be very interesting indeed. "You have a way with words Sally Yeh. They ring in my ears like the melody of a fine tune." Her response, "You should get used to the sound of my voice, you will hear a lot more of it, before the night has ended. We will leave here at ten this evening. Our aims, first of all, remove the obstacles of the guards. Then the test will begin in earnest." I am sure it will, I thought to myself. But as far as I was concerned, it has already began many hours ago. "Do you know the building that Phoebe is being kept in.?" "We can never be sure about anything, but it will only become apparent tonight, thanks to the person that has interwoven themselves among the rabble." I thought, this must be some brave and smart person. It was now nearing the time of our departure. Some people were tense, you could see it in their eyes. Reading what I had about these Triads, they didn't seem to take any prisoners. The phone rang in the background. Sally Yeh responded to its tone, picked it from its stand. She listened to it intensely and put it down quickly. She moved to the table and whispered something to one of the gathered few, around the table. They quickly got up and retired outside. One senior person spoke to the gathered throng, along with the inspirational Cho Yun. The latter evoked the spirit of their ancestors, to inspire them in their quest. He was dressed in a wonderful red kimono type cape, while small dragons dotted the entire cascade of red. He looked fierce and certainly put the fear of God into me. I don't know what he put into his attentive audience. Maybe it was Confucianism. They started to chant, it must have been some prayer. Thinking this was supposed to be a silent approach. The hum got louder and grew into a crescendo, then faded. Knowing this was the moment for us to move. I hadn't noticed Sally Yeh slip away, while all this was going on. Then she appeared out of the blue. She too had a ceremonial outfit, this of a lighter colour. It too had some indentations on the fabric, it was hard to make out from where I was standing. Feeing left out, just plain jeans and an ordinary top. Sally Yeh came over to me. "We will shortly leave Jason, you follow me." I thought, not to near the front of the throng. "Sally Yeh, I didn't mean for all these people to be involved." "You make to much out of so little. Our brothers are also being held there, so your friend Phoebe is not the common bond. It is our brothers who are incarcerated, along with your friend Phoebe. These people are willing to pay the ultimate price for their freedom. By doing this they cast away the shackles of repression. The Triads have been like leeches on our community." If they only knew at home what was happening to me now. I may never see them again and that deflated my spirit. I stood on the veranda, surveying the fields in front of me. Was I to return to this house and what's more with the freedom of Phoebe? Were these people to return with their brothers? The taxi driver came to my side and handed me a knife like object. "What is this?" "You take, you may need." This somewhat deflated the confidence in me. What would be the outcome? Cho Yun approached me. "Jason, we will liberate the one you call Phoebe and our brothers. You will be anxious, that is only natural. I and the people who lift up arms in this struggle will succeed." This huge man in my sight, spoke with authority and carried an air of grace with him. "I have learned the ways of these men and do not fear their threat. You will call upon your spirits, to protect you in the hour that is upon us." He took my arm, twisted his arm around mine and declared. "Let your God be on your side." I felt a power surge in my body, as if he transferred some of his strength to me. My spirits lifted and I knew than that I was in the presence of a great and good man. He had to attend to the rest of his followers, as he said the hour was nigh. My emotions were on supercharge. I could feel the pump of adrenalin run through my veins. Sally Yeh approached. "Jason, the hour is nigh, let you be at peace with your spirit." The only thing I wanted to be at peace with was a vodka and tonic. Sally Yeh, Cho Yun, our friendly taxi driver and myself headed for the jeep outside the hours. Cho Yun could fill the jeep himself. It looked like the taxi driver could drive more than a taxi. The people who had been in my sight earlier, had now disappeared. We were the last to leave. Cho Yun carried a sword by his side. It was gold and this did strike fear into the imagination. I thought, what is this good and peaceful person doing carrying a sword?

Then the thought struck me, as we were driving away from the house. What if in the past, he actually was a Samurai Warrior? This seemed more in line with the person that was sitting in front of me now. My spirits lifted once again. It certainly looked like he meant business. We were driving at a slow pace. This I thought, must have been to let our comrades in arms hit the outposts first and disarm them. It looked, from where I was sitting, that they have acted like this before. The jeep swung to the right and we turned down a laneway, to the entrance of the hostage takers. Cho Yun turned to me. "Get ready now Jason, we are approaching our destiny." This destiny I could do without. My thoughts ran back to my homeland. Where would I be now? Probably taking a stroll down by the sea. Well that isn't happening now, this is for real. This is the here and now. The jeep pulled up to a silent halt. The driver cut the engine and the lights. No aggressors were to be seen in the immediate vicinity. This isn't the way it is in the movies. Cho Yun jumped out of the jeep, sword in hand. I wouldn't like to meet him in a dark alley. His vision was not impaired by any obstructions. The driver was at his side by now. I was taking longer to get out. The smell of fear filled the air. Sally Yeh was at my side. Then from out of nowhere, there appeared about a dozen men. All of them dressed in black. It looked like a uniform of some sort. They camouflaged themselves to the immediate surrounds without much difficulty. I only hoped they were with us! Cho Yun signalled to them and they raised their arms in unison each carrying a sword, but in a hushed response to his signal.

I caught sight of Cho Yun rush towards the entrance door. Its wooden frame that had once stood in its rigid position, stood no more. With one thrust of his barefoot, he reduced it to a shell of where it stood. He carved through the scattering opponents that were running in his direction. Not one encroached on his wide beam. The quickness of his propeller like sword, quickly dispersed the onrushing horde. With slight of sword and quickness of speed, he was among the rabble that soon ceased to be. As I followed behind the rest of the troop, you could see the devastation that one man had unleashed. There were four doors facing us, what lay behind them? One of our troop tiptoed towards one of the doors. Behind him came the rest of the men in black, with sword like objects in their hands. As he slowly opened the door, everyone stood back. Nothing stood within the room it was completely empty. He quickly moved onto the next door, gingerly opening it in a slow movement. With each movement, everyone would lift their objects above their heads. If there was anyone coming out in anger, they surely weren't going far. Noticing that, Cho Yun had not been a party to this. He stood back and let them be seen to free their own brothers. But this was to no avail as it looked like they had made good their escape. I suspect the token few souls that we encountered, were left behind to entice us into conflict, with the soul purpose of slowing down us as much as possible. Their hands motioned in disbelief. Cho Yun took the centre of the floor. His frame cast a shadow over the area. He spoke to them in their mother tongue. I don't know what he said, but it lifted their spirits and with that it lifted mine. Confused now, as to what was going to happen? They all turned as one and slowly walked out the entrance they came in.

Sally Yeh was once again by my side. "Jason, as you can see, there is no one within the confines of the building. We will leave now and withdraw to our base. It seems that they had prior warning of our intentions. As we have someone immersed in their camp, it looks like they also have a mole in ours." An interesting scenario, how do they outfox each other? My emotions were drained, as the operation didn't come to the conclusion I had hoped for. "Do you think they have harmed Phoebe in any way?" "No, what would be the point?" came the defiant reply. I suppose she was right. "It would not serve their purpose, as they would cease to be a threat. They are a threat as long as they have a subject we desire." I wished to ask her if we had a chance of freeing Phoebe. "Do you think that you can find out for sure, where they are holding her and the rest of your companions?" "Not if we go by what just happened, they seem to be a move ahead of us." This wasn't too encouraging to say the least. "You know my fathers estate is to be read tomorrow. These so called Triads are trying to take away what he built up. Whatever about his methods, he never stooped to this level. The orphanage will also suffer, along with the new Medical Centre you are trying to build. How can we extradite her and the others from their incarceration, especially if we don't know where they are being held?" I was physically getting agitated at the thought of them holding her and the others for another night. This was with the exasperation of having failed to find them in the marooned hideout where we expected them to be. My brain was at a new low. Not able to think straight. My nerves were making me quite restless. Then came the words of this wise woman. "Come Jason, this is not the time to engross yourself in ones own self pity. These are not the actions of the son of my best and humble friend." I felt my whole body lift in reaction to what she had just said. I must have been in a slouched position. My deformed frame dwindling in the context of my imagination. "I and my brother will succeed in expelling these demons from your head. You need to be calm and wise under such circumstances. If the will is there to overcome such an obstacle, you will succeed in your task. We all will succeed in our task, to free and liberate our companions and your friend Phoebe." It seemed to me that every second, every minute, every hour, that passed, lessened the imagination of our own creativity. I could hear the words of her brother, but coming from Sally Yeh. "You also have a way with words, I suppose it runs in the family." We both gave a wry smile to each other. "This is not so Jason, you do have the gift to help or guide on the path. You help the one called Phoebe and not alone that, you help me in the pursuit of the orphanage. Not hesitating in these requests. You do these things form the goodness of your heart. This comes from within, not from words that are said, or thoughts, but you contribute to the community. This is the spirit of your late father. You have the sun in your heart, the light shines on the path of your journey. Why else would you choose to come to my country? This is the sign of a person, who can immerse and entwine themselves in the needs of others. Jason, your mind asks questions, searches for answers. You live life like your father before you." These words sunk deep into my whole being, into my soul, into every vein, every sinew and nerve of my body. The words she spoke, were words that I would cherish for the rest of my days on this earth. With these words, she uncovered the surface and peeled back the layers of the person beneath. She walked and talked with the person inside, not the skeleton, but the human being in the body, the spirit and soul of the person. I at this moment in time knew, why my father had come to this land. I was very quickly brought back to reality. I felt a tug on my shirt. "Come on, we must leave now." My mind must have drifted off, to a different place and time. Into a place where the mind and its thoughts are encouraged and creativity is at its peak. I ran for the jeep and sprang inside. Cho Yun was sitting in the front seat. "We have not failed Jason, we have merely put the inevitable off until a later date." I knew the giant of a man in front of me was speaking the truth. We moved swiftly and easily out of the confines of the lane way that a short time earlier we had raced down. Going to be the cavalry, coming to the aid of our compatriots. It was not to be on this occasion. Where had they moved them. Could we still rescue her before the deadline of the reading of the will? They know they have a powerful bargaining presence in the form of Phoebe. Let alone the other members of the community. When we got back to base, word had come through that we were unsuccessful in our attempt to rescue our companions.

Cho Yun came to me. "Jason, we have discovered where they have moved your friend and our own faction, but I must stress, take nothing for definite. If you are able and willing to continue, you may join us once again. If you wish, I will let you know when the time is near." I knew in my heart and soul, that I must go with them. "I will be with you when you leave." Cho Yun bowed his head, turned and walked to the people waiting for his presence in the courtyard. Sally Yeh had made some tea and she gave me a cup. As I took it from her, a small crouched man entered the building. Approaching Sally Yeh, I moved out of their way. He spoke in a quiet and soothing voice. Sally Yeh put her arms around the old mans shoulders. He walked quickly to the centre of the crowded courtyard and spoke to Cho Yun. Sally Yeh came to me and said we would be moving on in a few moments.

"Jason, we have a definite sighting of the one called Phoebe. We shall move in that direction soon. These people are still in the position they held earlier and we have this news, as you could see by the silent one." Pointing to the old man. "I have noticed that you all are readying yourselves to move again." "Yes, we are getting ready to move forward. Quickness to move fast, as you know from the previous time. So Jason once again, it is time for us to depart." Grabbing my jacket and proceeding to the jeep. In the jeep this time, there was no Cho Yun. "Where is your brother?" "He takes his comrades by a diverse route. We will go by road. Joining up with them at the exposed location." What was Cho Yun up to? He must obviously have his own plan. Leading from the front. Travelling at a slow pace I thought this to be so as we wouldn't be too far ahead of the group. Then we came to the meeting place. Hearing some noise like a wireless, coming from the front seat. The driver picked up a walkie–talkie and put it to his ear. Saying something back into the mouthpiece, with another echo reverberating back. It was all in their native tongue, so I couldn't make out what they were saying. We then stopped and pulled into a side road. Sally Yeh turned to me, "We will wait here until we hear from them." I sat quietly in the jeep. The time was slowly going by and I wondered had Phoebe been rescued. Even worse, had they failed in their attempt? Then a scrambled message came over the walkie–talkie. The driver responded quickly, with an equally garbled message back. We drove off at speed. Veering off the main road and about a mile down we entered a disused narrow lane. It looked like time had forgotten it ever existed. But obviously, other people hadn't forgotten about it. It led to an open field, with some outhouses surrounding it. It appeared to be derelict with no movement for us to see. Thinking to myself, had we come to the right place? Then from behind one of these outlying buildings came a foot soldier to the jeep. "Come we have liberated them."

My inner being soared, leaping out of the jeep I quickly followed him. Sally Yeh wasn't too far behind. Running to the side of the building and around to the rear, it didn't look very good at all. There were many bodies lying in clumps around the field. My heart immediately took a nosedive. What am I going to see here? Walking among what seemed to be dozens of bodies. But of course, there was only a handful. In this atmosphere one could see many instead of a few. Looking for the limp body of Phoebe among the many injured. She was nowhere to be seen. Turning to see Cho Yun walking towards me. "I am sorry young Jason, but it seems that they remove your friend before we arrived." Foiled again. I heard Sally Yeh's voice in my ear. "Jason, you and I will find her." I nodded in agreement, without looking at her. What am I going to do? Thinking to myself. Where do I go from here? There were people jumping around for joy. These were the lucky ones, the people who had been liberated. Feeling a wrench on my shoulder it was Sally Yeh. "Come Jason, we must depart, before we run into any more of these unsavoury characters. Don't forget she still holds great influence for them. She will not be harmed, come let us go now." Turning to survey the field once more, in case I missed her the first time. The rest of the assembled mass, were making their way towards the waiting lorries. Beginning to walk quickly as I thought what Sally Yeh had said about Phoebe. In my mind, the words were reassembling themselves. Trying to read the lines and vision a better outcome. Phoebe was their trump card, the one that could give them control over the jewellery business. Now I was thinking more clearly. Harming her, would loosen the grip they have at this present time. Hopefully she has come to no harm. I sat back into the jeep and we drove back to our base. "We will see these Trids later this morning Jason, at the reading of the will. You will know then how she is." My mind was rotating around in every direction. "I only hope you are right and Phoebe has come to no harm." Not knowing how long they would continue to help me. "Will you continue to help me endeavour to remove Phoebe from the clutches of these fiends?" She looked me straight in the eyes. "You have my word on this Jason. We will help you in your quest and it will be with a good heart." When we got back to the village, they were celebrating. Some of these people hadn't seen their families for up to two years. Cho Yun was in the middle of them he deserved all the respect. He gave them the spirit they needed to resist their own unbelievable thoughts. I looked at Sally Yeh, she was happy. They as a community had achieved the strength to break the strangle hold of these Triads. Now I sat and contemplated, would the picture of Phoebe being freed come to fruition? Sally Yeh looked at me. "Come Jason, don't be so dejected, you, I and Cho Yun will seek to help you in your mission." I politely smiled, but deep down I wondered. I headed for my room as I wished to gather my thoughts. As I slipped onto the bed, the thoughts of Phoebe crept into my mind. Was she in some far off God forsaken run down ramshackle of a place? Was she in good or nearly good health? Was she able to communicate with her captors? What was her frame of mind? These and many more queries re–emerged time after time. One question would fill the vacant space in my mind, as soon as the other departed. There was no respite, no letting go. She was part of my world now. The groaning of the deep pull in your stomach the fixation of that face you see everywhere you go. This was the mirror in front of me every waking moment. I should say, every moment as she appeared in my mind, whether asleep or awake. The thoughts of not seeing her again entered my mind, but would be blocked out by her triumphant return. Keeping a positive approach to her liberation. Even in this respect, the positive involved her liberation. The timing when I would see her and where, was yet to be set. My eyes opened and I immediately got off the bed. Looking out the window and saw people still celebrating the release of the brothers and sons. My mind wasn't in the mood for their generosity. So I kept to myself for the rest of the time. The hour was nearing for us to go to the Public Registrar's Office. Cho Yun came to me. "Jason, we will leave now." I didn't see Sally Yeh. Thinking she was in the jeep, but there was no sign of her. "There is no need to fear Jason, she will be there. First she has some unfinished business to attend to. You will see when we get to our destination." We drove at a moderate pace. This was a change to the previous encounter earlier that very morning. The building in the distance hadn't changed since the last time I visited it. Outside stood a figure with a satchel. Was it who I thought it was? The answer yes. Sally Yeh and in her possession was a satchel. This I am sure was the same one I saw her put away in the train station locker.

When we approached the steps of the building, she entrusted the satchel into my safe keeping. "Jason, you may need this, it is the documentation you were asking about." This was a complete surprise to me. "Is this the diary my father kept?" "Yes it is and it is in safe hands now. There is one more thing I must tell you. I do believe your father was murdered on that night. He was with some of the people you will come face to face with inside." That very thought sent shivers down my spine. "I do believe you are right. We will learn more inside, shall we go in?" Sally Yeh and Cho Yun nodded in unison. I opened the door and my heart started to pound that much quicker. The first few steps were the worst. What was to be unleashed in the next while, I was sure it would come as a shock to me. We came to the door of the Public Registrar's Office. I paused for a moment while gathering my thoughts. Am I about to come face to face not alone with my fathers' killers, but also Phoebe's kidnappers? The door opened and I walked inside. Looking around and I could see Susan and Anita–Mui. Behind them I saw Sun Yat Sen and two other people, whom I did not recognise. The blood immediately rushed to my head. I felt like I was going to burst open with rage. But then a calming hand on my shoulder was felt. Cho Yun grasped both my shoulders and said in a quiet voice. "Jason, we are here to help your friend Phoebe and learn the legacy of your late father. We owe this respect, with which I am sure you have within you at this present time." It looked as if these so called business people opposite were laughing in our faces, not physically but beyond their enterprising minds. I reached for the satchel, just to remind me it was in my possession. Promising that I will make you pay for what you have executed not only to my father, but also to Phoebe and the people of Lamma Island. This is the way in which I was thinking. My eyes were fixed on the two undistinguished people at the rear of the room. They seemed to be uneasy, in their movement and somewhat startled when Cho Yun walked in with us. This I thought was a good sign, the man carried authority with him. They stepped back and looked at each other. He just smiled at them. All having blank stares. A person came out from behind the glazed area in front of us. "Are you all here for the reading of mister Byrnes's last will and testament?" I wished my presence to be known. "Yes, I am the deceased mans son." She acknowledged me by bowing her head. I returned the gesture. Susan and Anita–Mui then put in their spoke. Sun Yat Sen and friends were obviously in a quiet mood, saying nothing. The will was read in the native tongue and at a very still moment in the proceedings Anita–Mui let a gasp. Seeing Sun Yat Sen and friends looking at each other. Turning to Sally Yeh and Cho Yun. She translated the offending piece to me. "It seemed Jason, that your father possessed fifty one percent and the controlling share of the company, but without telling the people opposite. If he has left the remaining shares to you, well then you will control the entire group and possibly their lives." This gave me distinct gratification. "I don't think that is quite right Cho Yun, as they still have Phoebe." He mused for a moment. "This is true Jason, but you may have the best hand." Sally Yeh then broke in. "She is now going to read what has been bestowed the family." The minor entities were banished with haste. Then I felt the heave of a hand on my shoulder. Knowing we were getting down to the nitty–gritty. "This is the interesting part, Jason," a voice in my left ear. Looking around to see Cho Yun and Sally Yeh intensely listen to the words spoken by the bearer of information. These words meant nothing to me as they were in the mother tongue. Seeing their eyes sway with every word spoken. Turning towards the speaker with acute attention. Cho Yun said. "Jason, this is the day you become part of us. Your name is now the controlling countenance in the Kingdom Jewellery business. This is a authoritative place for you to be at this present time. Feeling good within. Now having the trump card in my possession, with regard to Phoebe's wellbeing. Looking at some of the people whom I believed had an act in my father demise. It was now coming home to me, why he never trusted them with the majority share in the company. I had come from nowhere, to the position of power and possibly the influence to destroy their miserable intent. Only Phoebe had a immense part to play in the final outcome. My mind drifted to the contents of the satchel. As the gather few were leaving in a dejected state, one of the men who was with Sun Yet Sen came over and gave me a sealed note. He quickly departed with the rest of them. I could guess what was in the note. Looking at my fellow hod carriers. It felt like we were carrying the world on our shoulders. An extortion note just as I thought. It stated if I wished to see Phoebe alive again. I will have to voluntarily sign over my controlling shareholding to this Triad gang. Feeling the claws of the dragon reach out to grasp away the lifeline it had bestowed on me earlier. This may be the most distressing moments in my life, but for the fact of my late father was still playing a part in it. My body sunk into a slight slumber, the ebb and flow of this drawn out drama, was bringing about a crushing attack on my body and mind. I grasped for some comfort in my state of awareness. Still having the satchel bestowed under my arm. This didn't impart the uplifting effect I hoped it would. A voice rang in my ear. "Come Jason, let us take our leave of this place." Following the two of them down to the exit of the building. Having my mobile phone with me, I decided to phone home. "Will you excuse me for a moment, I wish to phone home," Stepping into a corner of the building I dialled the number. Sasha picked up the receiver. She asked how I was.

"I am O K. How is everything back there?" The reply was as I expected. Nothing too much happening on their side of the world. "No there is nothing wrong, I just have a sore throat." She must have detected a quiver in my voice. "I must go now someone is calling me. I will let you know when I am coming back. Its possible I may have to stay on a few more days, but do not worry, its only work. Look, I will say goodbye now O K. Goodbye." I ended the call. Thinking why had not my father estowed these gifts on us when we were growing up. I thought about phoning Bill a fellow technician that I had trained with, as he was working out in Asia, in Manila, but time was not on my side. Returning to the only people I could trust out here.

# Chapter

# VII

I asked myself. How do you find someone in a hurry out in this part of the world. I found a reply come back. Seek a helicopter. My mind was now working overtime. "Where would I be able to hire a helicopter in Hong Kong?" They both stared at me in bewilderment. "I guess you haven't your thinking cap on." The very thought of such a thing was beyond their comprehension. "We have never been asked such a question before." "Well you have now, so what do you suggest? Do you know of anyone or a place that has a helicopter for hire?" Cho Yun thought for a moment. "Not that I am aware of, but Sanyo Corporation may have a private helicopter for their executives." "That's a good place to start, lets go." They were both amused and baffled by my intent. "Lets go where?" I wished to get to the heart of things right away. "To get hold of a helicopter of course." Cho Yun was somewhat intrigued by my infusion. "What do you think they will say, here's our helicopter, do you wish to borrow it?" "I never mentioned the word asking them, did I?" Now their faces changed in appearance. "So you are going to steal it then?" "No, but borrow it I will." Their next question caught me by surprise. "Can you fly a helicopter then Jason?" "No, but I am sure you can fly one Cho Yun." "Well yes, if you must know. An old friend of mine, used to be a pilot for one of the big corporations. Unfortunately for him he got caught with one of the directors wives. It was a case of solo flying in the wrong position!" He was a bit of a dark horse. "I am not sure I want to meet this person, big brother." I quickly interjected. "This is no time for family squabbles, you two." "Lead me to this pilot Cho Yun." He thought for a moment. "I only hope he still lives in the same place. It's been two years since I last saw him." I pushed them out of the exit door. On our way to the jeep, we noticed two cars waiting our occupancy. I wasn't overjoyed to see them. "What do we do now? We don't need them on our tail." "Leave that to me Jason." Cho Yun got into the drivers side of the jeep. "Is it far from here, where your friend lives?" "No, not that far, but we will have to use a different route." At this point as we moved off, our heads turned to see the two cars follow us out of the area. Thinking, what if we could get the helicopter to find where Phoebe was being held? This thought lifted my heart again. They would not suspect an rescue by air, just as Cho Yun didn't think of the helicopter. Things were looking up again. Now, lets hope we can find this pilot, who may not live where he used to. Shaking off the tail of two cars was our first priority, then to borrow a helicopter. How are we going to get into where they keep the helicopter? That's another story. Driving swiftly off in the general direction of the port tunnel, passing the Wan Chai district and heading towards Causeway Bay. Suddenly, we took a left off Gloucester road up O' Brien road. The two cars behind began to put a spurt on to catch up with us. Holding on tightly to the dash of the jeep as we picked up speed. Then as suddenly as we had speeded up, we slowed down. "Just want to keep them on their toes. It may throw the weary traveller off the scent if we run through the long grass." This obviously made good sense to Cho Yun. We had settled back down to a steady pace now. Approaching the tunnel from Percival street, Victoria Park was in the distance as we entered the tunnel. The cars were still tailing us. On exiting the tunnel, Cho Yun pulled out a mobile phone from his inside pocket. Then it dawned on me that his phone must have had a vibration trigger on it. Talking for some time, he then put the phone down, then I heard, "Jason, we know that your good friend Phoebe is not on Hong Kong Island. But neither is she within the confines of the Kowloon district. This leads me to assume, that whatever path we take the river runs dry. The one good thing I can say at this moment is, that your friends intervention has opened slightly the door of the opportunist." Cho Yun was confusing me now. "Does this mean that you think the helicopter is a good idea?" "This is the idea of the one who wishes to be at peace with his soul." "But do you think it is a good idea?" "I may say it is the only idea worth thinking about. They may have her on the border line with mainland China, or on one of the small islands." Now more anxious than ever. "Lets hope your pilot friend still lives at this address." I gazed behind to see the two cars still there. "What are we going to do about our friends behind us?" "Jason, there is a time and a place for everything. We will deal with that at the appropriate time." These words seemed to be trickling off his tongue with ease. "Will it be hard to get into where they keep the helicopter?" Cho Yun was silent for a moment. "This we shall see when the time comes." I shouldn't have asked. Sally Yeh was very quiet in the rear of the jeep. Turning to her I asked, "What do you think of the idea of the helicopter?" She thought long and hard. Then came the reply. "I don't know if it is a wise move, but I do agree, it is the one idea that has merit and of course you cover such an area in a short space of time." I then asked her. "Is there many islands to cover, Sally Yeh?" "You will know soon enough, if your plan is executed in a measured form." Had I the distinction of sitting between two philosophers. I don't mind, as long as they help me get Phoebe out of her current entrapment and also help me put those who murdered my father behind bars. It was going to take some two to three days, to have everything properly documented. This being with regard to my inheritance for the legal aspect of things. This meant me having to wait until then, or giving us that amount of time to rescue Phoebe. Documents had to be handed over for the exchange of Phoebe. Anything can happen before then. Wondering what was going to happen at the meeting later this same night. They would know that the legal parts of things were now in train. What was the purpose of such a encounter? I doubt if it was for my benefit. The cars were further away now than they had been in the last while. Was this the occasion Cho Yun was going to loose the tail. It seemed not yet. We were heading into traffic, wondering what the plan was. Suddenly we came to a halt. "Is this where the pilot lives?" "No Jason, just a restful moment in our journey. It will help refresh our batteries. As we sat there Cho Yun`s mobile phone rang. A silence befell the jeep for a short period of time. Then came a raised tone from Cho Yun. This didn't seem to be the phone call he was anticipating. Turning to me with a exasperated look in his face. "They have moved Phoebe and the other European girl to Thailand, Bangkok! I have just heard from one of my contacts, who was sitting outside a well know hotel, owned by these people, when a car pulled up with two European girls. They appeared to be bound by their hands and were taken inside. "It sounds like they have taken Jill also, Phoebe's sister. But of course, that's what she told me, for all I know she may be another agent. These Triads don't mind who they upset, do they?"

"No, lets keep it as simple as we can for the time being. I will meet them tonight as arranged, but you two will fly to Bangkok later this very evening". I was now in no man's land. "This means you will still help me find her?" "This just means, more obstacles are thrown in our path. It does not mean that is futile to carry on". We turned our jeep around and made our way to a nearby house. Cho Yun knew the occupants and they made us welcome. He made some phone calls, to arrange the flights later that night. Sally Yeh didn't appear to know these people either, so at least I wasn't the only one in the dark in this situation. Cho Yun had disappeared and left a message with our hosts. Sally Yeh told me that we would be travelling to the airport in the next few hours. "The flight will be leaving very late". So we had a few hours to spare. Our hosts made us some tea. The time seemed to drag on. It was eight when we caught a glimpse of Cho Yun again, mind you only for a passing moment. He spoke to Sally Yeh by herself, and waved to me on the way out the door. She told me that things were moving fast and that we would see him tomorrow in Bangkok. My heart rate was fluctuating as the night wore on. Things were happening, we were making our way into the jeep. Then a thought struck me. "Sally Yeh, I haven't my passport". Now heading in the direction of the airport. She sat silent for a while. Then she bent over to the driver and said something to him. "It is all right Jason, I will have someone pick the passport from your luggage and he will bring it to us at the airport". This was a relief to my inner emotions. "These Triads will have some of their people watching the airport, so we will have to be careful. Taking measures so as not to be detected". These will be interesting tactics, thinking to myself. "What sort of measures do you mean, Sally Yeh?" "Jason, I am not that sure yet, but we don't want to be seen leaving the country if we can help it. This will alert them and they would move her again". The journey to the airport was one of a constant looking over our shoulders to see if we were being followed. Pulling into a side road not too far from the air[ort, we waited for some time. Then a car pulled up along side. I put my hand on the handle ready to alight at any given moment. Sally Yeh's voice responded to my momentum. "It is O K Jason, this is only your passport". I shook my head in response. Only hoping, that they hadn't followed our delivery person to where we were now. He gave the driver the package along with another package, then rapidly moved on his way. Opening the package and inside was my passport. "Right Jason, we can fulfil the rest of our journey now. Let us hope that we have no intrusions in this task." "I wish for the same thing Sally Yeh." We both looked at each other, with inquisitive eyes? The airport came into view. Would we make it and what was more important for us, would we get out of the country without being recognized This huge implication hung heavily on my mind, as long as it wasn't the other way round? The jeep slowed down. Sally Yeh and the driver were in conversation. Pulling over to the side of the road, we came to a standstill. "What is happening?" "Its nothing to worry about Jason, but we have to alter our appearance somewhat." This was confusing me more by the minute. "In what way would we do this?" "We are using this time wisely and to our advantage". Wondering how wisely. The driver got out of his side of the jeep and walked slowly around to the rear. He opened the rear door and took out a cardboard box which came along with my passport. The box seemed to be heavy, as he had his hand under it as a support. Coming around to the front passenger side of the vehicle and gave Sally Yeh the box. The question was running around in my mind, what did the box hold? Obviously they had an illusion in mind. Was it such a awful task that they didn't tell me about it? Was it guns, knives, or some other such unmentionable material. The box was open now in front of my eyes. It was worse than I thought, it contained hats, sunglasses and jackets. "Jason, you will put these on please." I felt like I was going to an ABBA concert. Putting the sunglasses on and a baseball hat and matching baseball jacket. It managed to cover my hair and obscure any facial extremities to the scrutiny of the public. Feeling like I was in a movie. Sally Yeh wore a baseball hat similar to mine, along with sunglasses and a denim jacket. She looked well in her attire. We both got back into the jeep and finished the final leg of the journey to the airport. My stomach began to rumble. The early warning signs of the advancing exertion, was engaging my stomach organs.

Stepping from the jeep like we were walking onto a picture set. Strutting our stuff as we approached the entrance. It was half an hour before boarding just enough time to get us through passport control and directly onto the flight. Approaching the counter with uneasiness, this would be a test of my nerve. I gave the ticket in and everything checked out. Waiting for Sally Yeh, and now the big one. Quickly looking around, nobody appeared all that bothered. Although in my mind, I knew that there would be someone from Triads group among the throng in the airport departure lounge. Walking as soon as I saw her in the corner of my eye. Approaching with aplomb and a cool manner. Hopefully not to chic. Handing in my passport, the guy looked me up and down for some considerable time. This felt uneasy, it felt like my feet were stuck to the ground. Then without a notion he waved me on. The sheer satisfaction of putting one foot in front of the other, was a great release as Sally Yeh just strolled through without a hitch. My nerves had settled down now, to a somewhat controllable level. We were in the departure lounge and over the public address system hearing the request for the boarding of flight number LH 4604. That was our flight. Looking at each other we began to walk to the departure gate. Continuously looking to the rear of me. Saying nothing to each other, only to acknowledge each others presence. Our main aim to get on and off the flight at the other end. We sat down keeping a weary eye on our fellow passengers. Quietly saying to Sally Yeh, "Do you think we have a chance of finding her in

110

Bangkok?" "Jason, there is always a chance. Otherwise I would have given up a long time ago. Only for your father we would never met and I would not be here today. That's not to say I had and wished to have met you under different circumstances." "I know what you mean Sally Yeh, its sometimes in the lap of the Gods." She seemed to understand my inference. "Something like what you say Jason." She finished our conversation rather abruptly. Being joined in our seats by another passenger. At this point I became tactile. The journey lasted about an hour and up to that point was uneventful. Now we had to go through a similar passport control, but with different people.

Lining up in the column that had formed and waited in the international passports section. Then out of the corner of my eye I caught a glimpse of Sally Yeh lining up in a column further down. In this column it read domestic passports. Walking up to the counter it was the same response as for the Hong Kong control. He looked at me then looked back at the passport. Quickly stamped it and beckoned me on. Walking to the edge of the steps that led down to the luggage pickup point. Sally Yeh was no where in sight. Not wishing to cause to much attention, I walked out the green channel to the exit hall. Outside looking all around to see if I could see her. Not a trace in sight. Sitting opposite the exit door my eyes capturing every movement from within. The time passed slowly. Did I overlook her, deciding to walk to the pavement outside where the taxis congregated. She was nowhere to be seen. Walking back inside my instincts led me to go up the escalator to where there was a K.F.C. No, not here. So back down to the exit door of the arrivals hall and back to the same seat. Clutches of people coming out, but not the one I wished to see. Some forty minutes later I was getting worried, so I went up to the tourist information desk. Wishing to enquire as to a place to stay if Sally Yeh wasn't going to be in my presence. Who would I notify if she doesn't show up. I haven't the phone numbers of Cho Yun or anyone else for that matter here in Bangkok. I was biding my time with the ever recurring saying. She will be here any moment. After the hour mark, my will and patience began to sag. But I still kept up the notion that, it wouldn't be in vein. Every opening of the automatic doors brought a response from me. A figure caught my eye. It was her, my eyes lit up. Slowly I strode towards her. "What happened?" "I don't want to say anything here Jason. Let us move to the boundaries of the exterior of the building." It was hot and sticky when we stepped onto the pavement. The air–conditioning had fooled me into thinking that the weather was quite mild. It hit me the minute I walked outside into the hot humid air. A taxi pulled up and we got in. Sally Yeh handed him a note. He nodded his head in agreement. We sped off in the direction of Bangkok City. She didn't say anything on the journey, so I kept my thoughts to myself.

We were on our way to an Apartment block down by the Chao Phraya river, on Roma road. Driving up to the entrance and the security officer opened the electronic gate. We entered and pulled up alongside the office. Sally Yeh got out and spoke with the woman who managed the apartment block. She beckoned to me, I got out and walked towards her. "Jason, you have a studio apartment on the right side of the building. I will take the apartment on this side." This was very agreeable to me. I went to see the apartment. It was well furnished and very pleasant, overlooking the pool. Not that I would be doing much sunbathing when I am here. Boiling some water and make myself some tea. I was disturbed by a knock on the door. Immediately putting the cup down and proceeded to the door, should I open it? Then I thought the better of it and decided to ask a question of the interloper. "Who is it?" "Very good," came the reply. "At least you are thinking first, this I agree with." This of course was the soft voice of Sally Yeh. She came in. "Do you want some tea?" "Yes." I poured her a cup. "I was worried, what happened to you at the airport?" She sat down. "They took me aside and questioned me with regard to some obscure jewellery deal. They knew whom I was all along. They obviously wanted to intimidate me. As you can see this Triad family reaches far and wide. We will be watched now, so take care wherever you are. We will go into the city shortly." She took her leave of me. This didn't sound too encouraging news with regard to freeing Phoebe. Would they move her again? I finished my drink and waited for word from her to call me. Some fifteen minutes elapsed. It was now eight thirty in the evening. She phoned me and asked to meet her in the car park area. I went out and a taxi was waiting. I sat myself into the green and yellow taxi. Sally Yeh showed the driver a card, with Emerald hotel on it. He nodded in concurrence. Making our way out the gate. The road was narrow and grey. It was hard to make out the people walking to the side as it was twilight. We both looked around to see a car pull out after us. This road led to the main artery to the city. Being on the outskirts of the city, well hidden away from any intruders. The many beautiful hotels intermittent within the grey surrounds of some of the old buildings lit up the city. "Jason, we will talk some more when we get to our destination." I nodded in response. Looking out the taxi window, seeing a multiple array of motorbikes on the road. A popular way of getting around as they also double up as a taxi. The sights of some of the finest hotels in the world were there in all their splendour. The illumination of the many colours at night was impressive. The neon sign of the Emerald hotel in the distance stood out. The taxi driver passed by and did a u–turn further up the road. Its pillar entrance spoke volumes for the opulence it generated in the area. This is the norm for such hotels here. We entered the foyer an the open plan view of the glass escalator facing onto the entrance and this was impressive. Heading for the restaurant, we were shown to a table by the window. Glancing around I noted what people were in our proximity. Thinking to myself, anyone here could be the key to Phoebes release. I turned to Sally Yeh. "Do you suspect there may be anyone here from the Triad family?" "Yes Jason, I suspect this to be the case. I have noticed a certain person, he is sitting at the entrance to the restaurant. Quickly I glanced around and saw him sitting there. "I see the person you are talking about. He doesn't look that impressive, I think his tailor could be called upon to rectify his dress sense." "Yes, that may be the case Jason, but that doesn't matter. It's what he can do, bothers me." This was the first time I had seen a chink in her armour. Beginning to feel uneasy now. This worried me, if she felt like this then what could be the matter. I decided to try once more. "Sally Yeh, what is wrong, do you have some misgivings?" She thought for a moment. "Our contact was to show up some fifteen minutes ago, but as you can see I am still in your company. This makes me feel in a delicate situation. I will go shortly to make a phone call." A waiter came to take our order. I ordered the Norway baked salmon. Sally Yeh went up to the buffet and picked her own choices. Sitting back down she still looked worried. We then just talked about life in general and the things we got up to when we were small. Her brother educated himself and then helped to educate her, it was a hard struggle, especially if you live among the Triads. "Jason we will if possible, with the help of the Holy ones, release your friend from her captivity. This in turn may release your heart of its chains." "Very profound I must say, what has lifted your spirit to this level?" Her reply was that of a well thought out scenario. "We must always have the strength to go on. My brother tells me this all the time. I have let this slip from my mind in the last while." This only proved that she was human. "This of which you speak, does happen to us all from time to time. This does not mean that you do not care, or have lost the will to carry on. It only means that you are human like every one else and besides, I feel that way on a regular basis." The profound logic must have been rubbing off on me. "Now look what you have me saying, Sally Yeh, you are giving me the gift of the gab." "What is the gab you speak of?" How do I explain this to her without offence? "It is our way of saying that you have a lot to say." "This is a good saying, I shall remember these words." She seemed to be relaxing more. "Do you think that they think, they are more secure here?" "Yes, this is a good point you make Jason. They may think that because they are on different soil, this will somehow make them less vulnerable to our attention. I will tell you Jason this is only in their minds, because we let them think such a thing. Trying to achieve this end, with the least amount of our energy or harm to ourselves and your friend." I knew she was talking sense, but my head had too many thoughts in it. It sometimes felt like a heavy weight suppressing them from getting out. My mind drifted for a while back to home. Wondering what they would be doing at this point in time. The inheritance which of course knowing what I know now of my father was not as straightforward as it seemed. Had me scouring the China sea, looking for someone that I had only met some days ago. What would they say to this back home? Little did I know that I would be physically

114

searching countries with a second woman friend of my fathers? Sometimes I wonder if this is not all a dream.

My silence was interrupted by the sound of Sally Yeh's voice. "Jason, we may leave soon. It doesn't look like our contact will show at this late stage and this is worrying." Now seeing a person who is normally docile to such events, being consumed with anguish. "What about your brother Cho Yun?" "I am not worried about him, as he may be even watching us from a distance right now." "What do you wish to do then Sally Yeh?" "I have a phone number, that I must call." "Is it safe to use these phones here?" Her apparent nonchalant answer was an indication of the fact she knew she would be listened in on. "It should not matter, as what I will say will not be understood by any other ear." Taking this to mean, that she would be talking in code. Well organised, I thought. "Jason, just wait here while I make a phone call." After she was gone from the table, I paid the bill. Glancing around at the rest of the diners. I then spotted the tail we had, get up and follow her to the phone. Watching her and the rather obscure little man stand there scrutinise her make the phone call. He pulled out a packed of cigarettes and lit one with a gold coloured lighter. This was intimidation, letting her know that he was there. Thinking to myself, what if she just vanished? What would I do? Make my way out of the hotel and go where? This began to weigh heavily on my mind. I should have a plan B ready for any such occurrence. I will speak to her when she comes back from making the call. Some time had elapsed before she put the phone down. Approaching she seemed more upbeat. Sitting down and telling me that she had been in contact with her brother. I interjected, "Is he here in the hotel?" "Not in the hotel, but yes, he is currently within the perimeter of the city." My stomach settled down somewhat, on hearing this news. "I take it, he is not too far from here. Does he know where they are holding Phoebe?" She was clear in her description. "It seems that they have her and the other girl, held in some hotel owned by one of the Triad members. It may be hard to get close to her without a diversion." Plan B had vanished from my mind. The news that Cho Yun knew where she was raised my hopes once again. But this time, I held some of myself back from being over optimistic. "Are we going to meet Cho Yun? Oh yeah, what happened to that guy that was supposed to show up to meet us?" "It seems that he was diverted to some other place and he knew that I would phone this number. Jason we must depart now. Our aim is to loose our constant companion. I am going to order a taxi. Wait in the lobby. This taxi will not arrive for some time we have arranged this. In the meantime, you have to go down the spiral staircase out the two doors into the entrance to the nightclub. From there get into a taxi. There will be a taxi waiting there anyway." She seemed to be sure of this. I only hoped she was right. "Wait for me in the taxi and make sure that when I arrive he takes off immediately." I understood the gist of what she was saying. Turning to me. "Do you follow my instructions Jason?" I nodded in response. We got up from the table and walked towards the lobby. Seeing our tail was getting up from his table and following us. Approaching the lobby, I then proceeded to the right. Seeing that our tail was confused. Which one to follow? Sure that it would be Sally Yeh. I was right. Walking down the spiral staircase, it led to another opening into the entrance to another bar and disco. My stride took me to the door and a waiting taxi. Getting into the green and yellow taxi I told him to wait. We sat there looking at the exit door. The taxi driver turned to me and said. "You wait for your lady?" "Something like that." Not explaining any further. Watching the door for any sign of movement. Then a shadow appeared at the door, it was her. She came running out and leaped into the taxi. Telling the taxi driver to put his foot down. Doing this, at breakneck speed. Nothing new here I thought. She was trying to think of the name of the street or road to go to. It wasn't coming. Then a flash of memory, "Luang road." The taxi driver recognised the name and we were on our way, without interruption. Looking behind to see if any cars were following. Nothing that I could see. "How did you loose him?" "It is not difficult, I get off the lift as he gets on. I wait for the right moment, to jump out the door. We go to see Cho Yun now, he may have some news on your friend." Hoping deep down inside that she was right. "I hope it is some good news." "I am sure the news he may bring, will be of the positive nature Jason." Sally Yeh was more buoyant now. "Hope you are right and it is so."

Speeding through the night, it was dark and we appeared to be travelling along back alleys. Coming to a halt outside a grey looking building. It certainly wasn't in the thick of things. Very quiet and misty sort of place, it sent a shiver down my spine. That's the effect it had on me from the outside. I dare not imagine what the interior looked like. Certainly it would deceive the multitude. Getting out of the taxi we went straight inside. High walls surrounding its exterior on all sides. Presuming to keep out prying eyes. As we entered, there was a individual on each side of the door. They didn't look like the type of person you would like to meet on a dark night on your own. Very stern faces and looked us up and down as we entered. Talk about radar, they didn't need one. Going from dark of the night, into a brightly lit room, made my eyes squelch. The room had a pine round table, with four chairs. It looked like they were expecting us, but who were the other chairs for? In a few moments the question would be answered. Just then Cho Yun sauntered in, two men accompanied him. The relief on my face must have shown. "It is O K Jason, these are my protectors. He shook my hand warmly. Sitting down at the table with us. "Jason, I have news for you." Not knowing what to expect, as he didn't say good or bad news. "We know where your friend is. It may take some time and effort, to extradite her and her companion." My heart was now pounding faster. "Do you think it possible Cho Yun, that she may be liberated?" "Let me tell you now Jason, it will be a hard task, as it is a very public place. This diminishes our chances of surprise." If he is feeling this way, I am glad I didn't lift my spirits up too high. "Do you have any plan as yet?" "This we are looking at. We need to know their weaknesses, where to hit them and when to hit. These things will take some time. I will have to take my leave of you both." He approached Sally Yeh and they spoke for a short while. "Until the next time we meet, let your God go with you." With that he was out the door. Waiting for some time before we made our way outside into the misty night. The same taxi driver was waiting. We left and made our way back to the apartment block. Pulling up outside, we could see a car parked on the far side of the road. Sally Yeh talked to the taxi driver. Seemed to have to do with the car parked opposite. Then she turned to me.

"Jason, it is time we moved on from this place. Get your belongings and meet me back here in the taxi." Again talking to the taxi driver, as I got out of the car. When I returned to the taxi, it would be another five minutes before Sally Yeh reappeared. "You make sure you leave nothing behind." I glanced at her. "This I have done." Making sure she knew I had taken her advice. "Good, we can now depart. Let us be in a position of strength not weakness." I took this as a reference, to the people watching the apartment. Driving out of the courtyard at speed, the driver hugged every corner and hit every bump, while manoeuvring the tricky side streets. My stomach wasn't feeling the best at this particular time. Not perceiving anyone following. The driver did the job asked of him. It was very dark on these side streets so it was hard to make out where we were going. No shapes to go by, no features stood out. Seemingly coming to a much more lively and bright location. Seeing the sparkling lights in the distance made my eyes dance. Slowly taking our leave of the side streets. The lights of the city beckoned. Stopping at a junction, I was able to make out the name on the nameplate. It read Phahurat road. Nearing our destination I assumed. Shopping outlets were abundant as we made our way slowly through the narrow streets. The driver appeared to be looking for an entrance. With the hustle and bustle in the background, it would be much more difficult to keep tabs on us. Arriving at the rear of a shop, the gates suddenly opened. We drove in off the road. Getting out of the car, I could make out some figures in the distance. A young woman came and pointed to a door. I hesitated before I approached, slowly turning the handle and pushing the door open. It swung inwards to reveal, what looked like a mattress on the ground. A dimly lit bulb showed how bare the room was. Hearing a voice. "You go sleep here." The woman spoke in broken English. Once again she spoke, "You sleep." It wasn't the most pleasant sight to see. "O K, I understand what you say." This seemed to please her. She left me in the room. It certainly wasn't anything to write home about. I suppose it served its purpose. It was late and I was tired. When my head hit the mattress I was out cold.

My dreams were all about Phoebe and finding her. Waking

up very thirsty. I got up and walked down the dull corridor. Finding a door open. The light hit may eyes as I opened it. It led to a balcony overlooking the street below. The sun was shinning down and the throng of people were rushing around. Looking at my watch it was now seven–thirty. Walking back inside and down the corridor. Catching a glimpse of a light coming from a room. My instinct was to headed for it. Upon opening the door I found myself in the kitchen. The young woman from the previous night was standing at the worktop. She said, "Hello," I greeted her back. Pointing to the kettle. Walking over to it I plugged it in. "You have troubled sleep, I can see in your eye." She was right. I brushed it off with a gesture of my hands. "Where you from?" she inquired. "I come from Ireland." Wondering if she had heard of Ireland. "Is this not a far away place?" "It is indeed, yes, very far away." Nodding her head. I was sitting down at the table when Sally Yeh walked in. "I see you have met Angkana. By the way, she will get you out of the country if anything happens to us." This wasn't the most reassuring thing to hear at this time of the morning. "What do you mean, if anything happens to you. Surely, you don't expect anything to happen, do you?" "You know the situation Jason. It might happen that you may find yourself in an awkward position. Be prepared to go with Angkana, if this should happen." It was somewhat confusing. "Have we any plans set for today?" Sally Yeh was always thinking ahead. "Yes Jason, we have some essential tasks to do. Why do you ask?" "Nothing, I only just asked." Finding the tiredness get to me. "We must meet Cho Yun later. This we must do without our inquisitors." My mind drifted for a moment. "Do these people know where we are?" Sally Yeh had anticipated their movement. "The may not know where we are at this present time, but they will pick us up at some time." Wishing to take time out for myself. "I am going to take a shower and a shave." They both laughed at me. I got up from the table and headed for the bathroom. As I was leaving Sally Yeh was talking to Angkana. Little did I know that she might be the person who plucks me from the arms of these tyrants. I shaved and washed. Thoughts of trying to escape from Bangkok with Phoebe filled my mind. Returning to the room they were still talking. Sally

Yeh turned to me and said. "I will go and get ready for our meeting." Wishing to know more about this young woman. "Angkana, how come you help us?" "Oh this question you ask is easy. My mother is from the same village as Miss Sally. I help cause they help mother." As good an explanation as any and a commendable one at that. "Have you lived here a long time?" "Me live here, most my life." Sally Yeh came back into the room. "Are you ready Jason?" "Yes, whenever you are." Looking at my watch it was nine–thirty. "We are heading off early. What time do we meet your brother?" "The hour will be twelve noon." Wondering if we were visiting somewhere else first. "Aren't we heading off a bit early?" "Ah Jason, this is not the only function we have to perform this morning." My mind began to juggle some thoughts, trying to balance the ebb and flow of my troubled mind. It did run deep. "It will become more clear in your head, when we walk." Heading out the door, with the words of Angkana drifting in our direction. "Do not let people from the island take you." The outside door closed and we walked to the nearby shopping centre. Sally Yeh began to talk. "Jason, we may need to be quick on our feet. I am sure they will have people looking for us throughout the city. We need to go to a certain street and collect some paperwork for Cho Yun. This we need to do without anyone following us." What was the paperwork, was it to do with extraditing Phoebe? We were walking casually through the shopping centre, when Sally Yeh tugged my shoulder. She looked at two people in the distance. I guess they were looking for us. Pulling out a mobile phone and ringing someone. We could see in the background, that these two people had taken to following us. Taking the phone away from her ear and turning to me. "Jason, let us get ready to move fast." She manoeuvred me in the direction of one of the exits. Looking around to see that our shadows were well immersed within the throng of people. Grabbing my shoulder she draw me with her. "Jason, it is time for us to fade away."

Finding ourselves running towards one of the exits. As we got there, two motorbikes pulled up alongside of us. "Get on Jason, this is our form of transport." I had no choice, as the two rogues were reaching our direction. At this point I didn't think they were the sociable type. We sped off in the direction of the city centre. Looking around I could see one of the guys throw something on the ground in disgust. We were directly behind Sally Yeh and her driver, hugging the curves and not doing the same on the far to frequent bumps. My body was being wrenched from the frame of the bike like a piece of paper. Aching bones and limbs and I was only on the bike five minutes. Like a spirit in the back alleys, flashing by. Then as we rode down one street a gate opened and the bike dovetailed through. As soon as we entered, another gate opened in front of us, as the other shut. Going through this and we were off in a different direction, a new street leading in the opposite direction. The mind boggled. On our way to our first meeting point. Well at least they seemed to be well organised, even if they are in a another country and seemed in control of the situation. Who was the meeting with and what information did they hold? Heading back now into the city, through side streets. Coming towards the Central Plaza in the region of Pinkloa. Slowing down we stopped beside the entrance to the shopping centre. When I got off the bike, I could see a bus station in the distance. I wanted to take in the surrounding landmarks in the event of Sally Yeh and myself becoming parted. At least I knew I could get back to the city centre on different transport modes. We moved up the steps of the entrance and through the doors. This led to an open plan layout on the ground floor. Some small mobile electronic units were displaying their wares. Moving towards the escalator and up to the floor above. Closely following Sally Yeh. Heading to the third floor, and eventually ending up on the fourth. I didn't fancy our chances of escape if we had to move quickly. Limited availability of exits imposed themselves. Entering the City Walk Pub and restaurant at ten forty–five. Noticing the clock on the entrance to the pub. As I suspected not to many clients in here at this hour, you know anywhere you are in the world, you always get the few. Sitting at a table by the window. A waiter came and I ordered a coke and a tea for Sally Yeh. "Jason, I noticed you looking about outside, that's good. Try always to get your bearings." There seemed to be a steady stream of people into the pub now. Our eyes were glued to the door. I don't know why mine was, as I didn't know who we were looking for. Then about ten minutes after we had entered, a slow old looking character with about two days of stubble growth on his face, walked by the table. As he did so, he opened his jacket and left a letter. He was the last person in the world I would have suspected. Sally Yeh put the letter in her jacket and got up to go. I did likewise. Making our way to the escalator and heading straight for the ground floor. Following right behind her, so as to ward off any interfering interlopers, which might stray into her path. We didn't say a word on the way down. Other things were on our minds. Was this the plan that finally would surface to rescue Phoebe? Getting off at the ground floor we headed for the side exit and as we did, I caught sight of a Caucasian woman with auburn hair. I could have sworn it was Kathleen, funny how the mind plays tricks on you. On arrival at the exit, no one was there to meet us and we crossed over to the other side of the road. I didn't know what to think. Where we left marooned? Being very exposed out in the open. The road was called Somdet Phra Pin Klao. Thinking I wouldn't want to be spelling that it in a hurry. Walking in the direction of Chao Phraya River. "Jason, we are here to see if they follow. We will get on the next bus. Do not worry, our friends are not far behind." This came as a relief. The bus approached in the distance. When it got up close to us I could see it was old with open windows, no air–conditioning here. Climbing on board to be met with a stifling heat. It was very humid and I hadn't realised it. Sitting near the rear of the bus. Looking to see if any cars were following? No cars or bikes at this time. As I sat gazing out the open window, to the right of the bus, a car suddenly drew up behind us. Quickly I tugged Sally Yeh's arm and indicated to her the advancing car. Taking a fleeting look around to see the car following. From within her jacket she pulled out a mobile phone and rang someone. It was a quick call. Before I gawked around again, she was putting the mobile phone back inside her jacket. "Jason, do not fret, this is what we were here to find out. As you can observe my judgement was correct. They follow, but not for long. You will be ready to leave the bus when I do. Do you understand this?" "Yes, that's fine with me." Waiting for some sign from Sally Yeh. "When we depart, we may go separate ways for some time. But this is only to confuse them. I may have to meet with

Cho Yun alone. So you may become detached, but not isolated. This is what we call a pack mule. You will be the one they watch, while I make my presence known to my brother. Is this implicit enough?" "Yes, I understand Sally Yeh, I am only happy to be in a position to help. If this facilitates in the overall cause of Phoebe being released." There was a stop coming up by the Royal Grand Place. Sally Yeh got up and I followed. Seeing the car pull up behind the bus. Behind them in the not to far distance I could see two motorbikes. Stepping off the bus, along with about five or six other people. The car came to a standstill. As soon as the bus pulled away, the two bikes came to our standing point. I got on one of the bikes. It turned completely around and headed back up the same road we had just come down. The car was in two minds as to who to follow. Sally Yeh had handed me a letter in full view of the cars occupants, before we diverged. Having this in my hand as I got on the bike. This was a deciding fact in their influence to follow me. We sped up the road swung right into Charan Sanit Wong road. Within a few minutes we were at the next junction, with our pursuers closing. The plan so far was working. Now swinging onto Krungthon Bridge and heading in the direction of the Dusit Zoo. Travelling at speed down the road towards the main intersection. Coming to Victory Monument we turned left. Never once leaving our pursuers to far behind, allowing them to follow. I certainly felt like a mouse on this thin machine with the force of the mousetrap behind us in the form of a car. Bobbing from side to side, the wind catching my face. At least it was cool riding on the bike. It had been twenty years since I was on a motorbike. This wasn't the setting I had anticipated it would be, being pursued down a highway in Bangkok. We were driving around now for at least twenty minutes. How long more was it going to last? Feeling the bike slowing down. In front of me stood Lardprao shopping centre. Manoeuvring the bike in and out of the parked cars. By so doing our pursuers were stranded in the middle of the car park. Making a quick exit onto Phahonyothin road and back towards what looked like the city centre. The driver was happy, he had led them on a wild goose chase and they had obliged. Hoping we would be meeting Sally Yeh and she had some good news. Coming to the junction of

Rama 1 Road and headed towards the Pathaya district. We flashed by the bus terminal on a very clammy day, down along North Pattaya road. The traffic was building up as usual. Then by surprise we turned off the road into a hotel entrance. Not noticeing the name as I was to busy looking at the traffic. The driver pulled up to the entrance of the hotel. He pointed for me to go inside. I got off the bike, with my feet shaky. Feeling somewhat disoriented, but within a matter of minutes I was in full command of my abilities. Walking up the steps of the hotel, not knowing why I had counted them. It must have been the bike ride or should I say divergence. Wishing to see if I was in the right frame of mind. What and who was here? No message greeted me as I entered the hotel lobby. Sitting in one of the chairs in the lobby, checking for any familiar faces. No one, but many visitors of similar complexion to myself in the lobby. Many tourists in the city, thinking it would be an ideal place to conceal some Europeans. Settling for a long wait, when out of the blue I got a tap on my right shoulder. Looking around with surprise, it was a face I didn't know. "Yes, can I help you?" "It is you I look for, your name Jason?" Not really knowing what to say. Be positive, I told myself. "It is indeed and who may I ask are you?" "I come from the one you know as Sally Yeh. She ask me to show you the way." Should I take the bait and run with it. Deciding to check out my newfound friend. "How do I know, who you say you are?" "I give you one name, that name is, I don't know if I pronounce it right Phe–be?" "That's close enough for me, lead me to her." Getting up from my chair and following him. It looked like we were heading towards the stairwell. Stopping to look around, no one following as far as I could see. Walking down the stairwell, my mind reacted to its natural inquisitive nature. Was this person the one whom I had initially thought he was? Uncertainties ran through my mind. Was I going to my own incarceration? Searching to see for any escape routes, if the need arises. If I am to meet Sally Yeh, she wouldn't be to impressed with my attentiveness of my surroundings.

The panic had set in as I walked down the stairs. Feeling the perspiration seeping out of my pores. Watching for bulges that might hide any firearm in his jacket. He was a well–built man, blocky from the rear and he moved with agility and speed. Finding it hard to keep up. A hard man to take down I thought to myself. I hope it doesn't come to that because I don't know what I would do. Flight or fight what would be the option? Deciding not to think of it, at this present time. The person in front of me knew where he was going and I didn't. That to was a worry to me. Now heading down another flight of stairs, when is this going to lead to? Down to the polar regions of the basement without a single person knowing where I am. Not looking good. Should I turn and run now? Picturing in my mind where the lobby entrance. Then a voice in front of me rang out. "It is not far now." Should I hang on for the last yard or so? Before I could make up my mind, I found myself in front of a greyish door. The person in front gave three loud bangs on the door. Not a whisper came from inside. Then about ten seconds later, I heard the sound of what seemed like a bolt opening from inside the door. It opened and a man stood there, he moved to one side as I passed by. Inside I found the presence of Sally Yeh and Cho Yun. This was a bonus to me. My two confidants stood up and greeted me with their traditional hands clasped and bowing movement. I reciprocated the gesture. They invited me to sit down at a table provided. There were three more people all of which I assumed were patriots to the villages cause. They had maps and plans on the table. The first words came from Cho Yun. "Jason, you know that you are to be in Hong Kong to sign for your late fathers estate tomorrow? I will see that you and my sister are taken to the airport later tonight. You need to fulfil this deed, as you know your friend Phoebe will not survive without you doing this. It had not crossed my mind as I was to caught up in events here. "Have you any plans for Phoebes rescue?" "We do, but these will take a day or two to put into operation." At least I now knew something was happening. "So this is the point with which my good sister and your good self will be as one in your fathers adopted country to confirm his possessions. You will be of that clan for whom we do kindly bestow good wishes." I took this to mean that I would be part of the overall family of these two people whom I have come to know. These feelings were good inside, filling up with pride. "You will go with my driver and you both will freshen up. This will be done in a room we keep nearby. It's a local hotel, so you shouldn't be noticed. You will be travelling light, as your stay will be of a short nature. You will go with our holy wishes, that you both return safely to our right hand side with great speed." This was beginning to sound a bit more than a mere formality. My spine was beginning to go somewhat rigid, to this revealing news, especially to the sound of safe return and holy wishes. "Jason, you are in the position of strength and with your fathers estate, a holy wish bestowed upon you. A great honour in our country, but as you see, it brings with it undesirable attention. We as your removed family, through my sister Sally Yeh and I will endeavour to fulfil your fathers honourable discharge." Quite a speech, I can see why he is a powerful force to be reckoned with. Sally Yeh said something and piled on the guilt bit. "You are somewhat caught in the middle, with a precious stone." She was right, a catch 22 situation. "I wish to say, that might be putting it mildly Sally Yeh." With her words ringing in my ear, we made our move. Leaving swiftly out of the basement to the ground floor. Plenty of people milling around. Our minder stopped us in our tracks. He beckoned us to wait by the stairs. This didn't appear good, especially after what Cho Yun had been saying. He came back in a hurry and with what I would say, some agitation in his voice. "You have to come with me down to basement." I couldn't figure this out, we were just after coming from there in the first place. We both complied with his request. Taking the basement phone in his hand and began to talk into it. Turning to us. "We must depart by a different route." I wasn't arguing with this. "Why is this", I interjected. "You mister Jason are the aim of these pursuers." I found myself repeating to myself. I am now the main aim of these individuals, I suppose it was only a matter of time. "It seems that these pursuers are from another Triad family. "Em, you see, they also want your gift from your father?" "You mean they are fighting the other family for my signature?" What next thinking to myself. "Yes this is the case." "Jason, this other family are sworn enemies of the ones who have your friend." "So what you are saying Sally Yeh, they are after me directly without having any pawn in their hand." "You are correct in this assumption, this is good." "It's not good for me or Phoebe,

126

now is it? If they get to me first." I was stuck in the middle of an internal Triad feud and I was the target of one family and Phoebe was the pawn of the other. I didn't think I would be able to phone them back home and tell them this story.

A car pulled up to the rear entrance, it looked like they hadn't spotted us leaving. The three of us jumped into our waiting car. We started off cautiously, surveying the car park for any unwanted bystanders. Gradually making our way to the exit. Then suddenly we tore out and the three of us looked back, no one following for the time being. Turning to Sally Yeh, "Is the hotel far from here?" "Not to far away, we will see anyone if they follow." Soon ending up in the traffic, no escape for anyone here. Crawling along when we came to a side street. The driver pulled into it and we moved a good bit faster. Seeing the neon sign of the hotel, it was soon within our grasp. Pulling into the car park, our minder got out and surveyed the entrance. Reporting back that it was safe to enter. Heading straight to the room, it was on the twelfth floor. The plane was leaving within the next hour and a half, so just enough time to wash. Not long after arriving we were on our way again. This new development had made a serious impact on me. Now I was the target of another Triad gang. Our minder knocked on the door. I let him in. "We must leave now." "Is there something wrong?" "No, but its better we leave now." Sally Yeh turned to me. "Jason, we will get to Hong Kong and you will sign for your fathers gift to you." I know it didn't sound that much, but having someone say that, at this particular time meant a lot to me and it helped to settle my nerves somewhat. Walking out of the hotel bedroom and heading for the stairwell. Not taking the elevator this time. Now I was watching every step I took. Noticing the exits and the people in my eye line. Taking time to watch for any unwanted attention. Nearing the end of the staircase, a person in the distance caught my eye. Tipping our minder on the shoulder and discreetly pointed the target out. Sally Yeh asked. "Do you see the one, that does not hold you in their gaze?" "Yes, he just takes a quick look at us, from time to time." She was impressed by my attention to detail. "This is your inner exploration coming to the fore Jason. You are becoming one of us within your thoughts and this reflection, will bear its fruit to the seeing eyes of the true believer." Thinking for a moment I was in a dream, but no. Our guardian came back to us with a smile on his face. Well it seemed that I had notice someone all right, but the person in question was on our side. "Well done, Jason." Sally Yeh remarks were apricated. "You are feeling the presence of the one who may do you harm, this is excellent." I was pleased with myself. Having picked out someone who had actually been there to watch us. Making our way to the side of the hotel, a car was waiting. Finding ourselves on our way to the airport. The difficult part was to get out without them noticing us.

As we were driving, I asked Sally Yeh, "How do you propose to get out of here without them spot us?" "Jason, we to have our contacts at the airport. It will not be easy, but I am sure we will go unseen. These prying eyes with unwelcome motives, shall see only what we allow them to see." "That sounds good in theory, but will it work in practice?" Her calm manner was soothing. "We will leave it to the Gods and the wisdom of the powerful interior forces that lie within us all." I was surprised by this. "You obviously have great faith in the powers of the Buddha." "Why do you not hold the faith of your God within you Jason?" "I do, but in smaller doses than you do Sally Yeh. There are many where I come from that abstain from any belief. I think they are afraid of what they would find inside themselves." She knew where her own beliefs took her. "This is the essence of our faith, belief. Not only belief, also belief in what we do is just and right for the many who have little." I settled back down into the seat of the car. Only hoping these people knew what they are doing. Having been taken into their extended family and shown their generosity. If I do survive this ordeal, I will see that the community on the island get the share that my father had bestowed upon them. There was movement in the car, I figured we were nearing the airport. It was in my vision. Slowly making our way through the maze of roads to get to the entrance. On arrival our guardian got out first and looked around, he then beckoned for us to come forward. The air was dry when I stepped outside. Within the terminal building, the air–conditioning calmed the protruding beads of perspiration from my forehead. Our guardian walked before us and had our tickets. Not realising until then that he was coming with us to

Hong Kong. Turning to Sally Yeh. "I didn`t realise he coming to?" The reply was precise and to the point. "Yes, it is wise." This makes me feel somewhat safer. It was ten twenty in the evening and we were leaving at eleven. The tickets were processed and we headed for the departure lounge. After paying our departure tax we moved through to the departure hall. Our protector was on constant watch, his eyes moving in all directions. The duty free shops were upon us and I straggled through them to pass some time. Bumping into Sally Yeh. "Jason, have you been keeping your eyes on the many that pass us?" "I at times have been engrossed in the items on display." "So I see, but if you had, you would have noticed the eyes which follow us now. They have been pursuing us since we entered the airport." I wanted to enquire to whom did she refere to. "Does these sets of eyes, come in the form of a man or a woman?" The question I posed brought a smile to the lips of Sally Yeh. "You have the quick brain and the eyes are in the form of a woman. This you will have to work out for yourself." My mind was executing its search engine, slowly filtering out the faces, that I felt didn't come into recognition. Remembering what she had said to me about eyes from afar. My radar scrutinized the upper tiers of the top floor. Was it someone with a uniform? If this were the case it would be hard to unmask the person. As there were so many within my eye level. This of course did narrow the framework of my observation. This I also did assume, who ever this person was, had the freedom of the airport. My eyes were focusing on the milling throng. My solitude was broken by the sound of Sally Yeh's voice. "Jason, we will move to the departure lounge now. Having the unseen ones eyes upon us when we land in Hong Kong." Letting it sink in and tried not to dwell on it to much. Of course we will have our own people there to. Entering the departure lounge we sat at the rear. Deciding to close my eyes and shut the world out of my thoughts. Immersing myself in my inner self. Relaxation, calmness and a quick re–energising of my depleted resources were filling the reservoir of my mind. Sally Yeh cruelly interrupted my inner thoughts. The tug on my shoulder caught me off guard. "Come Jason, we must check that you have not left your case back at the front desk." I knew this to be a ploy, as I did not have a case with me. Getting up I followed the two out of the departure lounge. Heading back into the main concourse. Assuming this to be a diversionary tactic. "You must realise Jason, that this other Triad family may try to have your hand in theirs. This by the time we leave the plane. Be on your guard, all the while we are at the airport. Be wary of those who sit next to you, or those who may talk to you." This had certainly concentrated my mind, on the immediate task in hand. Getting myself in one piece to the Public Registrar's Office was my intention. Needing to be with, the people that I am with now. If I have any chance of rescuing Phoebe from the untold hardship that she and her sister are going through. Their liberation from Thailand is the more important thing to me now and my own safety. My eyes were stirring in all direction, the cleaning lady and the person behind the counter selling stamps. My movement was fast and swift, leaving the other two behind. Hearing a still voice in my ear. "Jason, you are like a beacon that gives off the most light." My attention was drawn to the wise voice and I settled down into a gentle pace. Back in the main duty free shopping area. Our protector went to a counter and came back with a briefcase. Handing this over to Sally Yeh. She walked towards one of the seated areas dotted around the area. We all sat at one of the set of seats. Sally Yeh opened the briefcase as she had keys in her jacket. My mind jumped to the conclusion that she already was aware of what was to transpire. Opening the case and inside there seemed to be plenty of paperwork. Looking at me she said. "This will be of great interest to you Jason. This paperwork is in fact, a list of the payments to politicians and other Government sources. This of course is from the Triad family who hold your friend Phoebe. There is also a list of under the counter drugs that is supplied and I am afraid your late fathers network of shops in Hong Kong is on it. If we Jason, give you this list what will you do with it?" "Well it would be my intention to hand this valuable information over to the authorities." She was aware of my intentions. "I thought you would say this, but it is not our intention for you to do this. You and we also, do not know who is working for this Triad family, we thought it better if you used these papers to unbind the shackles that effect the release of your friend Phoebe." I didn't know what to say to her. "This is out of the blue." "What is this thing you say, out of the blue?" "Oh, it is a saying where I come from. Em, it means that this gesture was unexpected and I am humbly grateful for it. But I decline the offer, as it leaves you without an option to bring these Triads to their rightful decline." "No Jason, this is why we have some more papers, these would be sufficient to undo these people within the Government circle. We as I have said, would like you to make use of these for the pursuance of your good friend." This gesture was a significant outlay on their behalf. "I give in to your generosity. I commend that I as my father before me, gave to your orphanage the necessary funds and now I give my word of honour, that I will carry out the promise having made to you and your people." She seemed moved by my undertaking. "This is the word of an honourable person Jason." With those words she gave a slight bow. Thinking it appropriate to do likewise. We all moved from our seats. Walking I turned to Sally Yeh and asked. "What do we do about this current Triad family?" "This problem within our midst, is one that we will try to confine to the back of our minds for the time being. The task of getting you safely to Hong Kong is our main platform now. This is vital to all our aims at present. Move within the confines of the airport, so as not to give these people any chance of preventing our progress."

I had the briefcase now contained in my grip and we began to walk back to the departure lounge. Our protector was very cautious now with every step. Being in a confined place, so the thought of an attempt to remove me from my companions did cross my mind. Our eyes were trawling the cascade of colour and obstacles that confronted us. It was nearing the time for us to depart the airport, so we quickly made our way to the departure gate. The room was full and just about ready to board. The announcement came to board and a sigh of relief drifted through our bodies. Our energies were depleted and the extra drain on our systems had taken its toll. Being able to sit down for a long period of time and relax the inner tensions of pure raw emotion seeping from my functioning body. Was it the traveller within, whom I was urging to refrain from shattering, or overloading my system? My weary bones were beginning to ache. Whichever cog was being twisted, I felt the grip get tighter and tighter. The yearning for sleep, the false dawns of the previous attempted emancipation of Phoebe and the new and ever more threatening demise of myself was taking its toll. Then the sound of a chime came over the public address system. "Ladies and gentlemen we are now boarding the flight to Hong Kong." This lifted the attention span, which in turn rekindled the adrenalin flow. About to board the plane, kept swirling around in my head. "Jason, we will rest our weary bodies for awhile, on the plane." I just shook my head in agreement. "Your face has the sign of the child. You ask yourself why are you here?" I guess I knew that I was questioning the decision I had taken to follow my beliefs. Tired at this stage I did not want to dwell on this matter to much. Finding our seats we settled down. The journey time was going to leave us getting into Hong Kong early in the morning. I slept from the time I sat in my seat.

# Chapter

# VIII

Now I was removing myself from the aircraft again. "Time to keep a watchful eye on your surroundings Jason." Hearing this wise advice in my left ear. "This you must pay good attention to. As we will be going through a different passport control." I hadn't thought about this. The slight high I was on, was soon washed away with this insight. The pumping and the vibration of my heart began to drill in. My internal emotions were reaching the shallow vaults in the pit of my stomach. A slow trickle of adrenalin began to filter back into my body. The focusing mind became more aware of the limbs and this in turn made them less static. Coming to full awareness now and I needed to be on top of my guard. We walked towards passport control and uniformed guards were in my eyesight. My travelling companions walked past me, to their point of exit. I was confronted with a queue and slowly waited in line. At this stages able to see them both in a similar queue. Then it was my time to pass through control. The guard looked at me for some time without twitching an eye. Wondering are these people the same, all over the world. Then with a sword like action he stamped my passport. Following through to the baggage reclaim. Noticing at this point, that my two travelling companions were nowhere to be seen. A anxious state of worry descended upon me at this stage, not knowing who would be waiting outside. Plenty of taxis for the local hotels and the mingling of the advancing throng, heading for their destinations, but not my companions, no flickering glances, no eye contact, no one there. Looking at my watch, fifteen minutes had elapsed. Not wishing to seem anxious, so I looked around for a seat. Casually I took a paper I had in my briefcase and began to read it. Hoping it would look like I was waiting to collect someone. My thoughts were pressing me to come up with some alternative plan, in the event that they would not be joining me. How to make my own way to the Registrar Office, without being followed and possibly held hostage myself. Jumbled up thoughts raced through my mind. What if they were removed from the airport without me knowing? Looking around the airport to see if there were any friendly faces that would strike my gaze. The mass throng of a walking army, with a purpose in their stride, did nothing for my inner feelings. Getting up from the seat, just to make myself feel like I was doing something useful. As I sat down to that dejected feeling, the smiling face of Sally Yeh appeared in front of me. "Thought that we both would remove ourselves from these surroundings without your company, this I fear not Jason?" Curious to find out what had transpired. "Why did they hold you?" "We have been questioned by the local authorities about some minor thing. This is the doing of the one who holds your friend. We expected as much, that is why we took this early flight. We may have been rushing later this very morning if our departure had been delayed later. This way we are the people in control." I was sure what Sally Yeh was saying made sense, but it floated over my head. Our protector soon came to our side and we departed the airport. Finding myself now entering the community, which we had left not to long ago. They were in a happier mood, as their sons and loved ones had been liberated form their captors. These people would benefit from my late fathers inheritance. Hopefully I will be able to donate to the construction of the Medical Centre they are building. It was good to see that the Triads had lost their grip in this community. These people, along with the influence of Sally Yeh and Cho Yun, had started the long trek to breaking the corrupt cord of the oppressor and giving some dignity back to its people. Sally Yeh, the orphanage along with the proposed Health Centre, also proper educational programmes, would lead to this community

134

being able to stand alone and help themselves. This is why I have no hesitation in helping in any way I can. If that is what this money from my late father can do, then so be it.

These were the under privileged and the most vulnerable. The Triads had for centuries ravaged their belongings and decimated the community. The young were rotting in jails, having been forced to operate illegal activities for these barons of prey. It was now time to re–ignite the fuse of change. This was being fuelled with the help of Sally Yeh and her brother Cho Yun. These two people were a catalyst for the combined efforts of the whole community. In helping themselves through education and providing an orphanage and a Medical Centre. The money, which I can provide from my inheritance, will hopefully be the first step in many to come. Seeing the community grow even in the last few days. The release of their sons from the chains of the Triads had given them new hope. Finding myself resting from the journey. The elders were in session with Sally Yeh. In a few hours I would be able to sign for my fathers illegal ill–gotten gains. But this would be to the benefit of this community. How long would I be able to hold onto the inheritance, would not only cause me a problem, but the whole community. Would we reach our destination, would I see Phoebe again, would I see them back home again? In the space of a few days away from home, I have virtually been kidnapped and whisked in and out of back alleys on motorbikes like there was no tomorrow. Ironic me saying that, because this could be the whole point, there may be no tomorrow. I walked out onto the veranda, the morning was trying to emerge. Natural light shinning on the green vegetation, the hissing of the beating insects, the noise drifted above the foliage. My wandering mind had taken a shine to the far away Temple which adorned the walled yard not far beyond the complex. Finding myself being drawn by its enchantment. My legs had a mind of their own. I found myself being dragged in the direction of the Temple. Having a calm feeling inside as if to say everything will be O K. But I knew in my heart, things would be very different. These ordinary people milling around the complex. People making handcrafts and metal spinners shaping their wares. Watching a wood carver beginning the complex manoeuvring of his skill.

Smoothing out the pieces that formed in his mind. Thinking to myself, why couldn't I do that? The Temple was still in my vision, the pull growing stronger. I had walked beyond the gates of the complex, to see a three–layered canopy tiled roof on top of a red–bricked circular building. The pull was getting stronger. "Jason, where are you going?" Hearing a voice in my ear. Turning to see Sally Yeh follow me out of the complex. Turning to her I said. "I just felt like visiting the Temple." "Well don't, as you may or may not realise Jason. These other Triads, have people stationed in and around this community, who do not have the same concern for their fellow brothers and would gladly hand you over to the highest bidder." It sank deep down inside what she just said. Returning back inside. My faith lay with the telling influence of the leaders of the community along with Sally Yeh and her brother. Thinking that my late father tried to put some money back into the community. "We will make arrangements to move on shortly." She went back into the house, while I took another stroll around some of the workshops. Sally Yeh appeared once again on the veranda and walked towards me. "We will be using motorbikes later this morning. Taking two bikes and a jeep. In the jeep will be two people dressed to look like us. While each of us take a bike. This of course is to confuse our pursuers." My stomach was softly moving inside, with the hint of me sliding through back streets again. "Jason, we need to be there at eleven. Not wishing to take chances, so we will leave in half an hour." Heading for my room, as the sun came out. It was going to be another hot and sticky day. The pressure was now on to secure the share holding for the release of Phoebe and the welfare of this community. I want to be able to keep my promise to Phoebe and to the village. Needing to get to the Registrars Office in one piece. It was getting near the time for our departure. Observing the motorbikes enter the courtyard. Behind them came the jeep. Sally Yeh came out of the house and talked to the people on the bikes and in the jeep. Beckoning for me to join her. I did so. The two bike riders were very young. Plenty of banking at corners and moving across lanes, I thought. "It is the hour that we must leave." Getting on the rear of my bike. I was handed a helmet, hoping that it wouldn't come into contact with the ground in any shape or form. An elder came out and said something to Sally Yeh. With that we were off. Feeling the power of the bike pull beneath me as we sped off. The bike in front banked to the right and we swung to the left. Then came the jeep. So whoever was watching, would certainly be in two or should I say three minds, as to who to follow. The bike banked heavily first to the left, then to the right. My stomach was behind me somewhere. Both of us had the same type of leather jackets on. So from behind, you could not make out who was who. The jeep had two figures inside so it was also hard to make out the identities of the people inside. It looked like they were used to forcing the issue in such matters. I felt an air of calm come over me, for no reason. The air felt fresher. The destination, the impact it would have upon me. These sensations had overpowered me in the past. I was now focused and in control. Having a clear picture of my late father in my head and one of Phoebe to. A quick glance over my shoulder, to see if I was being followed. No one caught my eye. Then in the periphery of my vision, a car in the distance caught my attention and it was following us. Hardly noticed it. Tapping my driver on the right shoulder. Pointing to the car in the distance. He nodded in response. With that, my whole body was arched in a curve, as the bike sped off. Feeling the full surge of power beneath me. Within seconds, we were doing the things I had feared. Swerving from one side of the road to the other. Now interweaving between cars, buses and ordinary push bikes. Thank God, there didn't seem to be any pedestrians taking a chance of crossing the road in front of us. No sign of the car now. What if there was more than one car? Soon learning to dread those words. Looking behind me once again and what I saw didn't excite me. It was another motor bike in pursuit of us. Tapping the driver with haste, he saw the other bike. Immediately he reacted to the situation. Now, there was no time to hold on as we were virtually airborne before I looked back. The pursuing bike reacted in response. The faster we went, the more they responded. Beads of perspiration rolling down my forehead had hardly time to hit the ground. Who were the pursuers? The same people who held Phoebe, or the other Triad family? Were they after me, or just making sure we go to the Registrars Office? Our bike maneuvering was like turning on a sixpence. Our breakneck speed, had me holding on for dear life. They seemed to be catching us. Suddenly cutting across the traffic and into an open yard. Barely holding onto the driver. As soon as we passed through the yard, you could hear the screech of burning rubber. At this stage the gate had been shut, someone is keeping tabs on us. We sped off in the opposite direction on a parallel street. My driver was very edgy. I must admit, it did become scary at times. Not to long to dwell, our friends on the bike were back. Here we go again, it was getting hard to loose this bike. Feeling it swerve, as it hit the curbside. I felt the might of the bike take us along the road to a grinding halt. Rolling on the ground, we both got up quickly and we weren't hanging around for long. The other bike was nearly upon us as we made our way towards the shopping complex. "You take helmet off." Immediately responded to the request. Within a matter of seconds the helmet lay on the ground. Mingling with the throng. The driver pointed to the entrance of the shopping complex. Seeing in the distance, the other pursuer get off the bike and follow us on foot. My driver began to run, pulling me by the arm. Once inside the words of the driver was chilling. "You mister Jason must find your own way to office. I will bring him on journey to nowhere." "But what will happen to you if they catch you?" "I will be the safe one. If I can, miss Sally will know of you and our encounter." With that he disappeared out of my sight.

Now I had to find my way out and onto the Registrars Office. My adrenaline was in full flow, my heart was pumping faster and my blood pressure was rising. Looking to see if the other two were anywhere near my own space. I made my way towards the nearest exit. It was going to be an uphill battle to get to my destination. Who is after me? I had to assume that it is the family who want the inheritance at any cost. The exit sign getting nearer with every step. As I departed the shopping complex, I gazed to see if my driver was about. No, not to be seen. The heat began to take its toll on my body. Slower movements of my limbs, making it harder to grind out a path for myself. Finding my bearings, where I was on Kowloon? Knowing I wasn't far away from the ferry pier. Try to make it to the star ferry pier. I was on Chatham road. Knowing which direction in which to go. Figuring I was about ten minutes away from the pier. Moving within the throng, loosing myself in the sway of the movement of the crowd. Quick glances, many faces, movement carrying me forward. This was going to be a long ten minutes. My mind was focused on getting to the ferry. What to do after that was in the future. My emotions were pulling me all over the place. Phoebe, Sally Yeh, the driver, were they alright? The adrenaline once again began to flow, my legs felt lighter, my direction more assured. A sense of direction crept into my body. I knew what to do, where to go, who to see. Beginning to get my focus back, I thought criss–cross the road, to throw off any unwanted stragglers. Turning without thinking and running across the road. Creating scenarios with every step, it was up to me now, to fight the inner demons. Confusion began to reign, my tempo slowed down, I was on the back foot. My mouth was dry, the heat was once again taking its toll. Bumping into an oncoming pedestrian. A girl, she distracted me for a moment, but with positive results. What was I doing? Where am I going? These few questions in rapid succession, brought an air of reality to my plight. Looking at my watch, the time. Move faster, move direct, the calling of my fathers voice, rang in my brain. I am going to get there, I am going to reach the destination which I seek. Positive thoughts were creeping into my mind once again and swallowing up the demons. Colors, all sorts of colors, began to unfold in front of my eyes. Opening my mind up to the sea of people who reflected my inner emotions. I found myself standing on the opposite side of the street. To the ferry, how to get there was going to be a hard task. The point was, I had arrived at the first part of my journey. To continue on and come to a conclusion, was my biggest problem. By the rotation of the ferries, one was dew to leave within a short period of time. Standing to the side of the ferry terminal, to give myself a greater chance of deluding any unwelcome prying eyes. Assuming they would be watching the ferry pier. Having to get the Registrar's Office on Hong Kong Island. My chance was approaching. The ferry was about to dock and off load its foot passengers. The ferry was packed with people and this would give me a chance to board the ferry without being seen. The foot passengers were streaming off as

I fought my way on. I went to the bottom deck. Reckoning if I was inside, they wouldn't be able to throw me overboard. The toilets. The trip's duration was fifteen minutes. I could stay in the toilets that long. So without any further searching for the answer, quietly and discreetly I disappeared into the toilet. Feeling the tug of the ferry as it pulled away from the pier. Thinking that I may get to the other side in one piece. The ferry was moving at a steady speed. Thoughts already of landing on the other side, were forming in my mind. What tram to catch and where to go? My body could feel the tugging sensation of the ferry as it slowed to moor alongside the pier. The next big step was coming up. Having to open the door and hope no one was waiting to grab me. Pushing the door gently and the glaring sunlight hit my eyes. It was hard to see for the moment. But not feeling a tug of anyone's hands on my body. Walking out and off the ferry surrounded by many hundreds of people. From here I could see the tram station. Immediately making my way towards it. Feeling O K, if not altogether somewhat nervous. A tram approach the station and with that, I ran and managed to grab hold of the closing door Once inside the second part of my journey began. Feeling calm, focused and not downbeat. Reckoning if I can make it to the Registrar's Office, there would be someone from Cho Yun or Sally Yeh there. The tram was heading in the right direction and it wasn't to long before I saw the station I had to get off at. Sheung Wan district was my destination and it was upon me. The tram was slowing down and as it did so, I jumped off. No one, for the moment, following. Quickly ending up on the far side of the road. Taking from my inside jacket a card that had the exact address. Knowing which way to go from here. Crossing over to Morrison street and heading for Stauton street. Having time to spare. Out of the corner of my eye, I caught a glimpse of an object coming towards me. It was a motorbike, the one that had been following me on Kowloon. It wasn't that far away. I ran, my legs pumping, my adrenalin was on overtime, my heartbeat pounded like a drum. Quickly I turned down Lok Ku road. It was narrow, only wide enough for one car. As I entered I could see a car coming in my direction. I ran towards it and it slowed down, the bike was gaining on me. Managing to squeeze by the car. But the bike couldn't, then I saw a pillion passenger get off and follow me on foot. My heart pumped like thunder, my bones shook like rubber. Running as fast as I could. Approaching the junction of Ladder street I immediately turned right. Knowing this to be in the direction of the Registrar's office. Catching sight of the building in the distance. Its features stood out, as it was a throw back to the last century. My pursuer was gaining fast. The heat was now playing a part in my demise. The energy was being sucked from my veins. Seeing the entrance to the building, but I feared my hunter would be to fast. Then from nowhere a motorbike appeared heading directly for me. This is the finish thinking to myself, might as well give in. The rider pulled up in front of me and revved the machine. This in turn spun the bike around, now facing the Registrar's Office. To my astonishment, he grabbed my shoulder and pulled me onboard the bike. With that we sped off in the direction of the Registrar's Office. I couldn't work out what was happening. Then as we approached the entrance I saw Sally Yeh standing there. "You didn't think we would let you be late for such an important occasion, now did you Jason?" I smiled with delight and wiped the beads of perspiration from my brow. Rushing inside the entrance doors. Heading straight for the registrars Office. I wanted no more mishaps. "Did my driver get away?" "Yes, he did a Confucius on the remaining warring dragons." Smiling when she said these words. Two guardians plus Sally Yeh now flanked me, as we made our way up the stairs to the Registrar's Office. It was open until four thirty that day.

My mind drifted back to Ireland, whilst in the care of these people. Thinking it a strange time to think of back home. Maybe it was something inside me, trying to reassure myself that everything would be all right. My thoughts of the day I received the letter, secretly thinking of the travel and adventure. It sure has turned out to be an adventure, an adventure in more ways than one. Not thinking of the fact, that I would be the subject of kidnapping and attempts to endanger my life. "Jason, we as you say in the west, are not out of the woods yet." I didn't like what I was hearing. Here we were in the building of the Registrar's Office. "What do you mean, aren't we here in the building, what more could happen?" The silence coming from

Sally Yeh was deafening. "You have to realize that these people have friends in all kinds of places and that includes here." My heart rate had risen a notch. "So Sally Yeh, you think in your wisdom, that they may try something now?" "I am afraid so." My thoughts were awash with incomplete visions. "I do not see the journeys end yet." She followed on. Feeling myself suddenly looking around me for any signs of unwanted attention. My impatience was growing as we neared the office. "What would they gain, this other group of Triads?" "Their intervention would bestow you upon them and in turn would hold the key to their future." Didn't sound all that tempting. I knew inside myself, I was a willing challenger to an attack upon my being. This I had inwardly seen in the past few days. My thoughts were now focused on getting to another floor. Inside the words kept repeating themselves Get there, just get there. My eyes flickered from side to side, glancing at each doorway. The sound of footsteps got louder and louder, closer and closer. Catching my attention and what seemed rather out of place for such a quite place. We all looked around and I found my shoulder being tugged in one direction. "We must retreat this way." Now on our way down a side stairs. "But what about the signing?" Sally Yeh`s reply came in a calm relaxed assertion. "We will make sure you sign by end of day." Once again this was a different status to what I had hoped. The entrance door was upon us, only this time we were leaving in a gallop. Hearing the sound of our pursuers in the not too far off distance. Feeling like shouting ; I'll be back. As we hit the sunlight, into to view came a jeep and two motorbikes. Not that bike again, hopping not. My assumption was wrong as my frame was being manhandled and pushed onto the motorbike. The door swung open behind us, seeing three faces within our proximity. My driver left my stomach somewhere on the pavement, as we burnt rubber. It felt like as though someone had winded me, this feeling in the pit of my stomach. My fading memory was of the other group of people alighting from a car on the opposite side of the building and confronting the onrushing flock that we just avoided. It must have been the apposing Triad family, wishing to demonstrate their might. What is going to happen to Phoebe, will they ever let her go? We sped down another side streets, with the other motorbike following and the jeep drifting off in the opposing direction. Not knowing if Sally Yeh was on the bike or in the jeep, of course this was the object. I wasn't encouraged to look at the speed we were traveling at, as my head dropped to one side. The road came even closer to my face as we rounded a dangerous bend. Hitting a bump in the road, I went straight up into the air. My driver was lucky to hold onto the handle bars, as we slid from side to side. Thumping the seat with a wallop, which in turn put my heart in my mouth, along with everything else. The less said about that the better. From my internal grumbling I knew it hurt in more than one place. Feeling ourselves slow down, oh no I thought, what's wrong? The bike came to a halt behind a parked car. You wouldn't see the bike from the road position. As I got off I could see the problem. A rear wheel puncture, we must have hit the kerbside. My drivers immediate words were, "Not good, this area not good place." Less than encouraging, as I looked behind to see if anyone was pursuing us, not at the moment. "Me no can fix." Really sounding great now, here is my driver who is supposed to watch over me, afraid of what lies behind the walls. Mind you he's not the only one. "We need to get out, bad place." "What do you mean?" "This place no good for me, you." This area I guess is controlled by either of the opposing Triad families that are pursuing us. "Well, how do we get out of here?" "Me don't know." "Oh that's great, what direction do we go in?" He pointed to a narrow side street, I didn't like it. "No, I think we will go in this direction." I started to walk in the direction I had pointed. Hearing him follow quickly behind. Talk about the blind leading the blind. My stomach was churning inside, where to go? What to do? Questions sprang up, but little in the way of reassuring answers. Basic instincts of human survival came into play, flight or fight. The first option sprang immediately to mind. Seeing a taxi in the distance I ran towards it, waving my hand in the air. To my surprise it stopped, moving hastily it wasn't long before my companion and I were inside. On our journey, my driver spoke in his native tongue. The person beside me now looked much happier. We go back where we belong. Admitting to being somewhat unsure sure of the person beside me back there. Side stepping the main thoroughfare we proceeded to a narrow side lane. The car was unsuitable for the lane. But the driver duly delivered, stopping outside a battered wooden door. Getting out and looking around, it seemed all right to me. Where were we and whose place was this? Suddenly a thought struck me, an impulse. What if this person I was with was in fact going to hand me over to one the Triad families? The fear built up inside. My companion never tried to phone Sally Yeh when we were supposed to be trapped. What if that was the location that I was to be delivered to, in the first place. Suddenly he realized that I had copped on to him and knew I wouldn't be an effortless target. As the taxi was pulling away on an impulse I jumped into it. "Go, go, go," I screamed. The taxi driver sped off as I was dangling out of it. Left lying across the rear seat as the taxi swerved to avoid oncoming traffic. My traveling companion ran after me, but it was too late as the diminishing figure of him drifted off in the distance. This experience was a wake up call, now I was on my own, how would I find Sally Yeh and Cho Yun. Was it worth taking a chance and asking the taxi driver, or was I in the wrong Province? Knowing I had to get to Kowloon and out of Hong Kong Island, for the time being. Telling the taxi driver to take me to Victoria Harbour. I needed to catch the ferry to Kowloon. Noticing on our way that we passed by Happy Valley Racecourse, so we must have been heading deeper into the bowels of Hong Kong. I should think the principle of the Triad families, were rooted in this area. Seeing in the distance, the vast imposing building of the Central Plaza. I knew then we were approaching the ferry pier. Wondering what had happened to the driver I was with? Had he managed to alert the Triad family about my evading him, or had he vanished himself, not wanting to face the consequence of the impending and vigorous grilling he would have had to encounter from the Triad family? Time was of the essence, if I was to make the deadline later that afternoon. My conscious mind was working overtime, trying in advance to work out the best way to contact Sally Yeh. The ferry pier came into sight from the back seat of the taxi. Looking for odd characters, that didn't seem too interested in the ferry comings and goings, but in its passengers. Maybe the other driver had done what I had thought and cleared off. If this was the case, I had a chance of making it back to the Registrar's Office before four thirty. Now having to think of a way of getting to Sally Yeh. Paying the taxi driver I slipped quietly out onto the side of the ferry pier. Walking towards the boat I heard a thundering noise behind me. Afraid to look around, as I may not like what I saw. Knowing I would have to, so slowly turning my head and to my surprise, some people were pickup some iron bars that had come loose from a pallet near by. Now on board the boat in one piece. My conscious mind raced ahead to the next destination on Kowloon. What would I find there? Would there be a hostile committee of two Triad families or would Sally Yeh have someone there? All questions these erupted in my conscientious mind. Not noticing, but at the same time I found myself very calm, still and relaxed to a certain degree. It must have been my tape I been listening to. Many thoughts were racing around in my conscious mind, but it was though they were organized. At the same time I was able to deal with them in a logical manner. Of course this may not be the case when we get to the other side of Victoria Harbour. Feeling a lot more in control, although not fully. Wondering to myself, did this make sense. The boat was nearing its destination. Looking out across the river, not too many people around on our arrival. Docking at Tsim Sha Tsui District and the time in the region of twelve forty–five. Having until four thirty this same afternoon, to sign for my fathers inheritance. Feeling a rush of blood to my body, as I disembarked. Quick glances to overview the landing venue. Nothing of any interest caught my eye. Do I take a taxi or walk? The latter option appear the best, as I was already in my stride. Heading for Kowloon Park, which was already in my sight. Being able to sit and think there, if nothing else. The sun was beaming down from the blue sky above, as I walked towards Haiphong road entrance to the park. Reaching the park without any mishaps. Do I contact Lantau Island, but unsure if Sally Yeh was on Kowloon. Now other thoughts about Phoebe came into my conscious mind. Had they moved Phoebe, after what had happened at the Registrar's Office? If only I could contact Cho Yun or Sally Yeh. Will I be able to get back to Bangkok after I sign for the inheritance? Beginning to thinking positively, gathering snip bits from my subconscious. Do I go back to where it all started, at the Park hotel? Maybe it was to risky at this present time. My next move was going to be crucial to my future well being and that of Phoebe's. Not having anticipated this development. Trying to think logically and retrace my steps. What part of Kowloon would I find Sally Yeh? Then thinking about getting to the Registrar's Office by myself was giving me the mental strength to succeed. As I had seen earlier, they were waiting for us to arrive. Maybe they may not anticipate a solitary person. This thought was developing in my conscious state. It began to gather momentum, as the minutes ticked away. Beginning to envisage myself stepping off the ferry and catching a tram to the Registrar's Office. This time I would be more weary of them and make it more difficult for them to recognize me. If I could simply slip in the side door, without them taking any notice of me. This course was drawing me like a magnet. Knowing I would have to alter my appearance if I was going to carry this out to its full conclusion. Guessing they would be looking for the face they had become use to seeing. So my first endeavor would be to find a market to buy some different clothes. My plight was taking a new dimension. Earlier I had read about the market in Temple street. This was just off the north entrance gate to the park. Feeling myself drawn in this direction. My limp body leapt into action, legs pumping forward, eyes and head rotating with every step. The exit gate drew neared with every step. Approaching slowly I walked out and onto the pavement. Nothing to be seen. Then it came to me, it's a night market. I can't wait that long. So without loosing momentum I headed for one of the small side street markets. Able to gather what I needed from these stalls. Now where could I change? One of the hotels, or the easiest place I could think of, which was staring me in the face, McDonalds. Yes, thinking, this would do for the purpose I had in mind. Finding myself within its structure I headed straight to the toilet. Having purchased a small travel bag so as for the retention of my old clothes. Quickly I changed, and took a glimpse in the mirror. Who was this person I see before me? Thinking I had excelled myself. Continuing on my journey was now my priority.

As I stepped from McDonalds, I noticed a public phone. Walking across the road and picking up the receiver, I dialed the code for Ireland and then the house number. The sound of a ringing tone followed by someone picking it up. It was J.P. "Where is Sasha?" "She is gone out to the pictures, why? Do you need to speak to her?" "No, its just I thought she would be there. How is everything there?" "Its O K, nothing to tell you. When will you be back?" "In the not too distant future. Listen, take care of yourself and Sasha." "Is there something wrong, Jason?" I must have sounded tense. "No, why do you ask?" "It's your voice, you seem to be quivering." "It may be the phone line, being so far away, you know these lines. Well, I have to go now. Say hello to Sasha for me, good luck J.P." Putting the receiver down, with an empty feeling in my stomach. Digging deep inside for my inner strength again. Knowing that I had tapped into the power within and it was at this point I needed it more than ever. Standing back from the phone I breathed in a deep gasp of air. Holding it for three or so seconds and letting it out. Feeling the calmness re–enter my body. Now able to face the next hurdle, as my determination, my willpower and my inner confidence had re–emerged within. Now trying to focus on the task ahead of me. I headed back to the park. Sitting there I had a trial run in my head of what I was about to do. Get on the ferry and catch a tram to the Registrar's Office. Then the difficult part, get past those outside searching for me, without being recognized. It was coming together in my conscious state. If I didn't know me, I wouldn't recognize myself a good disguise and now it would be put to the test. Heading for the ferry the sun was making me very warm with this extra layer of clothes on. Feeling I was rather tall for just simply fitting in with the locals. So what I had prepared was, set myself up as a backpacker. This did not warrant any undue attention, but it was at the Registrar's Office, that's where the fruit of my labor would tell. Stepping from the ferry, back onto Hong Kong Island. Heading straight for a tram. It was now two thirty, so I had plenty of time. There were quite a few people about and this was in my favor. Hopping on the first tram. Now entering the lion's den and hopping I wasn't going to be their fodder. I was extremely calm, relaxed and in control of my inner thoughts.

My mind was a ticking nerve centre, of pulsating emissions, of positive emotive reactions, to the forthcoming events. Focused on the task ahead, entry into the Registrar's Office without being recognized. The stress level was in overdrive and I felt that the immediate task was achievable. Deep breaths were the order of the day. My sunglasses hid my eyes and the telescopic scan that I was making, every few seconds of my fellow passengers. Didn't get the feeling that I was being followed. The wide sweep of my eye level, gave me an advantage because of my height. The immediate passengers didn't seem to pose any threat to me. The tram was visibly slowing down as we neared the station where I wished to depart. No wishing to disembark to near the Registrar's Office, in case they had people at that station. As it was, a ten minutes walk or so, would get me to my destination. Walking up Pedder street, this led indirectly onto Queens road. Not too far away and I was out of sight from prying eyes. Hoping to enter the Registrar's Office from the off street side entrance. Plenty of traffic and people in the area, so I didn't feel as if I was fighting a lonely battle. My thoughts swung to Phoebe and what may be happening to her. Is Cho Yun still keeping the hotel under surveillance in Bangkok? If so, will they be able to remove the antagonists of their prize possession? gradually brining my mind back to reality and the present situation at hand. Trying to figure out, which was the chief road to take for my entrance. Staunton street, lead in the general direction, so it was in this direction I moved forward. At least I could be taken for a tourist with my knapsack, my hat and my sunglasses. The hat was doing its job, as it was a very warm and sticky. Coming into view was the imposing building of the Registrar's Office. My heart once again began to beat faster and I physically began to slow my pace down. On the odd occasion, turning to gaze into some of the shop windows, so as not to draw to much attention to myself. Now approaching Po Hing street and I had plenty to spare. Thinking that I could see the side entrance from my vantage point on the street. Small clusters of characters were walking in spasms in and around the building, at frequent intervals. This seemed to happen on a five minute basis, up one side of the building and then back down. Then they would, what I could make out two pairs of two people each, walk down the opposite side of the building as the other pair walked up. Turning to gaze in one of the shop windows from which I had set up a lookout point. A good vantage point, as I could see the reflection of them walking up and down. The good news for me at this point was, they didn't seem interested in the stranger on the opposite side of the street. I thought the camera around my left shoulder was a nice touch as it gave authenticity to my cover. Mind you, the all–imposing hat did have something to do with it. Not wishing to chance my entrance yet, as I felt I needed more time to explore the situation. Having to psyche myself into the correct frame of mind and I felt I had achieved quite a lot, in such a short space of time. It was time maybe to reinvest in my subconscious and take stock. Needing to concentrate now, on my ability to cover the ground to the side entrance. How fast could I move under this sometimes torturous sun. Quickness of mind, might not actually transit itself into action. My muscles were tensing, nerves becoming questioning, I didn't want this to last any longer than it had to. Digging deep within my internal resources I found myself calm and walking gently across the street towards the side entrance. As soon as I did, I felt all their eyes become fixed on me. It felt as though I had a sign pinned to my back saying. Here I am. This feeling did not ease as I crossed the street. Through my sunglasses, I noticed two protagonists walk in my direction. Internal thoughts were pressing me forward, calmly and in a relaxed fashion, not that I was, it just seemed that way. My subconscious mind was emanating the positive thoughts that I had installed in there on a regular basis. I kept walking towards the side entrance. Out of the corner of my eye, I could see these two surly guys were pressing their wide frames in my direction, as fast as I was heading for the entrance door. The sound of tyres screeching in the distance and the smell of rubber caught everyone by surprise. Looking around in the direction of the sound of the offending noise. With that the two progressing protagonists turned and bolted towards the oncoming motorbike. Keeping a calm resolve about me, I advanced to the side entrance. Pressing on and into the building and making immediately for the stairwell. Looking for the second floor. Turning to see if I had been followed inside. No one in view, so quickly I walked up the stairs. My mind for a split second turned to the commotion outside, who was on the bike? It wasn`t long before I began looking for the Registrar's Office. Seeing it in the distance the lettering became more into focus as I approached the glass–paneled door. Pushing open the door, to find a young looking woman behind an old faded desk.

I started with the most appropriate words I could find. "Hello, my name is Jason Byrne and I have come to sign some inheritance papers, which I believe are ready to be initialed." Not knowing if I had made myself clear. "You wish to sign now for papers?" This sounded progressive. "Yes," nodding in return to her question. A quick glance at my watch. The next words from her mouth were less encouraging. "I must speak to my superior first." Getting up from behind the desk and walking into the adjoining room. She had been gone for what seemed to me a long time. But in fact, it was in the region of two minutes. Reentering the room with my passport in her hand. Taking a look at the picture inside and then at me. She looked again. Thinking it's not too bad a likeness you know, keeping this to my inner thoughts. Beginning to feel anxious at this stage. My mouth was drying up, my breathing was deeper and I could feel a tingling in my hands. Next came the sentence that I wanted to hear. "You man in passport." Sitting back down into the seat she previously occupied. "I do up some documents for you to sign." Nodding in agreement. There was a small chair on my side of the desk. Pulling it to one side I sat on it. Glancing behind me on several occasions, not wishing the door to open, looking at my watch on a constant basis. Now I was toying with the thought, what if the Triad family were waiting outside. I would deal with that in it's own time and space. She was diligent in her work, going over every detail, handing me over some papers. "You sign papers now." "Hold on for a moment, while I read what it says." She seemed flustered by this. Maybe no one questioned their authority. Taking the papers in my hand I began to read the contents. It was interesting, as it also stated that I was the controller of a café on the island of Lamma, that of Sally Yeh's origin. "Do I get a copy of this here and now?" The reply was firm, "Yes, you sign now please." She was very demanding. "Hold on a wee moment, while I read the rest of this document." This caught her off guard. Handing me over the rest of the documents, with a kind of bemused look in her eyes. Assuming out here, people in authority are not usually questioned. It was fascinating to see before my eyes, the details of my late father's precautions, with regard to the family he had here. His reservations had to have some merit at the time. This unfortunately, is proving the point he was stating back when he made his will. His fear of this Triad family being interwoven into his immediate family here in Hong Kong, was an overpowering resolution that he saw a long way off. It also threw an unexpected benefit in my direction. It hadn't been stated that I now was also the new and full owner of the Café Reon on the Island of Lamma. Now that's a surprise, because Sally Yeh is from there and she never mentioned it. Is there some connection? Sure there must be. Everything here is connected in some form or another. Signing my name in full and then handing the paperwork back to the assistant. As soon as I handed the paperwork over, this young woman quickly stamped it. Excusing herself from my presence, as there had to be some official confirmation as to my signature. Sitting back in the chair and pondering the realistic chances of extracting Phoebe from the main Triad family. What was I going to do about this other Triad family? The young woman walked back into the open plan office with a copy of my inheritance. Passing the paperwork over to me and bowing in my presence, I reciprocated her gesture. I turned and walked out of the office. What was I about to walk into? The brown envelope contained the key to possibly a person's life on one hand. It also had my future in its destiny, as I could still benefit financially in some way from the transactions. A myriad of reflections stood before me. What path do I take? Phoebe's life was in my hands, also my own life, as this other Triad family didn't give a dam about how they came to have the control of the shops. Checking to see if it had an official stamp and all the paperwork was included in the envelope. All relevant paperwork was there. My next challenge was awaiting and this I did not relish. Putting the envelope away in my inside pocket. Knowing it had to be lodged with a reputable solicitor if I was going to stand any chance of seeing Phoebe alive again. Also I wished to gain some financial benefit from my late fathers inheritance, after all he was the one who suffered the most out of this. I was sure this Triad family had murdered him. My stomach tightened up as I began to walk towards the exit door. Glancing all around me, for that unexpected recoil from behind a closed door. My focus now was to get the papers to a solicitor, hopefully with the help of Sally Yeh and Cho Yun. Looking to see if I could use an alternative door? Taking a step forward and then turning on my heels I headed in the opposite direction. Can't afford to take any chances on either entrance. My father's death began to spring to my mind. Maybe it was the place and the circumstances, but it was poignant and having an effect on my internal feelings. My footsteps were of a short duration as I came upon the landing, leading down to the ground floor and possible mayhem. Not to many people stirring about, this didn't give me to much camouflage for my exit onto Square street. My options were limited. Beginning to breathe deeply, before I made my next move towards the exit door. Slowly walking down the landing stairs. I had two options, as there were two exit doors in my vision. Non inspiring thoughts of both doors being covered had seeped into my visualization. To seek inner resolve I affirmed my positive resolve and this in turn brought an immediate response from my conscious mind. Most people here in this building are wearing some sort of a uniform, what if I had one? This thought slowly crept further into my inner sanctuary. Scanning the corridor for anyone of my height and build. Not looking promising from my viewpoint. Glancing at the office doors in front of me. Searching to see if any of the door handles were unlocked? Walking to the top of the staircase, I didn't stop to think, I walked out into the sunshine of the day. The daylight hitting my eyes I felt the glare, as I squinted and put my sunglasses on to avoid the glare. Quickly walking across the street I could hear from behind a shout to stop. This was not my intention, nor did I do such a thing. Then hearing the pounding of footsteps in the background. Just at that moment, I saw a taxi pull up to let a passenger off. Immediately jumping into the back seat. "Move it, move it, the ferry pier." Hoping these words were making their point. He glanced in the rear mirror and took off like a bat out of hell. I was left sprawled on the rear seat. This didn't matter, as my objective had been accomplished. "They follow you, you in big trouble?" Replying in a harassed nature. "You bet they are, I bet your glad they aren't after you!" "Me no like these guys, they Triad style." "That's precisely what they are alright. Can you get them off my tail?" "I sure try, don't want them knowing me mister." He drove through side streets that I hardly thought you would get a car through. Thinking the following horde also thought the same, as no one was following us now. Coming to the ferry pier from the opposite side, as it appeared in front of me. "You got here at great risk to yourself." "No, no, you the one at risk." Looking at the ferry coming in to dock. "You get to your destiny, I know you capable man." Tapping him on the shoulder as I got out the door. Feeling calm and not as worried, as I thought I might be. My nerve was holding up. Needing to contact Sally Yeh as soon as I get to Hong Kong Island. The ferry was nearing its docking position, I slipped on as soon as the it touched the pier. Trying to figure out how to contact Sally Yeh and get the papers to a solicitor. Making for a quiet spot where I could keep an eye on those coming and going. The sailing time was fifteen minutes and hopefully I could refresh and tune my mind into a positive outlook for the coming hours. These would be of the most important for Phoebe and myself. I sat out in the pleasant sunshine as we sailed on the Victoria river. My name was now sanctioned on the paper of the National Government of Hong Kong. The only problem was, am I going to remain in some form of possession of the contents? The fight was only beginning. Noticing plenty of business people taking the ferry. Silently thinking that any one of these could be associated with the two Triad families. Keeping my mind focused all the time. Noticing a very good looking woman as I sat on board the ferry and once again, finding my eyes being manipulated by her charm. The pleasant thoughts of a smooth boat trip and the tranquil movement of the water brought a sense of regeneration to my impending troubles. Being curious as to where this charming woman was going. Was she off to her place of work, or coming from some well formed company? She didn't display a trace of any emotion, except for that gorgeous smile. My simple curiosity was getting the better of me. Bringing my mind back to the task at hand. Finding myself nearing my journeys end. Then my mind slipped back to this woman. Could she be part of the Triad family? Operating on automatic and first thing to think of was the Triads. Sitting quietly for a moment before getting up to depart the ferry. Regaining my focus and tweaking my mind to the task of achieving some productive end to my journey to this part of the world. Finding myself contemplating how to contact Sally Yeh. Had Cho Yun heard anything from the Triad family holding Phoebe? The tension was rumbling inside, but within my control.

Hong Kong Island was at my doorstep as I departed the ferry. It had now become a familiar sight, but I would wish it to be rather in different circumstances. Trying to see if I could spot any of Sally Yeh's people? No one to be seen as I lowered my head. Then I found myself searching again, in the distance I saw a car come close to the docking area. When it stopped, a woman get out, it was Sally Yeh. My internal emotions lifted. Making no gestures in her direction, just in case anyone was assessing my departure from the ferry. Having the signed documents was one of the major parts of this puzzle. My father's death was still to be evaluated. Firstly, I had to try to, along with Sally Yeh and Cho Yun, to seize Phoebe from these parasites. The woman on the ferry once again caught my eye, there was something about her and I couldn't figure it out. Back to my current worries, was Phoebe still in Bangkok? Another journey on the horizon. Finding my muscles now relaxing, as I walked towards the car. Sally Yeh was in the rear seat. Once inside, I told her that I had signed the papers and had an official document with me. But she already knew this, as I suspected. Anxious to hear any word of Phoebe. "Is there any communication from Cho Yun, regarding Phoebe?" "She is still in Bangkok and he is keeping an eye as to any movement." Now feeling in an in–between situation. "So, what do I do next?" Knowing exactly what was required. "Your papers, I believe, should be entrusted to a solicitor. This would be in your best interest." She has a good intellect. "Do you know of such a person that I could trust?" "We do from time to time have to rearrange some minor matters of importance and use a secure solicitor. Should you wish to deposit the papers with her,

I will transport you to this place." Wishing to remove them from my person as soon as possible. "Yes, I would rather have these deposited with her, if you don't mind." "This is your decision Jason and I respect this" With that, the car departed from the dock area. Leaving central district and now the time was getting closer to our immediate goal. The driver was a calm person, as we steadily drove through the traffic to the area of the solicitor. Would we be able to do some sort of deal with the Triads? There insistence on wanting all of the properties, maybe we could come to some sort of compromise? Hopefully I may still be able to hold onto one of the jewelry shops. Only time will tell and that time is running out. My mind was still and relaxed as we drove in the car, but I could feel the mounting pressure as we neared the solicitor's office. What would they say? "What will the Triad family settle for, or ask?" Sally Yeh was calm. "Well, I would say, we will hear from them within the next few hours." "Do you think we can manage to get Phoebe away from them, with some of the inheritance in tact?" "Well Jason, your luck is with you and in what you can achieve, we will help you. But if it is not to be, we can only reduce the loss as much as the Buddha will allow." "I understand that I have also inherited a café on Lama Island. Do you know of such a café?" "Yes, this was and is, an outlet for minds to rekindle and reenergize our cultural spirit. It is a centre to which we try to achieve the momentous task of running the orphanage and a co–op. Jason without the funds from this source in our small community, the orphanage and the community in general would have no ware to function from." She was an deft hand at focusing attention on the struggle of the orphanage. "These words that you speak, you utter them with conviction and pride and I try to understand your devotion to this institution." "Jason, we have to find new ways and means of withholding the grasp of these vipers on our community." I knew she put a lot of time and effort into this society. "I will help you in any way I can. Is there an action plan for Phoebe's possible hand over?" "That Jason is work in progress, this is why we head in the direction of the solicitor, as the person may hold a wider portrayal of what may happen." The sun was shining through the car window and was making me warm and sweaty. Beads of perspiration beginning to seep from my forehead. The car was slowing down and we turned off into a side street. Coming to a halt outside an undistinguished building. Sally Yeh spoke of the wise and solicitor we were about to meet. "This is the humble solicitors office of which I speak. This person, is in my thoughts when I speak of the orphanage." Getting out of the car we approached the entrance to the old structure. Sally Yeh turning to me. "Jason, it is my humble opinion that you embark on a journey that may bring great joy and sadness. It is said, that the Gods shine down on the one who is the sower of seeds. I believe you to be on this plain, as was your father before you." I took a deep breath of air and contributed to the momentum. "I take these things that you say to my heart Sally Yeh. There they are locked within the boundaries of my future thoughts."

Both pausing for a moment, before entering the building. Thinking both at that time, each of us had envisaged my father in our presence. Then more dialogue came from her. "Let us enter in the spirit of hope." Entering the old varnish door to an old graying building. It wasn't a big or opulent office, but was as befitted the people whom the solicitor represented, a small plain room, with little furniture, but the dignity to capture your troubled mind. The spectacle of this distinguished person behind the desk, bore the brunt of a woman who had championed the peoples cause for a great many years. An older distinguished person, whom grew along with the community in which she served. My inner thoughts gravitated to me thinking of a person whom had seen many great and many good days along with some very dreadful days. Being at ease within myself, as I stood there on a bare wooden floor. The graying hair and the craggy face just added to the age of the surrounds. Sally Yeh clasped her two hands together and bowed in respect to our host. Likewise I followed suit. It was met with an air of grace and elegance. The movement and poise of the person in front of my eyes, told me that, this person had been party to a well formed education, but held onto her inner beliefs. Seeing that the person enjoyed respect and gratitude from many. To me this was a warm smiling face, which expressed love, time and effort into her profession and her life. What abstract thoughts jump at you, when faced with a very serious issue? My tired body made a self responsive move to the chair and I found myself sitting down. With that everyone seemed to move to positions of comfort for themselves. The person now sitting in front of me brought an air of reality to our presence. The soft gentle sound of her voice carried its weight across the room. "You are most welcome, you are the one called Jason. It is my intention, for you to be relaxed in my presence." "And may I say you make me feel this way." A smile came across the face of the woman sitting in front of me. It was a comfortable relaxing assurance of the person opposite. "Sally Yeh and Cho Yun, have informed, nay enlightened me, on the one hand, good fortune, but doused with an assortment of Confucius, diluted the fullness of your fruits." My understanding of her interpretation was a symbol of my good fortune, laced with misfortune. "That is a fair way of putting it mildly." Her mild manner approach brought with it calmness and stillness to my inner sanctum. "It is your intention to remove the one you call Phoebe from her incarceration. Is this the position I am to understand from you?" I see Sally Yeh had already informed her of my predicament. "Yes, this would be my stance." She seemed to survey all within her reach and yet be able to convey the wisdom of her many years. "You have recently come into a family inheritance and these incarcerators wish to relieve you of that burden." My inner feelings were being exposed but with calmness and subtle aplomb. "Yes, that is the position I currently find myself in." The wise woman drew breath and again her vision reflected the inner well, which she drew from. "Your anxiety is a cloud, which keeps lifting and diminishing with the breeze of your emotions. We know that it is up to your good self, if you wish to lengthen the stay of your legacy in my presence!" The face of the woman sitting in front of me was passive. Knowing that I was in a dilemma, but her face was that of determination and resolve. She carried with her a hope, a commitment and drive to carry her stature and knowledge, to the very course of destiny itself. "If you Jason, wish to help to dilute the power of these demons within our society, you can do so with our help. Our endeavor is to help you, free your friend and allow the forward motion of your desired realization to be fulfilled. You do wish to deposit the inheritance papers with me for safe keeping. Is this so?" "Yes." I reached for the band I had around my waist and from within I removed the paperwork and handed them to the solicitor. Taking the papers from my extended hand she then went into another room. A few moments passed before she reappeared and bade us farewell. Turning to Sally Yeh on the way out the door I inquired. "What will she do with them?" Sally Yeh's thoughts seemed to be focused on our tasks. "The first task Jason, is to get a identical copy and by copy, I do mean reproduction of your inheritance. This will then be put to use in our next stage of progress. We shall be in a position of strength and this may gain the time needed to extradite information from the ones we rely upon. Hopefully Cho Yun may have more knowledge than before? It would be wise of us, not to be seen in this area. It may contain those who do not have the same interests as we do. Come let us leave with haste." The door of the vehicle opened and I jumped into the rear seat. It felt good to be in the company of people whom I had faith in.

# Chapter

# IX

M oving swiftly and comfortably in the direction of the centre of Hong Kong. It was a far cry from the events of reading of my fathers letter, it was here, it was now. Passing by Happy Valley Race Course, soon we were in the centre of the hustle and bustle of mounting traffic. The Wan Chai district was awash with cars and we were in the middle of it, along with people. Sally Yeh's voice brought my thoughts back to reality. "Jason, we go seek confirmation of your friends whereabouts. Maybe some information has seeped through and if so, we will act on it." The people thronging the streets didn't have a clue of the turmoil going on inside my conscious mind. My inner strength was churning and grinding the wheels of my thoughts and forward thinking. Seeing the path of the aggressor and in my presence was that of a smiling Phoebe. Imagining the release of Phoebe, the flight of her, as the vehicle came to a halt. Jumping out I stood there reflecting how far I had come. Heading down a side street, it was narrow and like the door we came to, it didn't exactly fit the building. Giving the impression it had been there for several years, but it was very heavy and this made me curious. In fact, it was made of steel, made to look old. What lay behind this door? Did it lead to another world? Was it another factor in the existence of a secret and untold flirtation with the people who barely touch the surface of the real world, as we know it?

Stepping inside, who was in the waiting wings? Who was

here? A well built person was watching our every move until the door closed behind us. A fragile old character, whose bones seemed to be double jointed, all bent and tangled, escorted us into another dimly lit room, which appeared to be a control room. Movement in all directions, a lot of people coming and going. The light was reflecting on some motorbikes in the courtyard. My mind working overtime. Where we in the nerve centre of an elaborate and well concealed smuggling operation. "Jason, this is where myself, Cho Yun and these good people of our community run the orphanage and part of its finances from." My inner thoughts had once again got it wrong, but at least it was kept within the confines of my mind. "We conduct a legitimate courier parcel service and this helps us keep in contact with what is happening inside the different ethnic communities that we serve. We hear and know of the many different movements of certain people in and out of the islands and some of which is not public information." Certainly impressed by the efficiency of their network. "You seem to have a flair for business Sally Yeh." Her confident attitude was a guide to the calmness of her smooth running of the business, combined with that of the orphanage. "It is in the blood, but I and my brother Cho Yun choose to use it to the advantage and for the use of our comrades in our community. You will have to forgive me Jason as I have to attend to the many and varied tasks and also I have some phone calls to make." With that she wandered from the room. Now finding myself in the kitchen with some of the workers. They seemed to be having a break. A seat was pulled out from under the table and a friendly smile from the woman to my right greeted me. Walking over I sat down. Hearing the pot boil I turned to this lady. "Do you work for the orphanage?" Her soft voice was charming and I am sure had a reassuring presence in the company of the children. "Yes," came her reply. "I work part in the orphanage and I study in college at night time, along with helping out here." Her vigor and her eagerness to get on impressed me. "Very good, what are you studying?" "I study Economics, but my work is mostly here. I put back into community, the help I receive from here." "That's a good basis to start from." I tried to contribute to her optimistic outlook and enjoyed talking to this young woman.

160

My eyes kept returning to the open door, where these people worked. She had noticed my roaming eyes. "Your eyes see the other room, where they bring letters." Quick to realize my curiosity. "Oh, you mean the courier business." This was me being my usual self. "Yes, this business also helps with the daily running of the orphanage, but also has to contributes to the daily upkeep of services provided to our comrades. We all help if the need arises. It is often the case." As I sat there, I wondered had any news filtered though to Sally Yeh from Cho Yun. At least the inheritance papers were in safe hands now. The door opened and Sally Yeh beckoned to me. Getting up from the table I bowed in respect to all the people in the room. Walking towards the open door I stepped inside to where Sally Yeh was ruminating. "Jason, I have been in contact with people in Bangkok. Your friend is still in the place of her incarceration." My first words were that of an inquisitive interloper. "Is she O K?" Her answer slow and deliberate. "This Jason, is in the hands of her captors and I wish not to be the bearer of news that has a negative outlook. Later tonight, we will meet with the Triad family who hold her and then we will have more information. You of course Jason will be in our presence." My inner thoughts were an obvious cause for my concern and the possibility of her rescue from these unwanted agitators. "When do you expect us to be departing?" Sally Yeh took her time as she replied, not wishing, I presume, to over state the delicate situation we were in. "It will take some hours yet Jason, but I should think around eight in the shadow of the moon." Deciding to get some air within the confines of the courtyard. "I am just going to take a stroll in the courtyard for awhile. It may ease my thoughts." Stepping outside I found myself in the courtyard. Then hearing the voice of Sally Yeh. "Jason, you will be accompanied by this person." It was the girl from earlier. Why was she accompanying me? Did they think I might not be in the right state of mind? "What is your name?" Being interested in this young woman and why she decided to give her time and patience to an unselfish cause. "It is the name Loraine." "That's a very western name." She smiled and told me the story of how her parents had been watching western movies. "Yes, it comes from the movies. It was while watching such a movie that my parents discovered this name I have. It gives me a warm feeling inside." The mist began to fall in the courtyard, but at least it was out in the open, with a slight breeze. It also gave me the chance to discover the shadowy figure that I had observed earlier. This figure still monitored my footsteps as I strode in the courtyard. Who was this person and why were they keeping an eye on me? It had an unearthing impression upon me. The outline feature of the figure was not a clear indication of whether it was a man or a woman. This intrigued my conscious mind, because of the lack of opportunity to gain access to the very same building. As it shared the dividing line between both buildings. All doors had been locked and this was somewhat confusing. But then as soon as that thought left my conscious mind, another more intriguing thought entered. What if within our midst, there was a collaborator? As I recall on an earlier occasion to gain Phoebe's release, the captors already knew we were on our way. Could this be the same person by my side, as she maybe fishing for information and could the person in the shadows know this? Suggesting that we go back inside. Walking with a nagging feeling in the back of my mind. The feeling of being not alone, being watched, did not sit well with me. Pressing the handle of the door I opened it, this leading into a bright fusion of color. A voice cried from the far side of the room. "Would you like something to eat?" My eyes lit up and in response I nodded my head, they seemed to be a very flexible people. Seeing the door, which lead to Sally Yeh's, what looked like her office. A figure, which sat at the table, looked at me and beckoned me to enter the room. Immediately I walked into the room and thought, had any news come from the Triad family about the time to meet them. Sally Yeh was writing on a pad and while still writing, she enlightened me of the latest developments. "Jason, we have had contact with your friends captors. They say she is in good health and in the fullness of time this will only be known." I didn't like the sound of what she was saying. "They have made fresh demands upon your inheritance, as you know it requires you to sign it, for the contents to come into effect. Hopefully in our wisdom, we will have a substitute document in time for our departure. Hearing the word departure must mean we are traveling somewhere.

"You Jason, do understand that you will have to sign a forged copy of your inheritance?" "Yes, I gather that you would ask me something like this. I fully understand this." She had thought of things that didn't enter my mind. "They will very carefully examine this paper, in very minute detail. The craftsman we will use is one of the best and can be relied upon to ensure that the quality of his imitation will be a masterpiece." Quickly interrupting. "Well it better be." Her staring eyes was a reminder of the esteem with which she held the people she toiled with. "I assure you Jason and it is my belief, along with my brother and the community that we shall endeavor to remove your friend from their grip. This may be completed by withholding of your fathers inheritance, until they feel safe to deal with us. We have to wait and see. It is a wise person who can see the path to the edge of the forest." Only hoping these people had all the information at their disposal so we could bring this to a peaceful conclusion. From what had happened before, I wasn't filled with over confidence. Sally Yeh gave her thoughts on our struggle. "We will now forge our thoughts on your friend in Bangkok, along with these Triads we are meeting tonight. We must have the torch in our hand when the flame needs to be lit." At this time I needed to voice my opinion. "I gather by what is being said, that as we meet with Phoebe's captors, there may be an attempt to rescue Phoebe. Far from me to suggest what to do, but isn't it a bit risky to attempt this while we are talking to her captors?" Sally Yeh's words were aimed at keeping another option open. "Jason, we have to look at all points of view, as I am sure you will agree. You talk with the vision of one who has a precious stone and wishes to keep it from the harsh winds. It would be wise of us to cherish this thought, but it is in the hands of the Holy One now." My inner zeal was more settled and could see her intention. "I see your situation Sally Yeh, but not wishing to have come this far and not see the stone shine in my hands." At this stage, while Sally Yeh and myself were dissecting the merits of the situation a person came into the room, moved to her side and whispered something in her ear. Writing something down on a piece of paper, gave it to the messenger and he departed. "It is wise you think in the way you do Jason. As you see I have had some information brought to me that concerns the movement of your friend." Thoughts of her being moved again sprang to mind. "What's happened, is she O K? Where is she?" Sally Yeh was calm and deliberate in what she said. "This is the point of my communication with my brother. It seems that in anticipation of our meeting later tonight, the captors have once moved your friend into a new location. It would be unwise of us to break the hand that binds the spirit of your friend. It is an indication of the information they receive, which we believe come from within our movement. It may be much wiser to remove the petals from our fountain and follow in the footsteps of what we know." My gut feelings at this stage didn't seem to be functioning in any great shape. "What I think you are saying is, that you think or you know, that someone from here in this compound, is feeding the Triads information about our movements!" Her sharpness to my interpretation was once again exposed. "Once again Jason, it is befitting of your capabilities to use your mature wisdom in not seeing from your eyes, but that of an impostor. This is good, my own such thoughts may descend to the very same picture that you see. The larger picture has yet to be portrayed, as we only have an outline of the elements. Jason, we now must abandon the mission of our surprise. You must get your thoughts together and meet me in the room that we now sit, within the hour." With that she moved swiftly out of the room. Heading for the bathroom, I wished to bring myself back to full awareness. The heat of the sun had taken its toll on my frame. It will be important for me to seem strong and steady in the company of these Triads. Needing all my inner strength to become the force that I will need to be. Wishing to forge my concentration and focus upon the task in front of me, I headed for the bedroom and lay down. My eyes closed and I brought myself down into deep relaxation, there I focused upon the sight and the part I could play in this encounter. Being confident and strong in manner, but also willing to hear what they wished to say. Not alone with their words, but also with their body language. Needing to show this without fear in my eyes when I face these Triads. Now knowing I was more focused and confident in the way I would approach the up and coming situation. My inner strength was forging a path to my conscious mind. My subconscious was

164

giving me the resilience to carry on, to move forward, to be able to make a positive contribution to the ever changing landscape of our problems. It looked now as though I will be in eye contact with some of the Triads who were responsible in my mind for my fathers death and Phoebe's abduction. These very same people who drive the wedge between their very own. I need to be at one with my spirit, my mind, my body and self. Now entering a deeper state of relaxation. Using my subconscious mind to bring together the emotional and creative part of my mind. Whilst I lay there, I envisaged the emancipation of Phoebe. Deepening my thought patterns and relaxing my entire body of the tension it was holding onto. It was time for me to return to the reality of our problem. With that I brought myself back to full awareness. My outlook was that of a positive nature, not lacking in creativity. Lifting myself from the bed, my conscious mind began to flood with pictures of alternative ways to liberate Phoebe. She was still in Bangkok, but having moved her, it was back to the drawing board for us. My mind frame was excellent and I was in a positive mood as I strode across the courtyard. Feeling calm and relaxed on entering the room. As I did a messenger passed me on his way out. Wondering was it good news that he brought. Sally Yeh was sitting at the table. "I have just received news on the whereabouts of your friend. They have moved her to a more central location in Bangkok. It makes it much harder for us to gain entry to their constructive retreat." Searching for the right words to say. "What do you think will happen at the meeting later tonight?" "We are about to receive the duplicate of your original document and we shall let them see this. While withholding this document until they are prepared to hand over your friend." My stomach succumbed to a sinking feeling. "What if they want this document tonight?" Her initial hostility to this idea gave vent to her outburst. "This Jason cannot happen, if so they will be able to check out the document. Hopefully while we are talking, my brother and his comrades will obtain the exact location of the hiding place they hold your friend." Being inquisitive was second nature to me. "Do you think it will be a difficult task to achieve from your brothers point of view?" Her confidence in his ability to seek out and find the whereabouts of

Phoebe struck me. "This part does not worry me, but tonight with the Triads, is the most demanding mission. That is to say Jason, to hold onto the paperwork and by so doing withhold the origin of where it came from. It is within our powers and the prevailing Gods to shine on our venture. With this, you will agree, Jason?" "Yes." Came from the body within. "It will not be long before we commence our journey." She sat back in her chair as her words entered my conscious mind. Concentrating on the activity ahead. I picked up a English newspaper that was lying on the table and began to read, my mind jumped to a picture of where, possibly, Phoebe could be. Closing my eyes I was now concentrating on Phoebe's picture in my mind. "Have you a map of Bangkok Sally Yeh?" "It is within your reach Jason," pointing to the crumpled up paper on the side of the table. Lifting my body from the comfort of my chair I walked over to get the map. "Do you Jason, know a place of where they may hold your friend?" My sixth sense is beaming some images to my visual thoughts. "I think it may be in the Sukhumvit area, as there are many tourists in this area, or is it a local area with little access to the general public?" Sally Yeh was interested in my line of thinking. "This is possible, I will immediately let my brother know of your inner feelings. This is a good momentum, you have the gift of your late father. He had a gift of being able to express movement of many precious valuables of our ancestors. We in turn were able to liberate precious items from these Triads, who in turn were seeking to gain monetarily at the expense of our ancestors." She was very interested in my internal flirtation with my inner thoughts. "Tell me where did you see this area?" I remembered it had registered in a dream. "In my dreams, I could see Phoebe been held in this tiny room, pretty dark and obscure. It seemed to have faded curtains and an old window." As I spoke, she was writing. "This is good Jason, as your vision may hold vital information in our quest to free her. Jason, will you sit in this chair and recount your thoughts on paper?" I could see Sally Yeh was very interested in my dreams. Thinking it might have something to do with their culture. The vision in my dream may manifest in reality. Intuition and instinct is highly considered in this part of the world. Was I succumbing to the more natural ability to develop my mental powers of innovation and creativity? What's more important is, we all have these powers, but under use them. As I had known the power of the mind is the most important feature in your makeup. Well back to my dream, it's as though I was in the room with her. My mind was galvanized by these visions, these images, the movement of limbs. It was as though she was transmitting her thoughts to me telepathically. I gauged that I had written down all that I could remember on paper. "Tell me the wisdom of your dream Jason?" So recounting my dream to her. "The images you see are real in your dream and therefore real to you. These come about from your inner flow of energy to your friend. This is a good thing, as she may be able to send you some sort of mental picture. When we come back, you must focus your mind on her thoughts and it may be possible for you to send a message through your thoughts. We believe this to be true and you will try this." Beginning to feel out of place, talk of sending messages through telepathy. She now took on the role of leader.

"We will depart now and arrive at our destination in good time. This will allow us to be prepared for any variation they may have planned in their minds. The night was closing in and it became darker and misty, as time went on. Complete darkness had fallen when we swept out of the courtyard. We exited in a dark colored jeep, a car and two motorbikes followed us, as I looked back to the trailing cavalcade. "I see we are going well prepared." "As you have seen in the recent past, we do need to be well prepared. All may not be as it seems!" I was curious as to whether we were bringing along the forged documentation. "Have you got the documentation to show the Triads?" Sally Yeh was a step ahead at all times. "This document is in the hands of our driver, I should make sure of this." She spoke in her native tongue to the driver, I could see him shake ahead in agreement with her. "Yes, it has been confirmed to me, that we carry the said document with us." Curious to find out what actions we would take. "What will be the procedure when we get there?" "This Jason, will not be the benefit of hindsight, but it will play itself out in the fullness of time. We shall endeavour to have our own custodians in positions of readiness in anticipation of the unforeseen. This of course is in the event that we will not be in total control of the situation. You must take my lead Jason, watch, observe and you will read the unfoldoing events. I feel Jason, you have an inner understanding of the workings of our body and mind. You must look deep within the confines of our restrictions, to engage your inner strength. Changes will occur in my movement, if I feel the thunder of the Gods, or the intrusion of unwelcome intruders. It will be vital that you remain near to me on all occasions Jason. These poachers are not to dissimilar to preying mantas, just waiting for a lack of anticipation on our behalf. They wait in the wings to pounce, to take this opportunity to catch the bigger fish. You Jason will have to be on your guard. Your own presence will be an added bonus to these creatures." Sally Yeh was certainly being forthright. "You must realize that our custodians will not be in view all of the time and may be distracted by the opportunistic elements of this evil and dangerous band of people. The same can be said of the ones who hold the dagger to the throat of the precious bird of prey they hold within their grasp. It will be wise to go unnoticed, to hold your tongue, until the time is given for such a task." Sally Yeh draw a deep breath, before she carried on speaking. "I will gently lower my face, if it is a wise time to speak. This is why you must have my vision within your gaze on all occasions. These people do not show nor do they endeavor to treat with respect, the way of our customs. Sometimes they strike first, with the element of surprise in their favor. At this stage Jason, it would be unwise of you to move in my direction. If this should happen, unless the movement be swift and to the point, you may find that these people will have the upper hand. So be wary of every such movement, but keep in close attendance of me and this will be to your advantage. I shall be cautious of your movements and your need to be nimble on your toes. If we create a duel movement, this will increase the depth of our opponents thinking and reserve of their response. It is wise now to be at one with our minds and our bodies. So be wise in your response to these inquisitors. These people shall be looking for signs of weakness in our body movement and that of our mind. You show the courage and the calm stillness in your resolve and this will in turn be instilled in your character. This will be the vibration of inner strength flowing between your mind, body, spirit and soul." I took a moment to instill this vision into my minds eye and she noticed that I was indeed absorbing these vital facts. These facts that could mean the difference between life and death, between the ecstasy, or the abandonment of my wishes. "Your positive movement will be the outcome of our actions. I know and wish that the knowledge is within your being and the exploration of this knowledge will come with the fullness of time. Jason you have the gift your father had, also his inner strength and attitude." I was very suspicious now of the true reason behind their willingness to talk to us. Also I have this sneaking gut feeling, that they knew our every move before we made it. "Do you suspect Sally Yeh there may be one among us transmitting inside information? If so are they with us on this encounter?" My question was a mere frustration, with the recent outcomes of our deeds. Her response, was that of a person who knew it was not the time or the place, to deflect from the focus of our plight. "I cannot respond in the manner you wish Jason, as I limit myself to the task ahead." I knew of her concern and didn't wish to exasperate her any further. "That's fair enough. I am sure you will discreetly let me know, if I speak out of turn, in the company of the one that does not hold his tongue." Respecting the position held by her. "This Jason, may not be the case, if indeed the person whom is the suspect, may realize our response to be negative to their inquires. This task alone of finding and removing the transgressor without upsetting the seed of trust will be in itself a major task to accomplish. This is why our positive thoughts must be focused on our instant captivation of the facts at our disposal" Sally Yeh, certainly knew what she was about. "Are we in any danger of being kidnapped ourselves Sally Yeh?" "This thought has occupied my mind and it is a burden that we place upon our shoulders. It is my belief, that it would not be in the best interests of them to conjure up such a maneuver, but as in the confines we find ourselves in, this may prove to be a not so wise thought on my behalf. The result would be a holy war. This would diminish their monetary income and expose them to incursions from not alone ourselves, but the many other groups who have the same vested interests." My inner thoughts were awash with jumbled up mayhem of diverse emotions. "I understand what you are saying, so if they are after money, this thought would serve no purpose." Posturing in the back seat of the jeep, as we glided our way through the narrow streets. "Where is the meeting point?" Inquisitive to the point of being very nosey. "It is in the heart beat of an area, that is of equally less, or little significance to both traditions. We shall as I have said, have our own custodians within sight of our gathering. As you can see by our friends following, if there is any need for us to move with haste, we can do so in the spirit of time and with swiftness on our side. The seeds of our harvest must be sown and reaped." At this stage she looked around to see if everyone was in position to move on her signal. "We need to gently and calmly reduce the suspicions of the individuals we talk with. Their minds must be altered, so that a smooth and gracious flight of their fears may occur. The craftsman who duplicated the documentation is that of a local artist and these documents that will carry the burden of our fruit." Feeling I had to say something. "Convincing these people that it is the genuine article will have to be carried off with grace." Being a wise woman, along with clarity of mind. "This point has reached the desired depth in your deeper mind and this is good Jason. Not far from our destination now, so caress your mind and body into a binding rope, that holds the strength of the inner spirit." Seeing the tall structure of the New World Harbor building coming into view. It stood tall among the many other skyscrapers that filled the skyline. Thinking are these Triads trying to prove a point. This is the very building that was the headquarters of the trading firm that my late father had worked for some years. Sally Yeh, contributed, "It is a place that your late father knew well." Wondering if she knew what I was thinking? "Are they trying to make a statement?" "This is so Jason, they wish to let us know that they embrace people of power and influence. Then by their sheer arrogance, think it will have some impact upon our resolve. This Jason, is the year of the Tiger at its worst." For a moment I drew breathe and digested what she was saying. "As they say in the West. You can't see the forest for the trees." "In some ways this is what we have here. These unseen people never venture far without their mask of concealment. The face you see, is not without its uncovered blemishes, but not detectable to the adorning eye. You see Jason, we know we have learnt and can conquer the unwinding path to justice in our land." The jeep came to a halt. "We have reached our destination. Now it is for us to observe the movements of the ones who care to remove your fathers desires." Sitting in the jeep and glancing at the throng of people crossing our path. "Are we far from the meeting point?" Interjecting in a somewhat pessimistic way. "It is view of our eyesight." This was a statement of little encouragement to me, as many people and a vast array of buildings were in my vision. My mind and my sight homed in on one area beyond the World Harbor building. Making out a cluster of neat and smart buildings beyond the harbour area and the ferry crossing terminal. These people were smart and they knew all vantage points, keeping their options open and everybody else guessing. Down the road was the underground tunnel leading to Kowloon and Mainland China. The situation was beginning to get to me and the beads of perspiration came rolling down my chest. Now my face was dripping like a sponge. Grabbing a towel, which I had brought along for such a situation. Figuring it would be a sweaty and sticky night. Attention was drawn to our driver, as he sprang up.

Sally Yeh reacted immediately to this. "What is it?" My voice rang out. "They are ahead of time. These people are the protectors of the ones we meet later. They are many and they do bring the hostility of their masters." Beginning to think what does this mean? Are we going to be lambs to the slaughter? "It is wise for us to know the enemies strength and what positions they hold. As you may observe, they seem to be forming a circle around the area we meet in. I think Jason, it is time to disarm their ability to close the gate of retreat." At this stage she spoke in her native tongue to the driver. He handed her a mobile phone. My mind racing now, what is she up to? What is she saying to the driver? Dialing a number and waiting for a reply, while gesturing to me to be still. When she spoke, she spoke with authority. Her voice was crisp and strong with an element of composure. Forcibly engaging the other person in a deep conversation and this ended abruptly. Speaking to the driver we sat patiently in the jeep. Not wishing to say anything. A tense shadow was apparent in the jeep, it felt like a glass cage. The silence was broken by the sound of the mobile phone ringing. It rang three times before she answered it. Again speaking in her native tongue, the conversation was terse. Suddenly everything went quite. "Jason, we have moved the location of our meeting, to a more flexible and fluid environment of the surrounding landscape. This will leave us much less open to a hostile atmosphere, as is the case now. These people will not have the potential to establish their protectors in the immediate area. We will be much less open to containment." Wondering why the sudden change, as she knew about the meeting place earlier. "Why have you moved the agreed meeting place, as you knew where it was all along?" "It will now be on the river and only the main characters will be on board the vessel we have chosen." Feeling very nervous now. "Forgive me for asking Sally Yeh, but how many of them will be there?" "They will have five, but only two will confront us and we will be the other two passengers." Not sure as to how this equated. "Does this not hand them the advantage?" Her answer, as always was a contradiction in terms. "The odds have reduced greatly in our favor. The movement of the tide diminishes their motion." Finding this a bitter pill to swallow. "That may be so, but we are not facing water." "This is only a metaphor, but the meaning behind it is the same." "If you say so, Sally Yeh. I suppose we won't be overrun, but who will be piloting the boat?" "The boat we meet in will be one of the many that sail in the harbor. The family we gather with does not protect these people. The turbulence is much less than on land." With that, our driver started the engine of the jeep and we moved on. Unsure in some ways of what advantage we did have, now that the meeting had changed. Sally Yeh had in her possession a walkie–talkie and she gave instructions to the ones we could not see. Thinking it rather ironic that we were bargaining for the life of a friend, with the same people whom I believed murdered my father. Our direction was still within the area of the Aberdeen Floating Harbor area. My internal organs were recoiling to the trigger that had been put into my mind and body. I knew Sally Yeh didn't wish to say anything to me, as this was the place where my father died. My own inner strength was proving to be a capable potency in my hour of need. Breaking the ice. "Are the others following on their motorbikes?" "Yes indeed Jason, we will not be out of their vision for any great length of time. As you can see by the ease of maneuverability of the motorbikes, it is a wise choice of transport if the need arises in difficult circumstances. Visualizing this mentally. "I must agree with you, it is a wise especially in the event of an crisis." The streets were narrow and awkward to get anywhere in a hurry. "This vessel in front of us will be the one we trek to." At this point she pointed to a boat tied to the jetty. A cascade of colored lights of the Aberdeen Floating restaurant was upon us. The glare of sparkling fusion seemed to trickle into view. The symphony of lights was dazzling as we edged our way through the narrow streets. Feeling my blood pressure rise, along with the flow of adrenalin, the rush of the blood, the heart beating quicker, the pulsations of my emotions all were bringing me to a higher level. My eyesight cradled the massing throng that veered in and out of my vision. The jeep came to a sudden halt. "Jason, from here we go on foot. Keep within my view at all times. Our guardians are watching us from afar as we walk. From within, our nerves should be that of a silent whisper, only there when the need arises." My internal emotions were with me, but, I feared I was not with them. "Well it's not my nerve that bothers me, it's just simply!" Her calm reassurance was timed to generate a most simple approach. "You Jason, have the power within to steady and direct your destiny on the course you wish." At this point I didn't know if she was talking about me, because I really felt nervous. "You are wise without being old and less afraid of the people we now face. You have learnt that from within, you do not allow the faceless demons to reap the rewards they seek." Walking with distinction on the path of destiny. The boards beneath our feet creaked with the spirit of my father's steps. He may have taken the very same path that I now tread upon, but with a very different outcome. My movement was swift and sharp. My posture upright and focused on the task ahead. I had summoned from within, the strength and guile of a person who had unlocked the tomb to a hidden treasure, the real me, the person who could cope, who could deal with the unexpected. Seeing a figure standing at the pier side as we approached the vessel. A tall and broad figure, was this one of the Triads or a friendly foe? "Jason, be calm and be responsive to my requests. This will have a great bearing in the way they perceive our union. They seek to divide, so as to withdraw the firm footing of the ones whom come to relieve them of their precious stone. This firm standing is the will of your friend and the atonement of your fathers life. We shall seek and we shall strive to see the light at the end of the tunnel." Sally Yeh was a rock, a mountain, all rolled into one. Her energy, her drive, made her the daunting hurdle these Triads had to overcome. "They will seek to destroy any confidence that they may perceive to be a threat to them. This is precisely why I choose to be on water. You Jason are familiar with the flow of a wave, the ripple of the ocean, the sway of your emotions, as this is in your bloodline. This movement will entwine our thoughts and so redistribute our inner strength in a more positive manner. It will harness the forces of our forefathers. Let us be the strength and the will of your friend Phoebe. It is now that we must stand and conquer the ocean that casts a shadow over the unforgotten grave that exists." We both strode forward towards the pier. Not seeing any visual characters or unusual happenings within our scope of vision. It would be impossible for us to move with any great freedom, even if we so choose to. Sally Yeh was slightly ahead of me as we walked towards the boat. Looking around on several occasions discreetly, but could not detect any intrusive eyes upon us. As we walked the sound of laughter filled the air, many people enjoying the surrounding amalgamation of good food and music. She slowed down and I nearly bumped into her, my eyes were converging on a different target. Movement of energy was reduced to the capacity required. My heart rate quickened as I came closer to the two characters stand guard outside the entrance to the boat moored at the jetty. The tension built up as I stiffened upright and pretended to be strong and sturdy, while walking beside me, was this calm and resilient looking woman. Her words were direct, "Jason, this is the quarry that up to now we have had no face to visualize. Now as you may see, they send their scavengers to feed off the dying prey. Let this be their

174

greatest mistake." Striding slowly and with purpose, towards the waiting boat.

# Chapter

## X

The first person we encountered said. "You will go below be seated and wait for the ones you have come to see." Sally Yeh said nothing, boarded the boat and I followed. No words were spoken between us as we sat down. Then two sullen looking characters appeared in our midst. Their first words were comforting to me. "You bring the wise one with you," looking at Sally Yeh. The first words out of her mouth were sharp and to the point. "You have the detainee of my friend here under your control, do you not?" There was a silence for a period of time. "We are here to talk and see your companions reassurance of the genuine documentation of his inheritance. Do you carry such documentation in your possession?" Looking at Sally Yeh, it was she who spoke. "It is my companions intention to furnish you with this documentation, that perturbs us mutually. This of course will only be granted on my comrade knowing that his friend is in good health." The reply took me back somewhat, as these two men didn't seem to be interested in anything else except the documentation regarding my fathers will. "This is not our concern, only that of the documentation." "Your wisdom, is of a limited nature or so it would seem. If my comrade's friend's health is of no concern to you, well then this meeting no longer takes up our precious time. If you do have something to say with regard to the woman friend, then we may progress." At that Sally Yeh got up and I quickly followed. This caught our two surly characters by surprise. "No, no, you must wait." We stood still, while one of these signaled to the person standing on the pier, to bring him something. "Sit, sit." We sat back down. "You shall have the proof, only if you have the proof of ownership of the Kingdom Jewelry." This statement of intent came from the people who controlled the freedom of Phoebe. The previous evocative movement had been the catalyst for our next move. Now we sat in a deep mire and only the craftsmanship of originality would bring the relief I sought. The two faces opposite were of middle aged and business like in appearance. Two well dressed men in suits, preferring the anonymous plausibility of a dinner engagement, to the transaction of that of a extortion extraction. Both had thinning hairlines, one of grey and the other a mixture of grey and brown. Their noses were off centre, the trait of a boxer. One had a thinning moustache, the one with light brown hair. The other had a goatee like beard. Again one was balancing out the other in build, one medium and the other muscular. At this stage Sally Yeh had retreated the scroll from her jacket. She was now about to reveal the diluted version of my late fathers estate. My breathing tensed up as she removed the forged copy. I was very, very tense now and had to admire her, as she coolly and calmly opened the scroll laid it out in an open position, for these two Triads to look at. My breathing became even more acute, as one of them picked it up in his hands to look at it more closely and microscopically. My thoughts began to express a wide and varied outlook on our health. Two Triads in our present company, but how many lay in the dark shadows of the eerie night? My eyes were like gaping golf balls, as I tried to determine whether or not the craftsman had replicated the original. My eyes were still wide open at this stage, as they began to minutely inspect the scroll. For one instant the grey haired man picked the scroll up and held it to the light. At this point my internal organs were doing a dance. The pit of my stomach was churning, as they talked quietly among themselves and in their native tongue. Then with a calm and demonstrative manner, they returned the scroll back into Sally Yeh's hands. My inner system was pumping blood at a quadruple rate. Feeling my inner intestines move with fear as we heard the words from their mouth.

"We see that the signature is that of the one who sits beside you. This document holds the key to the Kingdom Jewelry, but not only that, alas to the flame that burns in the heart of his woman friend, the one who now sits in a place of restful turbulence. Does your friend here choose to reduce the barrier that holds the pulsation of his companion?" Sally Yeh chose her words with care. "You wish Jason to make a contribution to your advancement, such as the remaining share holding in the Kingdom Jewelry. This would see the flight to freedom of the wayward interloper, that you have captured." Their refusal to directly involve themselves in an admission that they were the instigators who had spirited away Phoebe. This was a penetrating indication of the lack of compassion they had for their fellow humans. "Let us just say, that we think that this business should remain within the family of our brothers and sisters." Sally Yeh did not mince words with them. "Once again, your judgment and misguided abuse of the common good have somehow been swallowed up in your deceitful empire of greed and envy. It is the God's who will have the final say. I will not be the resistance in this case, as my friend has mush more pressing matters to think about. Where and when, shall we see the fruits of the generosity of my friends sacrifice fulfilled?"

There slow and oblique answer was less than informative. "The physical sight of your friend will be revealed with the next moon, until then we must depart." The two wriggled their way around the circular table to the point of exit. The quickness of their departure was a sign that pleased me in some ways. My first words to Sally Yeh were, "Do you think they thought the scroll was original?" She sat still for a moment and seemed to dip into her inner mind. "This Jason appears to be the case from the first reactions I saw, but I do have reservations. You see, I am sure they will seek out the government official, who did witness you signing the document. His recounted recollections will be the key to the opening of the door of your friends' incarceration. May the God's shine on our seizing the opportunity to free her from her captors." With that she rose from the table and made her way off the vessel. Following slowly behind, trying to envisage the mental state of Phoebe. As we walked on the wooden bedecked pier the jeep came into view. My eyes were scanning the margins of the masses, the open doorways, the small side walkways, as to a clue if we were being pursued. It did my mind some good, as it had a focal point to home in on. Arriving at the jeep with ease of movement, arching our bodies into the jeep. "Jason, you know we will have company on our journey." My instinct was to turn around and glance out the rear window of the jeep. She knew I would do this. "This may be a vain cause, as they move well within their capabilities." "For what purpose do they follow us now, Sally Yeh?" Her authority stood out, as she ventured her proven skill at judging the opportunists that stood between Phoebe and us. "They see themselves with the upper hand." I was somewhat lacking in faith, the thought that these Triads would be deceived by the forgery and I passed on this feeling. "What if they just took this scroll from you and left us there without any notion of handing over Phoebe?" "They would still have the agent of the British Government. Yes, we know Phoebe is an agent of the customs department. One of their ploys could be to try and exchange her for the informant within our own organization. You see Jason, these people do not stand on ceremony. They take the opportunity if it is there. This is why you travel with me and my fellow colleagues, so as not to make you too easy a target." She was bringing home the realities of this process to me. I was as much a target as was Phoebe. "You are not alone in being the target, myself and my brother are also on this list." More confused than enlightened by Sally Yeh's elaboration. My words were a direct question to her. "So why don't they try something now?" Her calm, resilient manner was in contrast to my confused state. "I suspect, that they do not know if the scroll is genuine or not. Until they can ratify this situation, they will wait and see. This is why it is important that my brother finds out if they can seize your friend." Her interpretation of the current situation seemed to confuse what my conscious mind could decipher. Then she divulged the course of events that would unfold. "We will loose sight of their prying eyes when it is to our advantage." The bustle of the people made it difficult for anyone to disengage anyone in this situation. I suspected that they chose this time, so as we couldn't rush away from the area. Thinking that our resources may not be the bottomless pit that these Triads had, but cunning and a will to succeed were our main resources. This was enough to overcome any struggle in life. It wasn't that I was impatient, but I questioned Sally Yeh once again about our chances of succeeding in liberating Phoebe. "Do you think, we can rescue Phoebe from her incarceration in Bangkok, by the time the paperwork has to be furnished." The reply was slow to come, yet with a velvet lining. "We must let her see the light of the sun, before we encounter these people again. My brother Cho Yun will be the catalyst for her and our emancipation." The vibration of my inner thinking was reducing as she spoke. Her liberation can not be guaranteed, but it would act as a beacon in our midst. An even greater focus was needed now. "Jason, we once again need to be in Bangkok." Once again my heartbeat was pumping with adrenalin. "When do you intend to leave?" Her quick response was an indication of the urgency of the situation. "As soon as the pathway we have chosen is laden with the element of surprise. It may be on this very night." Once again, the ever changing circumstances, was triggering events which in turn, put us in much danger. Our speed had increased and the pace at which we arrived back at the courtyard was transfixing. It seemed as if time had stood still. Sally Yeh made her way to were the others assembled and I retired to my room to retrieve some items. Taking my time back to the room Sally Yeh was waiting, she had just got off the phone and had received a message from her brother Cho Yun. "Jason, we will leave in the next fifteen minutes, as we fly out in the not to distant future." Sitting myself down at the table I tried to remain calm. The roving from one place to another and the intermittent adrenalin rush was having an effect on my internal organs. They didn't know if they were coming or going. Suddenly the jeep drew up in front of the door.

Winching myself into the front seat I waited for Sally Yeh to follow suit. Coming out of the inner office, across the paved courtyard and sat herself into the rear seat. Carrying with her, both a radio and a mobile phone in either hand. The jeep tugged off into the night once again. Heading once again for the airport and God knows what the outcome would be. The journey was quiet and solemn, no time for inner reflection. The lights of the airport drew closer and closer. "Our tickets will be waiting for us as we disembark from the jeep." Her voice very subtle. Nodding in response to her. "You have your passport with you Jason?" "Yes", came my response. "We do not wish to be exposed in the entrance of the airport, so speed is our guide. The minute we stop, remove yourself from the jeep and into the confines of the airport." Again a silent nod of my head was my response. The jeep pulled into the side of the footpath and our driver got out. At this stage another person secured his pace in the front seat. The driver walked around the side of the jeep and opened Sally Yeh's door. I jumped out and walked towards the main airport entrance. Heading straight to the check in desk. About half way down, a stranger, to my eyes, met us. Handing Sally Yeh some paperwork and left straight away. Turning to me she gave me my ticket. The three of us checked in and we moved on to the departure gate. It was as one would expect, a glut of people milling around. "Jason, no doubt we will be monitored as you may have noted back there. So we do not sit together on this trip. My friend here will be with you at all times and I will not be to far away." He seemed to be as nervous as me. She then decided to start the final leg of the journey. "I think it is time that we parted company, until we see each other at the other end. We do not want to give these concealed eyes, an even easier target than we do at this present time. My brother has made the appropriate arrangements, to pick all us up at the other end. This may mean that I will be behind you, so as to give these a target other than you. You will take the fabricated document with you. It is good to have something to bargain with, in the event of another course of action, other than the one we choose." This was not the most optimistic outlooks to fill me with confidence. The last few hours had gone swiftly. It was a hard chore and had taken its toll. Now beginning to feel rather tired. "Jason, we will rest our body on our journey and at its conclusion, head straight to our associates on the outskirts of the city. They may have some information on the possible liberation of your friend Phoebe. It would be wise not to talk to anyone who may seem friendly." Glancing at Sally Yeh with an inquisitive look. "My driver here will be with you at all times. We shall separate now and diverge into isolation until we reach Bangkok." With that she drifted away. Looking at my watch, the flight was at eleven thirty and it was ten fifty five. Deciding to waste some time, by walking around the duty free shops. Not able to make out if I was being pursued, but it was most probably the case. Stopping to look in a window and scrutinize the reflection. Thinking at one stage I could detect two people monitoring me. The driver was by my side as I turned around quickly the immediate impact this had, was to dupe the two people into turning in the opposite direction. When this happened, I now knew there was maintaining a watch and brief on me. Turning to the driver I told him that we had a tail. He became more vigilant and within a minute it had become obvious to him. His remarks were. "We shall remain within this area, as these eyes will not be upon the one who can make contact with our brother's in Bangkok." I only hope this left room for Sally Yeh to be in a much more free role. We floated around the duty free shopping area, until it was time to go to the boarding gate. Keeping my eyes on boarder control that is to say, I scoured the immediate area of vision for the two who had been on our tail earlier. My deeper emotions were being brought into play as I slowly and calculatedly brought my focus onto the people within my view. The call for boarding came over the public address system. It was time to take one more step into the realms of unsolicited demands. The plane would be crowded by the looks of things. Catching a quick glance of Sally Yeh, but refraining from over doing it. I looked at my ticket, we were sitting near the front of the aircraft. Noticing that one of the people following us earlier on was on the same flight.

Feeling somewhat nervous getting on the plane. Wondering what the rest of the night or morning would bring. Beginning to breathe deeply, to regain my focus on the less than positive attitude, captivating my inner mind. What were the odds of us getting Phoebe out of Bangkok before the original papers had to be handed over? We moved slowly towards the boarding desk, glancing behind our tail was still in attendance. I couldn't see Sally Yeh. Hoping that she had contacted her brother Cho Yun and that he had some more information for us when we landed. Being quiet as we approached the departure desk. Handing in my ticket and receiving back my seat stub. Getting nervous and my stomach was churning, my mind flicking back and forth between pictures of home and Phoebe being released from her captors. Moving forward I began to seek out my seat. The driver beside me was a very quiet and silent type. Not to much would distract this person, thinking to myself. Finding myself next to the window. At least, I would be able to see the magnificent symphony of lights, as we soared above the skyline. Opening the English speaking newspaper I bought before departing the airport building. Beginning to unfold the tightly wrapped sheets I separated them into a thin fold–over lap top. I began to flick through the uninteresting pages in the newspaper and then something caught my eye. Gravitating towards a specific headline. It read ; "Grisly find at rear of hotel in Bangkok." Immediately I sat up and began to read the article with furious attention. As the words appeared in front of me, my heart began to sink back in my chest. "European white female discovered hidden in a black bag. Body found beneath a rubbish disposal unit at the rear of this hotel." I was afraid to read on, but my unconscious mind told me to forgo my expectations and press on with the gory details, which I was about to read. Her throat had been slit and she had been carefully concealed, so as not to cause any interest for another week or so. This was the estimated time when the disposal unit would be collected. Had they lured me to Bangkok to capture me? This was the sort of thing that rushed through my conscious mind for a short period of time. Breathing deeply and refocusing my mind. The authorities were searching through the hotel registers to see if they could name the person. All of this information had seeped into my unconscious before we had even taken off the ground. "What if its her? What do I do?" These thoughts rumbled through my conscious mind. Will I get off the plane in one piece? My thought pattern had been knocked once again into a frenzy of disjointed fragments. There seemed to be no logic to my functioning mind. Was I being naive to the printed media? Does my subconscious relay the fear out of my inner frustration of my emotional turmoil? Or was it an unconscious desire to reduce the adrenalin building up inside me? The jigsaw in my mind was slowly forming a pattern of images that I could fit together. This story had caught me completely unaware and thus threw my internal system into turmoil. As my breathing began to eat into me, my focus was conjuring up images of rescue once again. Having to continue with the mission I had started out on. The mirror image of me standing in the morgue with a picture of Phoebe lying on the slab was slowly diminishing from my mind. My inner well–being was taking over and forcing a more positive image into my visual mind. The sap that tore from the layer of my inner strength was bringing me to breaking point. From reading the story my emotions were drawn to a new low, but knowing that I had to carry on. Sure that Cho Yun would have got word to us if it wasn't safe to travel. Again trying to push this story out of my mind was an arduous task. The sound of the humming of the jet engines being revved up broke through to my conscious intellect. The plane was about to take off. The wheels began to speed up, building into a crescendo of power. The well–cushioned interior shook as the maximum vibrations began to filter through to the living souls occupying the seats within its frame. The slow but deliberate upward jolt of the aircraft released the many tingling feelings in my stomach region. As we climbed into the night air, these feelings began to ease. One hurdle had passed and another was about to become reality. I was trying to concentrate on positive images. Taking the paper back up to read the other items of interest. At times, my mind would flick back to the other article, but it diluted with the infusion of new information.

The journey seemed shorter than the allotted time, as we swooped down towards Chiang Mai Airport. Touching down on the apron and instantly began to focus on the assignment ahead. My destination and safely getting there, was uppermost in my mind. As the plane cruised down the runway with its brakes squeaking, the thud was a culmination of behind the scenes activities. The door opened for disembarkation, Sally Yeh was behind us. Walking to the exit door, my stomachs unease was further vibrating when the driver was held up at passport control. The rumblings in my inner organs were even more intense, as the thought of no driver to help me find my way to our destination. Was he in the hands of Thai security, or the people we had come to negotiate with? My instincts were to go to the exit door and wait. These I followed and wondered how long a wait I would have. Was I a target at this present time, or was it a cruel turn of events that such an incident could happen when I needed this person more than ever. It looked like I now had to get to whatever destination by myself. Standing waiting I heard my name being called over the public address system. Walking over to the reception desk I inquired as to the cause of me being summoned to the desk. A note, which had just been left for me. It read, "Go to the Plaza Hotel on Central Pattaya road". I folded the note and put it in my pocket. Heading straight to the taxi rank, I asked to be taken to the Plaza hotel. The airport grew smaller and smaller as we made our way towards the centre of Bangkok. It was now one thirty in the morning, but the streets were still buzzing with people. Now we were on Pattaya Beach road, turning onto Soi–6. I could see the hotel from the taxi. Pulling up outside the entrance to the hotel. Paying the driver I exited the taxi, hovering outside this impressive hotel for a short time. My conscious mind questioned the validity of entering this hotel. What if the message was a ruse from the Triads, just to get me into the hotel. My inner feelings were confused to say the least. If this message was from Cho Yun or Sally Yeh, they would have met me outside. Walking into the reception area and over to the front desk. "Is there any message for mister Jason?" The girl behind the desk, looked down under the counter below her. I followed the movement of her head, as it rose to an equal eye–line with me. In her hand was an envelope and on it read mister Jason Ireland. She hesitated for a moment and then asked me for some identification. I had taken the precaution of making a color copy of my passport. Producing it, she closely looked at it with great care. "You seem to be the person whom this letter is for." With that she furnished me with the letter. As soon as I had it in my hand I crossed the foyer to a seat by the entrance window. Planting myself down on its soft interior, it had been a while since I had such a soft landing. Slowly opened the back of the envelope, each little rip unfolding the contents it had some object inside. A key and a short note was contained within. The note read: "Be wary and follow the instructions, as it may give you the opportunity to speak to and see your friend again". They certainly weren't keeping all their eggs in the one basket. Approaching the reception desk I asked the girl behind the desk, "Did you see the person who left in this letter?" "No came her reply, I didn't expect anything less. Looking at the key number, 72. "Could you tell me on what floor is room 72?" Her smile was a halfway approach to a welcoming greeting. "It is on the third floor." Shaking my head in response to her answer. Heading for the lift. The impressive lobby, was a forlorn thought to the hasty unknown physical and mental apprehensions that lay within my mental cage. Entering the glass rimmed lift. Pressing with hesitation the button to floor three. Taking a deep breath and sighed. As it rose closer to its destination, my stomach began to feel heavier than it weighed. The lift stopped and the doors opened. Staying within its limits for a few seconds. Thinking it wise to do so. Giving me the extra seconds to withdraw from the scene, in the event of somebody wishing to extricate me without my consent. Slowly emerging from the lift with that sense of a grim determination. I'm here now, lets see what is thrown at me! The palpitations of my heart began to beat louder as I neared the room. My intake of breath drew deeper and deeper as I put the card into its receiver. Proceeding to turn the handle slowly and delicately it gradually reached its maximum revolution. Taking a step back, as little by little the door opened. Thinking I heard a faint noise. Having now revolved to a ninety degree angle. Switching on the lights I found the space in front of me empty. The bright spark engulfing the room didn't hold any unwelcome guests. Quickly entering I headed for the shower and no one or nothing appeared out of place. My breathing came back to its natural rhythm. Looking at the glass table at the end of the bed. It had an envelope on it. Picking it up and dissecting it. A was short but a revealing one, exhorted me to a meeting the next morning at ten thirty in the nearest shopping centre. Being very tired at this stage and I headed to bed, alerting my own internal alarm clock to wake me at nine, but just in case I dialed in the appropriate code in the phone, just to be on the safe side. My eyelids were quickly tight together, as my subconscious worked out a plan for later that morning.

The following morning my eyes gingerly opened, looking at my watch. It was eight thirty–five. Quickly getting out of bed and straight into the shower. My conscious mind was now working overtime, as the beads of water ran down my light brown skin. The crisp touch of the luke warm water splashing onto my face, helped to rekindle those positive thoughts. As the water rushed onto my body it felt like a breathing ground for interchangeable positive thoughts. As the force of the droplets hit my face and ran down the rest of my body, it seemed to forge a new and more eager positive thought pattern. The cascade of water felt like a liberating emancipation of my emotional capacity to unwind the clever, but flawed reasoning of the Triads imprisonment of Phoebe. Thinking that this would lead me to cut my ties from this great land, would I think, be a misfortune that they may come to regret. My inner strength was growing stronger by the minute, as I stood under the fast but furious water droplets. Deep intake of air was a sign of the workings of my subconscious mind, rearranging the internal outlay of a working plan for the forthcoming events. As I choked the water supply and stepping out onto the mat I grabbed the hairdryer by the sink unit. With the hot air hitting my scalp, my inner mind was formulating a plan that would see me alive and in one piece by the end of the day. Putting on my clothes I began to scribble some words on the paper pad left on the glass table. Writing down the phone number of this hotel, also what room number and what time I arrived. Also the name of the shopping centre, the place and time. I would leave this at reception and putting Cho Yun's and Sally Yeh's name on it. Finishing this task and now for the final frontier. Walking out of the room at nine–thirty and handing in the note to reception. Asking her for directions to the shopping centre. I left through the main entrance and turning left onto a small side street, leading down to the main shopping centre by a side entrance. Coming to an opening between some buildings where I could see the shopping centre. Standing there and looking at the main entrance and also a side entrance. As I stood there, a black car with blacked out windows approached and slid down by the side entrance. From my vantage point I could see the first person out was that of a well built guy in a smart black suit. The next person was a woman, in fact a blond European woman, by the name of Phoebe. I wanted to call her name out, but the forces within held me back. Quickly stepping to the side of the building I was standing at. My conscious thoughts were being overrun by well meaning objectives. I felt like running over and removing her from the perils of her captors. As soon as these thoughts hit the reasoning logic of my brain, a blank picture reoccurred in the quagmire of my mind. Watching from the distance I slowly walked with my hand resting gently against the building. Keeping the targets in my eyesight, as another man got out of the near door and strode quickly around to hold Phoebe by the arm. Gripping her by both arms and proceeded then into the side entrance of the building. Watching them go up the stairs and then all of a sudden disappear out of sight. Making my way towards the building I quickened my stride and saw the obstacle to my quandary. It was a small side door, it looked like a service entrance. This would suggest that there were some more unexpected entrances not visible without straining my eyesight and safety. Among the throng of people, so it would have been hard for them to observe me. My inner feelings had me in a quandary, should I go, or should I stay. The question echoed in my mind and no positive answer were responding. The difficulty of how to approach this situation at this present time, was weighing heavily on my mind. If I choose to stay and had been seen by her captors, then I really don't know what the outcome would be. My instincts were telling me to move on and wait till the time of our meeting. I mingled with the rest of the people and had noticed a KCR eatery within my gaze. Heading for it and once inside I swiveled around and could see the intersection at which the meeting was to take place. Ordering some food I took a seat by the glass paneled window overlooking the meeting point. It was five past ten, twenty five minutes to go. I still had in my possession the imitation copy of the inheritance that Sally Yeh had made. At least I may have something to give them in exchange for her, if only a very good copy. Looking straight at the intersection, this was having an unsettling feeling, as I only hoped I could carry on with the encounter. It would be my inner thoughts that would have to stand up to the forthcoming events. Trying to focus more on these positive thoughts and the possibility that I may be able to pull it off, without the help of Sally Yeh and Cho Yun. My mind was now racing as the time drew near. Watching from the window towards the corridor. In the distance I could see faint figures approach. Yes, these figures grew larger as they got closer. The blonde hair stood out among the bastion of mostly dark haired people. Four people now accompanied her I rose from my seat, with trepidation building up within the bowels of the volcano I was becoming. My heart pulsated to the flow and rhythm of my surging blood. Feeling red faced as I approached the corridor. Now five people stood between me and Phoebe. Walking forward to be greeted by the arm of one of the interlopers. The voice of the commanding figure spoke with authority. "You remain on that side of the line. Only when you hand over the paperwork, may you cross the threshold." He then pointed to the dividing line in the square tiles on the floor. The next remark grated in my inner dimensions. "Let us see the papers?" The words, What do I do? kept running in circles in my mind. Breathing in and with one foul swoop, removed the false document from my inner coat pocket. "I am not handing this over, till Phoebe is on this side of the line." I must have sounded convincing, as the one holding by the arm let her go, on the instruction of the one in charge. She ran to my side and grabbed hold of my arm. "Are you O K Phoebe?" "Yes," came her feeble reply, squeezing my arm tightly. I handed over the document and the one with authority looked closely at the parchment. He seemed to be taking forever, as his eyes scrolled up and down the signed pages. "You have chosen to do the right thing, it is the wisdom of the fair one." The next sentence was a joy to hear. "Let us depart these settings." As he and his men turned to leave, I felt the tug of an arm withdraw from the stillness of my support. Phoebe had removed her arm from under the protection of mine. Moving in the direction of her captors. My stunned look at maybe her wanting revenge on these characters. "What are you doing Phoebe? Let them go and lets get out of here." She spun around with a faint smile on her face. "But I am going in the right direction Jason." I was feeling somewhat confused. "What do you mean Phoebe, you are going in the right direction?" "You see Jason, I am the one who thought this whole thing up." Even feeling more confused now. "What do you mean thought this up?" "You must not deceive yourself any longer Jason, I not alone thought it up, but I am the one in the dark suit." Pointing with her index finger to the

189

person on the right of the four men. "I am his wife and the mother of his children." My stunned silence and statue like figure must have left the numbness coil within. My inner volcano had been stopped in its purest form by the feeling of a tightening of my upper arm. "Jason, are you O K?" "What?" In front of me stood the people who cared for me. "What has happened?" I said with open palms. With that Sally Yeh said, "You have been fooled by the one you call Phoebe. We had confirmation come through late last night. Come Jason and sit with us." We all moved into a nearby café. "You see, the one called Phoebe is really the wife of the main Triad leader." My heart sank with despair. My inner emotions were a volcanic eruption. "What do you say to me, Cho Yun, she is the Triad leaders wife." "I am sorry Jason, but this the truth." "You mean I have nearly been killed several times by these people, trying to convince me to hand over my fathers controlling interest in the Kingdom Jewelry business." Their deceitful grasping antics, left me with a pounding in my head. "Yes, they needed the premises to expand into their own brand of business. Not alone that Jason, but your late fathers wife of Hong Kong origin, is a blood relation of this Triad leader." My head was spinning in disbelief. Where was it going to end? "Jason, did you give them the copy of your fathers inheritance." "Yes, I thought it only wise, as I figured it would give us time. Us I am saying us, what a fool I have been." " Jason, there is no time for self–pity, we must get you to the airport and on a plane back to your homeland." With that Cho Yun took me by the arm and he and Sally Yeh led me to a waiting jeep. Cho Yun was on the mobile phone to someone, arranging a flight for this same morning. Sally Yeh looked at me. "Jason, you have the strength to move forward from this encounter. You have learned many lessons and you can still keep your late fathers wish to help the orphanage by way of contributions on a quarterly basis, as we still have the original inheritance." Smiling to myself. "I must say Sally Yeh, you all have a great capacity to carry on under all trying circumstances don't you? Here you are thinking of the future of the orphanage." "Yes Jason, but you must not forget, that it was your father who bestowed upon us the idea and the financial backing, to purchase and maintain the orphanage. So you may see in your heart, that this is a gift that you and your late father have in common?" I sat back in the seat of the jeep. "How would I go about maintaining the contribution to the orphanage?" This was a question that I posed to Sally Yeh. "We will open an account in your name Jason and have a sum transferred every quarter to the orphanage." "This is alright, but I would like to have a quarterly sum transferred to my mothers account also. I can say that it comes form an insurance policy that my father had taken out." Cho Yun quickly interjected. "But, is this not the case, did not your late father not provide for such an event as is now? I am sure he had not the wisdom to foresee what events would unfold from such an astute and vital plan." Sitting quietly in the jeep as it approached the airport. "Jason, you must leave now for your homeland without the baggage you came with." This was the last thing on my mind. "You can say that again." I could see they were somewhat bemused. I explained the meaning of my interpretation of Cho Yun's remark. They both smiled quietly to themselves. Sally Yeh put her arms around me. "You go with the peace of our brothers and sisters and the orphanage." She kissed the side of my cheek. Cho Yun put his hand forward and I shook it. "Let me say before I depart, it has been a privilege to meet and know you both. I shall return sometime in the near future, to see how the orphanage is coming along." "Jason, it will be our privilege to see you and to welcome you as the man who fills our hearts with much joy." Cho Yun handed me the plane ticket at the departure desk. I strode away with precious memories and very eventful moments of my journey here. One last wave as I paid my departure tax.

I walked through the open glazed door and wondered, will I ever make the return journey some day again? Turning, I read the departure gate number and headed on my first leg of the journey home. Gathering my thoughts I smiled internally, this is one trip I will remember for a long time to come............

Printed in the United States
107675LV00001B/33/A